Always a Body To Trade

K. C. CONSTANTINE
Always a Body To Trade

A Mario Balzic Detective Novel

DAVID R. GODINE · PUBLISHER
Boston

This softcover edition published in 1993 by
David R. Godine, Publisher, Inc.
Horticultural Hall, 300 Massachusetts Avenue
Boston, Massachusetts 02115

Library of Congress Cataloging-in-Publication Data
Constantine, K. C.
Always a body to trade.
I. Title.
PS3553.0524A79   813'.54   82-48700
ISBN 0-87923-952-2

First printing
Printed in the United States of America

Always a Body To Trade

Before the mayoralty campaign Mario Balzic had never heard of Kenny Strohn. Apparently, neither had a lot of other people in Rocksburg, because early in the campaign Strohn had felt compelled to place an ad in *The Rocksburg Gazette* affirming his residency requirement: the ad displayed a facsimile of Strohn's first wage-tax statement to the Rocksburg Treasurer. It was six years old.

Four-term Democrat incumbent Mayor Angelo Bellotti two days later placed an ad of his own which showed a facsimile of the voter registration rolls that plainly evidenced Strohn to be a Republican. Bellotti had joked about that with anyone who would listen because Strohn had proclaimed himself to be something else, taking as his slogan, "It's Time For A Strohn Independent Leader," the emphasis, of course, on "Independent." And with Democrats outnumbering Republicans four to one on the voter rolls, Bellotti seemed to have good reason for his ridicule.

Balzic was thinking of these things as he sat opposite

Mayor Kenny Strohn in the office Bellotti used to occupy, an office Bellotti vacated on the weakness of two votes for him for every three cast for Strohn.

This new mayor was not yet thirty-five and he ran in marathons and he didn't smoke and he boasted of a pulse at rest that beat fifty times a minute. Worse, it seemed clear to Balzic, his face had the youthful and excited flush of a zealot. Soon into the conversation, Balzic's first private one with the new mayor, it became obvious that not only was the mayor in the peak of cardiovascular health but he believed without question that everyone else could be too if only they put their feet to it—especially the members of the City of Rocksburg Police Department.

"How many miles a week do the members of the department run?"

"Run?" said Balzic.

"Yes."

Balzic was trying to think fast, but his mind had sidetracked. He had been trying to comprehend what all those Democrats had seen in this man that all the political observers—himself included—had not seen, and so he was stammering his reply.

"Well, I think, uh, I don't think I know how many they run. We got a couple guys run a lot. But there's never been a program, or a policy, or anything anybody had to do."

Mayor Strohn sniffed and chewed his lips and made a triangle of his fingers and thumbs as he swiveled from side to side in his chair. "The volunteer firemen have an outstanding fitness program. Fire Chief Sitko believes his men should be healthy for their own sakes as well as for the department's sake. In one of their stress tests they discovered a fellow who needed triple bypass surgery. I don't think there's any doubt that man's life was saved and that he'll lead a long, healthy, productive life—thanks to the fire chief's foresight and leadership."

"No doubt," Balzic said.

"And that's my point. Why are volunteer firemen so involved? Why do they—who are not remunerated—why have they got such a program? I hope you don't mind my saying so, but clearly it's a question of leadership."

Balzic put his tongue over his upper teeth and looked over the rims of his glasses and waited.

"Leadership, Mario—you mind if I call you Mario?"

"No," Balzic lied. He minded a lot.

"Good. Mario, there's got to be effective leadership. Under the third-class city code, the responsibility of the police department is the mayor's. Mine. And I intend to lead both by word and by example."

"Yes, sir," Balzic said, nodding.

"To that end, I'll lead conditioning runs every weekend of at least ten-thousand meters—that's six point two miles. I know the volunteer firemen will stack up. And I know your department will stack up. I mean, we can't expect anything less, now can we?"

"How many miles, Mr. Mayor?"

"Six point two."

"That's what I thought you said, sir. . . . "

At his first opportunity, Balzic fled to Muscotti's to try to overcome the self-pity nibbling at him. At the bar among a dozen patrons stood a stiff and sullen Mo Valcanas. Balzic went and stood next to him and, in spite of himself, blurted out what he'd just heard from the mayor.

Valcanas stared morosely at the backbar. "Change is painful," he said. "Getting a new boss, hell, that's, uh, that's painful."

Balzic shook his head and looked at his shoes. "He wants me to run! One foot in front of the other—fast. He's gonna lead by example. He thinks I'm gonna be followin' him. You know how long it's been since I've run anywhere?"

"Sounds to me like he's looking out for your health,"

Valcanas said, tossing down the last of his gin and smiling wickedly.

"Hey, Greek, this is only the beginning, this running number—"

Valcanas ordered another gin for himself and a draft beer for Balzic and after Vinnie the bartender brought them and went away Valcanas said, "Listen, I know you're not having any fun with that dipshit mayor, but listen to this one."

"I'm listening."

"I worked a divorce for this woman, oh, five, six months ago. I held her hand through the whole thing. She wound up with the house, and he wound up with an obligation to pay the mortgage in lieu of child support. They have a kid under his majority. So she comes to me today—not an hour ago—and she tells me to get some kind of court order or injunction, she didn't know what the term was, you see, and I'm to get this order or injunction or whatever to stop her ex-husband of five or six months from writing checks on their joint account.

"Now, this is not some envelope-stuffer from the rehabilitation workshop. This is a woman with a master's degree. I mean, this woman has gone through the American educational system from kindergarten to graduate school, and five or six months after her divorce she is still maintaining a joint checking account with her former spouse!

"And when I asked why she didn't close that account and open a new one—mind you, she's just asked me to put in motion some legal instrument to stop her husband from writing checks on that account—she said, and I quote, 'Oh, I don't want to do that. That's such a bother.'

"For all I know she's still sitting in my office. I said, 'Excuse me, I have to go get a drink.' I think she thought I meant water.

"The trouble with you, Mario, is for the last sixteen years you've had a boss who didn't know what you were doing—and the only time he cared was when your people were getting ready to strike. And now you've got a boss who thinks it's not only necessary that he care, but essential. Only trouble is, he doesn't know how to care. Or what to care about. But I have jerks like that for bosses every day." Valcanas motioned to Vinnie for a refill.

"And you guys come in here and I got both of you," Vinnie piped in. "And what a couple of pieces of work you are."

Iron City Steve shuffled up behind and between Balzic and Valcanas. "Excuse me, gentlemen. I couldn't help overhearing your conversation."

"You couldn't help overhearing!" Vinnie shouted. "You hear everything except, 'Gimme the money!' That you never hear."

"Let the man speak," Valcanas said.

"Thank you," said Iron City Steve. "All I mean to say is this: proceed carefully. You go in circles no matter which way you turn."

"See there?" Valcanas said, holding high his glass. "Out of the mouths of babes and boozers. A drink for my friend."

"Go sit the fuck down," Vinnie said to Iron City Steve. "Go in circles—go and sit the fuck down in circles in somebody else's joint!"

"Jesus, do you have to shout?" Valcanas said.

"Loudness is rightness," said Iron City Steve. "And nobody is righter or louder than my friend—"

"My friend, huh," Vinnie said. "My pain in the ass."

"That too," said Steve. "Let him among us who has neither ass nor pain come forward."

Balzic threw up his hands and walked to the other end of the bar for something to do. The phone rang, and he reached under the bar and answered it, waving Vinnie off.

"Muscotti's."

"Is Chief of Police Balzic there? This is the mayor."

Balzic stifled a groan and looked at the ceiling.

"Speaking."

"Uh, Mario, there's been a burglary—"

"A what?" Balzic was incredulous.

"A burglary. Didn't you hear me?"

"Oh, yessir. I heard you."

"Well. Okay. The thing seems to need your attention. Your Detective Carlucci—is that his name?"

"That's him. Yes."

"Well. Detective Carlucci thinks you ought to, I don't know, supervise the investigation I suppose. If you can get away that is. You can get away?"

"Oh sure. Yessir."

"Uh, Mario, are you often at this number during the day? To be perfectly candid, it sounds like a bar. Is it a bar?"

"And grille. Yes, sir. That's what it is."

"Well?"

"Well what, sir?"

"Are you often there during the day?"

Balzic chewed the inside of his lower lip. "Yes, sir. I am often here during the day. I get a lot of information here."

"Oh. Oh, I see."

"Yes, sir. Now where's Carlucci?"

"Uh, he's at 540 Winter Street. He says something's very unusual."

Balzic said thank you and goodbye and hung up. He walked back toward Valcanas and Iron City Steve, who was still haranguing Vinnie, apparently over a loan.

"What's the matter with you?" Valcanas said.

"What's the matter?" Vinnie said.

Iron City Steve, his shoulders twitching and jerking

up and down, his elbows flying, peered up at Balzic expectantly.

"Well?" said Valcanas.

"The bastard wants to know if I'm at this number a lot."

"What bastard?"

"The mayor."

Valcanas shook with silent laughter and motioned for Vinnie to fill his glass and Iron City Steve's. Steve's eyes brightened at the prospect.

"He calls me to go check out a burglary and wants to know if I'm at this number a lot, and is it a bar 'cause it sounds like one."

"Serves you right for answerin' the phone," Vinnie said. "He's a fuckin' bullshitter anyway. He knows this number."

"What? What're you talkin' about?" Balzic said.

"I said he's a fuckin' liar."

"I know what you said. What'd you say it for?"

"What I said it for was 'cause in football season he calls here every week to get his bets down."

"Oh yeah?"

"Absolutely. All football season, he knows this number. He calls for Soup. 'Is Mr. Scalzo there?' he says. Shit, he's a three-dollar bill, that guy."

"You sure you got the right guy?"

"Certainly I got the right guy. Ask Soup. He'll tell you. We was laughin' about it the other day. He said he was gonna put him on tape so the next time he got busted he'd have something to make a little deal with, you know."

"Is he heavy?" Balzic said.

"Nah, you kiddin'? Ten bucks a game. That's it. Five, six games. But he's good for it. Soup never had to chase him."

"He ever been in here?"

"Nope. I wouldn't know him if he fell down right here. Strictly a phone jockey. No Ma Bell, he don't ride."

"Back to me," said Iron City Steve.

"Back to you. Yeah. Back to you," said Vinnie. "I guess you think you got money comin' for crissake. And you get short in a couple weeks? Huh? Lean on your lawyer here, he thinks you're so goddamn cute, maybe he'll lend you the money."

"Cute? Was that the word you used—cute?" Valcanas said sourly.

"Oh shit, I'm leavin'," Balzic said. "Between you guys and that mayor I'm gonna be ready for the laughin' academy."

"What the hell's so important that you got to call the mayor that he got to call me and get me out of Muscotti's?" Balzic addressed Detective Rugiero Carlucci.

"Hey, Mario, honest to God, I didn't know that mayor was gonna answer the phone. How was I supposed to know that?" Carlucci's voice was thin at best and squeaky at worst. He was easily excited and quickly agitated when confronted with administrative or political quandaries; otherwise, he was soft-spoken, reflective, curious, and composed. His Anglicized name was Roger; his fellow officers called him "Rugsy."

"I don't know what that clown's even doing down there in the duty room," Balzic said. "But it looks like he's gonna be there a lot, so we better get used to it."

"Well, Jeesou, how was I—I mean, I wasn't calling him, I was calling you—"

"Okay, forget about it. What's so important here?"

"What's important here is, uh, the guy that got burgled didn't make the complaint. And I couldn't figure that one until I saw a state narc pull up across the street after I got here."

Balzic looked around the apartment. They were in the

hospital district, a hilly area of mostly old, mostly large, single-family residences that had been turned into two-, three-, and four-unit apartments.

This particular apartment was on the ground floor of a stone house built probably in the 1920s. The apartment was—or had been—exquisitely furnished in three colors: white, burgundy, and black. The wall-to-wall carpet was white and deep-pile. The couches and chairs, whether upholstered or wood, were either black or burgundy. The drapes were burgundy velour. There were also many mirrors and much chrome.

Balzic did not have to imagine much to visualize that this apartment had been beautiful; he had only to glance around to see that it was destroyed. Everything had been turned up or down or inside out.

"You talk to the narcs yet?"

"Yeah. This one was on their active sheet. Name's Thurman Burns. Nickname Red Dog. Moved from Pittsburgh in the last eight or nine months. Ton of surveillance, couple of arrests, nothing past a magistrate's hearing. College educated, twenty-four, very hip dude—for a white guy in the trade, that is."

"Uh, what trade is that?"

"Pot and coke. Mary Jane and snow. See how fast I learn the lingo?"

"I was just gonna say—uh. That's marijuana and cocaine, right? I mean, you got to spell it out for us old folks."

"That's it."

"Well where's the narc, one, and two, who reported the burglary, and three, where was the narc when it was burgled?"

"In reverse order, he was gettin' something to eat, the lady across the hall, and the narc's probably trying to explain to his boss why he was eatin' at the time he was eatin' instead of being here."

"Lady across the hall still here?"

Carlucci nodded. "She's a nurse. Working eleven to seven this week and the commotion woke her up. Having a hard time sleepin', she says. So her peephole looks out onto this guy's door and she saw the number, uh—"

"What number?"

"I'm coming to that. A female at the door, complaining about wrecking into his—Burns's—car and one guy on either side of the door, all white, one of them with a piece, she thinks maybe it was an automatic, she's not sure but she's seen some like it on TV, and she—the female at the door—coaxes Burns out to check out the damage on his car and exchange insurance information, and as soon as he sticks his head out his door, the guy with the piece sticks it against his neck and away they all go.

"Then, enter two males, white, approximately five minutes later and she—the nurse—can hear them tearing up this joint. She gets scared, doesn't know what to do, finally after twenty minutes or so, they leave, and she calls us. I get the call and come up here and listen to her story, and then I see the narc drive up and I call you, and get the mayor, and here we are."

"Yeah, here we are," Balzic said, rubbing his face. "It used to be a lot easier than it is now, Rugs, you know that?"

"Uh, I don't follow."

"Hey, we never used to worry about dope here. Anybody used dope—no matter what it was—they went to Pittsburgh. They disappeared in among all those people. They never hung around here. All we had here was drunks. Every once in a while we'd get some nigger hyped up on sweet wine and speed or we'd get some smart-ass out at the community college on diet pills and beer—hell, those were big numbers. No more. Uh-uh. Now everybody and his daughter is smoking something, inhaling something, swallowing something."

"What can I say?" Carlucci said. "We hit the big time."

"Some big time," Balzic said. "I never spent so much time in high school lockers. And the only reason we get away with that shit is the kids don't have a Bill of Rights. They're the first ones to tell you that."

"What're you gonna do," Carlucci said with a shrug. "What d'you want to do about this?"

"What are we supposed to do about it? The guy who lives here isn't gonna complain. We tell him about the lady across the hall and he'll tell us she's been spending too much time alone or not enough or too much time not minding her own business. Then what?"

"Look, I just thought you'd want to know about it, I didn't—"

"Take it easy. Sure I want to know about it. I'm just telling you we may as well go talk to the narc. He might tell us we can do something about it. On the other hand, I doubt it."

"I doubt it too," Carlucci said.

"Oh, before we do that, d'you get descriptions from the nurse?"

Carlucci nodded. "And she swore she'd recognize all of them if she ever saw them again."

"All of them? She swore?"

"Yeah. She said she was going to some kind of art class and she was really studying faces lately. Bone structures and stuff like that. For what it's worth, you know."

"Uh, d'you find anything here?"

"Nothing. Whoever it was scored. They didn't leave a penny. Or if they left it, he hid it in places I never thought of looking. Course, you know, if he's what the narcs says he is, maybe he really knows how to hide things."

"Hey, Rugs, look at the quality of the furniture here. You think this guy is an amateur? Those drapes must've cost a thousand bucks. And what d'you think this couch cost? And that chair? And this table? Huh? And I'll bet you he paid for everything in twenty-dollar bills."

"I agree. He's no amateur."

"So then why does somebody think he's an amateur?"

"Huh?"

"Hey, whoever pulled this number, they look like the amateurs. They didn't score anything here 'cause there was nothing here to score. I mean, ripping this place up like this, you got to be an amateur. Who the hell hides something in a couch?"

"They might've ripped it up just 'cause they took the heat."

"That's a thought," Balzic said. "Now, the question is, did they rip it up 'cause they were beginners or 'cause they were mad?"

Balzic nodded in answer to his own question. "That's what I think they were. Real mad. Well, let's go talk to the narco."

Carlucci coughed. "Uh, I think I better tell you. This guy's a real piece of work. He got an attitude from here to Cleveland."

"Oh yeah?"

"Yeah. I mean, what he don't know ain't worth knowin', know what I mean?"

"Then maybe you should go talk to him. I don't need to listen to any more answer-men today. This new mayor, this Strohn guy—remember his posters? Huh? 'Time for a Strohn leader.' Remember that bullshit?—Well, he's really in there pitchin'. Is he ever in there pitchin'. So maybe you should go talk to the narco. One clown with an attitude is enough for me in one day.

"Course, on the other hand, I really suppose I should find out what the narco has on our resident here—what's the name again?"

"Burns. Thurman. A.K.A. Red Dog."

Balzic sighed and motioned for Carlucci to follow him out of the apartment and out onto the street. Less than fifty yards away, on the other side of the street, Balzic spotted the dark blue, four-door sedan with black-wall tires. He set off quickly toward it, and Carlucci hurried to catch up.

It was the mildest January in three years. The last two had been cold in the extreme, with heavy snowfalls. So far, this winter had been like a brisk autumn compared to those past two winters. The temperature had fallen to five above only once, and never lower. There had been two snowfalls of consequence: one of one inch and the other of two. Snow was still on the sidewalks from the last, but the streets were clear and dry.

Balzic tapped on the window of the dark blue sedan and roused a young agent from the Bureau of Drug Enforcement, who had been faking that he was asleep and looked up at Balzic and tried to rub sleep that wasn't there out of his eyes.

"Come on, come on, for crissake," Balzic grumbled. "Get the fuckin' window down. What d'you think this is?"

"What's your problem, Mac?" the young agent said, suddenly alert, hostile, and defensive. He rolled the window halfway down, then decided to get out.

Balzic prevented that by putting his hip against the door.

"Hey! What the fuck you think you're doin'? You know who you're messin' with here? Huh?"

"Hey, Mr. Undercover, Mr. Stakeout, Mr. Narco, whatever the hell you think you're playin' here, you got the most obvious car parked in the most obvious place, and you're trying to come on like you're asleep—hey, your subject's gone. Bye bye. Pffft. Out of the barn. And you don't know who I am and you're asking me if I know who you are?"

Balzic stepped back and kicked the car with his heel, putting a deep dent in the door.

"Hey, smart-ass, do I know who you are? When did you ever stop in at my station and tell me you were conducting an investigation here, huh? You think you can just ride in and park anywhere and not tell me what you're doing or why or when—you asshole, that's rudeness! That's impolite!"

Balzic delivered another kick to the door of the car, making another deep dent.

"Grade school kids—white kids—know this is an unmarked state car, you klutz. And you're gonna park it fifty yards away from your subject's residence and then you're gonna fake sleep when I come out of your subject's residence after—AFTER—one of my men already told you there's been a burglary in your subject's residence, and you sit there and ask me if I know who you are? Shit."

Balzic stepped back from the car. "You got any information you think I should know, you better get out of that car and tell me about it. And before you ask, who I am is the chief of police here. And I've already had trouble with your boss, so don't throw his name at me. This is just one more on him. He's got no manners and he teaches you guys no manners. Get outta the car, goddammit, and tell me something!"

"You, uh, under control or you going to start kicking again, uh, if I get out?"

"C'mon, out. Get out. I'm tired of bendin' over to talk to you. And I'm tired of standing in the street."

The state narc eased out of the car apprehensively. "Uh, there's not really much I can tell you."

Balzic led the way around the car to the sidewalk. He

threw up his hands. "Will you come on? Not really much you can tell me! When the hell were you assigned to this—yesterday? C'mon, let's hear something for crissake. What's your name?"

"Gensheimer. Frank."

"Okay, Gensheimer. How long you been with the bureau?"

"Six months. Actually five."

"And while you went to get something to eat, your subject got burgled. Huh? Is that it? You didn't bring lunch? Huh?"

"Dinner. No. I didn't think I was gonna be here this long."

"Hey, Gensheimer, you know the motto. Right? Be prepared, huh?" Balzic clapped Gensheimer on the shoulder. "So whatta you know about these people?"

"Nothing. Really. I don't."

"Hey," Balzic said. "Listen to me. What do you think I'm gonna do—screw your case? Huh? Hey, your case went out the door while you were out to dinner. That dude—what's his name, Rugs?"

"Burns," Carlucci said. "Thurman 'Red Dog' Burns."

"Yeah, him. Old Red Dog. He's gone. He's not coming back. Never mind you, Frank. Never mind us. He's not coming back because he's no novice. He knew he was in a jackpot as soon as he stuck his head out the door. And there's only two ways he's going, Frank. He's either going to the morgue or else he made a deal. Either way, we'll never see him again. Not at this address. And there's nothing in there. So what're you doing here, Frank? Huh? I mean, you had to figure this out for yourself. So what aren't you telling me?"

"I'm not—hey, what—why should I be holding something out on you? I don't have anything to hold out—honest," Gensheimer said.

Balzic rubbed the drips off his nose and peered intently at Gensheimer. "You trying to bullshit me, huh?"

"Why? What for? Why would I want to do that? I mean, that's crazy. I just don't know anything. And I'm really just waiting for orders, that's all. I called in a long time ago—when your guy here told me what happened—and nobody called me back to tell me what to do. I'm just—shit, I don't know. I'm just waiting here, that's all."

"And you're waiting here and you don't know anything about the two guys who went in afterward and turned the place over? You don't know anything about them?"

"No. Honest. Nothing," Gensheimer said. "I didn't really know much about this Burns guy. Except what he looked like. And he was a dealer. Pretty heavy dealer. But that's all. But, hell, these dealers are always ripping each other off. That's the name of the game. Get the stuff for the lowest cost, the lower the cost the higher the profit, and there isn't any lower cost than no cost at all. Rip it off and the profit's a hundred percent."

"You paying attention here, Rugs?" Balzic said over his shoulder. "This is the short course in how to deal in contraband." Balzic looked back at Gensheimer. "So?"

Gensheimer shrugged as sincerely as he could. "I don't know what you want from me. I don't know anything else. Honest."

"Okay," Balzic said, wiping his nose on his glove again. "Okay. But if you should happen to remember something, I would like to be told, okay?

"Come on, Rugs, let's go get warm. Christ, winter. My nose always runs like crazy in the winter."

"Everybody's does," Carlucci said, as they walked toward Balzic's cruiser.

"Nah. I mean, mine really runs. You know, when I was a kid some old guy scared the piss right out of me one time. He told me that this stuff was my brains leaking out of my nose and if I wasn't careful and didn't hold my head back, by the time I got home I'd be an idiot. You know, completely stupid. So I walked home from school with my head back. Jesus Christ, did I have a cramp in my neck when I got home. Tripped and fell down twice, ripped my pants. My mother gave me such hell you wouldn't believe it. Every winter, my nose runs, I think of that. And I can't remember the guy's name who conned me. Anything like that ever happen to you?"

"You mean really dumb like that?"

Balzic frowned. "It wasn't that dumb."

"It was pretty dumb."

"Okay, okay. So what happened to you?"

"I don't think nothing like that," Carlucci said, after a moment's reflection.

"What d'you mean, 'nothing like that'?"

"I mean I never fell for anything that—uh, like that, that's all I meant. But, uh, I—I think it's pretty funny."

"What're you telling me—you were never conned when you were a kid?"

"I don't ever remember it if I was. But maybe I was. Probably I was. I just don't remember it, that's all."

Balzic wiped his drippy nose on his glove again and got into his cruiser. "Hey, listen, Rugs. If you think of anything you fell for when you were a kid, I'd like to hear about it, you know? It's sort of a hobby of mine. It's kind of—I kind of get my jollies figuring out what people fall for, you know?"

Carlucci didn't respond. He stood there stamping his feet and punching first one palm and then the other. "Well," he said finally, "if I think of something I'll tell you. Uh, in the meantime, you want me to—what d'you want me to do about this?"

"What would you usually do?"

"Not much. Let the nurse look at some pictures, that's

about it. Not much else to do. Maybe run Burns through NCIC, see if they got prior addresses, relatives maybe. But how far can I take it? I mean, what's the point? Nobody's gonna make a complaint until somebody wants to make a deal. That could be months—or never. Hey, Mario, I'm getting cold. What're you asking me this stuff for? You know what I'm gonna do. You taught me. You're sore 'cause I don't have a con story for you. Well, I can't think of one and, anyway, I never saw you get sore about such a little thing before, you know what I mean?"

"Hey, Rugs, go get warm. See you later." Balzic closed the window, put his cruiser in gear, and drove off, leaving Carlucci staring after him.

Balzic went back to the station and busied himself looking over bids and specifications on a new four-wheel-drive vehicle to replace one that had been wrecked a week ago, probably beyond repair. He winced, looking at the figures. He wasted many minutes trying to figure out whether it had been four years ago or five that a vehicle very similar to the one specified in the bids he was studying cost half as much. The bids he was looking at now had not one among them under five figures. A few more years of inflation like the last five, and the city of Rocksburg was going to have to open a casino or strike oil or, better yet, figure out how to turn solid waste into natural gas because, if property taxes remained at their current rate—and nobody in city hall was talking very audibly otherwise—then the city was in for a severe reduction of services.

Balzic looked up to see the mayor getting ready to knock on the open door. Balzic cleared his throat and invited the mayor in.

"Those wouldn't happen to be the bids for that new

four-wheeler, would they?" Mayor Strohn asked.

"They would," Balzic said and thought, so the bastard's been snooping around in here. That's just wonderful.

"I was looking at them earlier—I hope you don't mind—" Balzic didn't answer.

"—and, uh, well, in looking over them, I really think that's a luxury we should see if we can't live without. That's an awful lot of money, Mario, don't you agree?"

"I do. Yes, sir. But we only have two four-wheelers, and one of them was wrecked last week, and it may not be fixable. And if it isn't, and we don't get a replacement, then that's gonna put a hell of a strain on the other one."

"A strain? I don't understand. What kind of strain?"

"In this kind of weather, those four-wheelers start a lot of cars and push a lot of cars up hills and so forth. They're really invaluable."

"But why should the police be starting cars and pushing cars up hills?"

"Because, Mr. Mayor, one car stuck in the middle of Main Street northbound can tie up six, eight intersections in nothing flat. And you can't wait for somebody to come along and push that car off to the side—hell, we used to have to do that before we got the four-wheelers, and it was crazy. You know what tow trucks charge?"

"I see. But couldn't we make some kind of contractual arrangement with certain towers to be on a retainer? It seems to me it might be a whole lot cheaper than the price these people are asking for a new vehicle."

"Well, Mr. Mayor, if you can swing that kind of deal, that's fine with me."

"Do I detect some skepticism on your part, Mario?"

"Not some. A lot. We already got tow-trucks on retainers to clear the streets and roads after a wreck. You're not gonna believe their prices either."

"Well, I'll have to look into that, I suppose."

"I suppose you will, yes, sir."

One of the lights started blinking on Balzic's phone. He depressed the button, excused himself to the mayor, and answered the call.

"Chief? This is Fischetti. I got a really funny thing here."

"What's that?"

"I got a burglary reported by a neighbor, but nobody knows the occupant. I mean, nobody's ever seen the occupant. And I can't find the landlord."

"So what's the problem?"

"Well, it's no problem. It's just there is this beautiful goddamn apartment—and I mean beautiful—and it's just destroyed. I mean, I'd like to have the money they put in draperies."

"Wait a minute. They wouldn't be burgundy-color, would they? Burgundy velour?"

"Yeah. Yeah! No stuff. Wine-colored velour, man. I never saw anything like 'em."

"And the rest of the stuff all black and white and chrome and glass? Huh? A lot of mirrors?"

"Yeah? No stuff. How'd—I mean, is there something going on I'm supposed to know about?" Fischetti was always afraid something was going on that he didn't know about.

"No, no, no, no, nothing like that. It's just that I just came from a burglary that Carlucci called about. Practically identical to what you're talking about. Listen, why don't you call him about it and, uh, the two of you take care of it. Okay?"

"Yes, sir. I'll do that. You want to switch me to the desk?"

Balzic switched Fischetti's call to the desk so he could try to make a connection with Carlucci.

Mayor Strohn watched open-mouthed as Balzic hung up.

"Two burglaries in the same day," the mayor said. "Isn't that unusual?"

"Unusual? In what way?"

"Well, two in one day, that seems . . . "

"No, sir. Two in one day is, uh, a mild day. Usually there's a lot more than that."

"A lot more?"

"Yes, sir."

"Oh, really, Mario, a *lot* more?"

"Well, sir, a lot more depends on what we mean by 'a lot.' But, two burglaries in one day is a long way from 'a lot.' "

"What is 'a lot' of burglaries?"

"Reported burglaries?"

"What other kind are there?"

"Well, for instance, neither one of these was reported by the victim, sir. Reported burglaries, sir, I'd say average about ten to twelve a day. That's a fair day, yes, sir."

"I don't believe this," Mayor Strohn said, putting his hands on his hips and pacing about, his lips severely pursed.

"Uh, what don't you believe, Mr. Mayor?"

"My God, Mario, how long's this been going on—ten to twelve burglaries a day—my God, this is outrageous! We have to put a stop to it. At once!"

Balzic slid his glasses back up his nose and rubbed his temples with his thumb and the middle finger of his left hand. "Mr. Mayor, I think, uh, I think I should explain something, sir, if you don't mind."

"Explain what?"

"Mr. Mayor, you don't stop felonies—what I mean is, sir, the police, we don't, the police do not stop felonies or misdemeanors. We, the police, in felonies, we work ninety-nine percent of the time after the fact. I mean, sir, what I'm trying to say is, uh, I think you got a not really accurate idea of what the police function is, sir."

"Well, by all means, Mario, please tell me what the police function is. I mean, is it the police function to—to, uh, somehow feel gratified, as it were, that a fair day—was that your phrase?—a fair day was ten to twelve burglaries—"

"No, sir, no, not gratified, no sir. Gratified was not my word. No. What I meant was that ten to twelve burglaries a day was an average day. I'm not gratified by that at all, sir."

"I should hope not. But tell me about the 'police function' —was that your—were those your words?"

"Yes, sir. Police function, those were my words. Well, sir, in felonies, it's pure and simple. Unless the police become agents provocateurs, well, they simply react to a violation after the fact. I mean, that's just the way it is."

The mayor was aghast. "This is ridiculous. I mean, for God's sake, what place does prevention play in your work? I mean, in the police function, is there no thought given to prevention?"

"Well, sir, prevention's a very good word for, uh, say, editorial writers and TV commentators and social workers and so on, and even some politicians have made a lot of moves with that word, sir, but the truth is, sir, uh, prevention's pretty much bullshit. I mean, if somebody wants to murder a president of the U.S.A., and it has been done, even with the best-trained security people around, I mean, those Secret Service guys are like a second skin on a president, and if somebody wants to kill him, why, sir, they just go ahead and kill him. And if that can happen, sir, why, hell, a burglary's almost a one-to-twenty cinch."

"But that's different."

"What's different?"

"An assassination. Completely different."

"Uh, beg your pardon, Mr. Mayor. But that's my point. If somebody can knock off a president with all those security people around, then just what do you expect this police department to do to prevent burglaries? In all fairness, sir, there isn't one goddamn thing we can do to prevent 'em. I mean, short of apprehension in the act, there isn't a whole hell of a lot we can do. D'you have something in mind?"

The mayor started to pace and purse his lips and rub his chin and pace some more. "Well, I'm not sure what I have in mind, Mario, but I intend to give it some thought— a great deal of thought. We ought to organize block, uh, block prevention groups."

"Sir?"

"You know. What I talked about in my campaign. Block parents to assume the responsibility for each other's children."

"That's a fine idea, yes, sir."

"Well then I think we should implement it at once. Why delay? And then we can go from there to organizing a crime watch in each block."

"Yes, sir, we got to cultivate our informants."

"Not informants, Mario. Informants? No, not at all. That has such an odious ring to it."

"An odious ring?"

"That's—yes! Why are you repeating me? Are you mocking me?"

"No, sir, Mr. Mayor, I am not. But to be blunt, sir, what you're proposing is very close to vigilante law and that, sir, scares the hell out of me."

"Nonsense. You're not understanding me. Vigilantes! My God. I'm talking about neighbors caring enough about their neighbors to report suspicious persons. To look out for each other's children, to look out for each other—how can you confuse that with vigilantism?"

"I don't confuse it at all, sir. But, uh, I'd just like to, uh, bring to your attention the simple human fact that there are lots of neighbors out there who hope their neighbor's car doesn't start in the morning, who are tired of stepping in their neighbor's dog poop, who are fed up listening to their neighbor's kids screaming and running through their yard—I'm not explaining myself very well, sir, but the point is—"

"The point is it's our job to make them care!" said the mayor hotly.

"It's our job?"

"I mean what are we here for, Mario? We're here to serve the people. And what better way to serve the people than to make them aware of their responsibility to each other? What better way than to make them know how important it is to care?"

Balzic rubbed his forehead again and then his temples. "Uh, Mr. Mayor, how do you think you should go about doing these things?"

"Not just me, Mario. You. All your men. All of us in public life. You spoke earlier about the 'police function.' Now I'm speaking about the 'public function.' What all of us in government should be doing."

"You'll have to be, uh, a little more specific, sir."

"I've already told you, we can organize it along the lines of block parents. Each parent assumes the responsibility one day a week to watch out for the kids. We do the same thing with a person looking out for other persons, for property. Why is this so hard to understand, Mario? Your face, your expression, is utterly pessimistic."

"Mr. Mayor, you're gonna have a hard enough time finding block parents. But there are time limits involved with young children. I mean, after a certain hour of the day—early evening—people can relax. The kids are home. The ones that are coming home, that is. But houses, cars, apartments, they're not the same. They don't go to bed. They stay up all night. You think there are people out there who are gonna stand guard around the clock? Sir, that's what cops get paid for."

"But, Mario, that brings us back to ten to twelve burglaries a day! 'A fair day!' Your words! *If* the cops are paid for this, Mario, then how can it go on?"

Balzic leaned back in his chair and silently cursed this young mayor with a heart that beat under fifty times a minute at rest. Balzic wanted to get up and grab Strohn by the shoulders and shake him and say, "Hey, numb-nuts, this is the world here. Where you been?" But he said nothing and tried to make his expression as open, as attentive, as willingly subordinate as possible.

"I suppose you think that was not fair on my part," the mayor said. "I suppose you think I had no right to expect anything else. But it is loathsome to me to have ten to twelve burglaries a day characterized by you as routine. I don't care whether you think I'm being unfair. It is loathsome to me. It is outrageous to me. No burglaries would be a fair day. Ten to twelve burglaries is hopelessly unfair to me—an unfair day! Totally unfair. Totally unthinkable."

Balzic leaned over and scratched his side and then sat upright again. "Mr. Mayor, I don't want what I say to be misunderstood or misinterpreted. But I do want to be heard. And I don't want you to mistake me for some bleeding heart. The facts are these. And no matter how much we like to forget about the facts, we can't 'cause they won't go away.

"This is the county seat in a county that's got the second highest unemployment rate in the state among white males. It's damn near eight percent. We have a large black population, and unemployment among black males is half again as high. Among black male teenagers, it's almost thirty percent. Those are official numbers. The truth is probably ten percent higher.

"Mr. Mayor, we'd have to put a cop in every residence and two on every block to stop all the burglaries, but thefts from autos and residences, and auto theft, and shoplifting—Mr. Mayor, have you any idea what the rate of individual bankruptcies is around here? Are you—"

"What's your point—what's the point of all these facts?"

"Mr. Mayor, if I was unemployed through no fault of my own and I had run out of options to find honest work, I would soon find dishonest work. The fact is that unless you are born rich it takes money to live in this society, and you have to get it one way or another—I don't care what the WCTU thinks of how you do it, or the PTA or the DAR or the AMA or the ABA. You got to have tickets to ride, and not too many people care how you get the tickets. Just so you get them."

"Mario, I'm not at all sure I can even find it in me to say that I can tolerate your attitude. I'm, quite frankly, I'm astonished that you could be saying what you're saying and still call yourself a police officer."

"Mr. Mayor, I, uh, I resent that. I'm trying to tell you how it is around here and you're trying to tell me that I have a wrong attitude. I don't like it at all. There are things cops can do and there are things we can't and nothing gets a cop or a whole department in trouble faster than trying to do something it can't do.

"Mr. Mayor, unless a beat patrolman or a patrolman in a cruiser sees somebody going through a window or jimmying a door, or unless one of our silent alarms goes off here, there is not one way in hell we're going to prevent even one burglary a day, no, sir."

The mayor stopped pacing and put his hands on his hips. He began to rock forward and backward on his heels and toes. "Tell me, Mario. Do other police officers share your opinion on this matter, or is this more or less your own opinion?"

"My opinion that prevention of felonies is pretty much bullshit, is that the opinion you mean?"

"Exactly the one."

"I've never taken a poll, Mr. Mayor. I really don't know what most police officers think about it. All I can do is guess. And my guess is they would agree with me."

"Your opinion, Mario, your opinion and your attitude are both reactionary and defeatist. And I urge you, as strongly as I can, to review your opinions and your attitudes and see if they're not due for an overhaul. I'm dismayed, Mario, I truly am. I have to leave now, but I want to continue this discussion. Soon. Very soon. I have no doubt that given the right information you'll come around to my way of thinking on this matter. Ten to twelve burglaries a day in a community the size of ours is not tolerable. And prevention is the key. Education. Prevention. I'll start drafting proposals for city council to act on in the very near future—and I'll want your cooperation. Despite your attitudes."

"I'll cooperate in whatever way I'm able, sir."

The mayor started out the door but came back. He shook his head forcefully from side to side. "You can't hedge like that. This is too important to hedge on. I want your word you'll cooperate. Not just in ways you are able. Not at all. No. I want your word you'll cooperate in implementing my prevention plans."

"Sir," Balzic said, rising slowly and taking off his glasses to rub his eyes. He put his glasses back on and looked squarely at the mayor. "Sir, I will cooperate in whatever way I am able. That is not a hedge. That is the only reasonable statement I can make at this time.

"All I ask is that, before you make some plans that, uh, well, before you make any plans and present them to council to act on, you do me the favor of getting other opinions from other police officers. On every level, sir. I think that what they'll all tell you is that the only prevention possible is in crimes where victims don't complain. And prevention there is really not prevention at all, it's just temporary interruption."

"All right, Mario, I'll get other opinions. I will do that. But in return I expect you to rethink your opinion."

"Fair enough," Balzic said. "I'll think about it some more. But just let me tell you a couple more things. One, I'm sure you're old enough to remember the John Kennedy assassination."

"I am. Vividly."

"Well, sir, I have no idea how many law officers of every kind there were around Kennedy when the first shot was fired. There may have been fifty within two-hundred yards of Kennedy, there may have been five hundred. The point is, not one of them was able to prevent the second shot from being fired."

The mayor did not respond.

"The second thing, Mr. Mayor, is, have you ever been in jail or prison?"

"No, I have not."

"Well, sir, there is no more controlled society anywhere. There is absolute gun control, for example. There's prohibition not only of alcohol but of every other controlled substance. There are frequent searches of residences and of bodies. There is no Bill of Rights to protect anybody from anything, from illegal search and seizure to cruel and unusual punishment."

"What's your point, Mario?" the mayor said.

"My point, sir, is that crimes happen in prison. Lots of them. Right under the noses of guards. And you'd think that would be the easiest place in the world to prevent crime. And it should be, but it isn't."

The mayor looked with utter dismay at Balzic for a long moment and then left. Balzic slumped back into his chair and swore. He felt the frustration turning his neck muscles into a dozen tiny spasms that were growing into larger and larger spasms. He opened his desk drawer and took three analgesic tablets and swallowed them with cold coffee. Mo Valcanas was right: change was indeed painful. . . .

Balzic was at home finishing dinner and kidding his daughter Marie about the boy his daughter Emily said Marie was very interested in. Balzic had poured a glass of wine and was getting ready to kid Marie some more when his wife told him the phone call he had refused answer because it was probably for him was indeed for him.

"What is it?" Balzic grumbled into the phone.

"We got a body," came Desk Sergeant Vic Stramsky's reply.

"What kind?"

"Female. White. Early twenties. No ID. Shot with a large caliber gun in the face. Left on the sidewalk on South Main in front of Angelo's Barber Shop, apparently where the shooting took place. Two citizen calls on the gunshot at 6:15 and 6:16 P.M. One citizen call at 6:17 P.M. that there was a body. Fischetti was in the first mobile at the scene and he confirmed at 6:21. State police, CID, and the coroner all been notified. I think that's everything."

"Okay," Balzic said, sighing. "Shit."

"What's the matter?"

"Aw, nothing. I just thought I was goin' to have a pleasant evening with my family. Now I'll be lucky if I see them tomorrow. I'll be down there."

"What's the matter?" his wife said, passing him in the kitchen.

"No luck today, Ruthie. New mayor all afternoon, new body tonight. No luck at all today."

Balzic got out of his cruiser at about the same time the photographer from the state police CID began taking pictures. Coroner Wallace Grimes was getting up out of a crouch from beside the body. Blood was still oozing over the sidewalk into the curbside gutter from the woman's head, which was in the middle of the sidewalk. Balzic did not see any necessity to go around and look at the back of the woman's head. He had already noticed that another trooper from the CID was examining the empty storefront next door to Angelo's Barber Shop, where the woman had been standing. The impact of the shot had thrown her back against the bricks, and she had crumpled to her right and fallen on her right side. There was hair, blood, bone, and brain matter splattered over the bricks.

Balzic turned away because he knew that if he didn't he'd lose his supper.

Lieutenant Walker Johnson of the state police and Coroner Grimes approached him from different directions.

Grimes began talking first. "From the condition of the entry wound, it was a very large caliber fired from less than a couple of feet away. From the hole in the bricks behind where she was standing and from the size of the exit wound, I'd say it was probably a .357 Magnum, but I'm just guessing now. I'll see if any of it stayed inside, but I doubt it. Every time I've seen exit wounds that size I've never found anything inside. Could be a first though. I'll let you know tomorrow. Good night." Grimes walked quickly away, his slight frame hunched over against the cold.

"There's an efficient man," Lieutenant Johnson said. "No wasted motion, no wasted words, and never tells you he'll deliver if he can't. So how you doin', Mario? Don't mind my saying so, you look like hell. D'you throw up yet?"

"Cut it out, Walker. Christ."

"Okay, Mario, okay. So, uh, what's happening to old

Rocksburg here, shit, bodies in the street. Christ, what's that new mayor of yours gonna think?"

"Hey, Walk, cut it out, will ya?"

Johnson's lips quivered and he dropped his gaze. "I'm sorry, Mario, but this is the fourth pile of blood and brains I've looked at today, and, uh, I just thought three was enough, that's all. So I'm talking like an idiot."

"Oh," Balzic said, commiserating at once. "What happened?"

"Head-on job when I was coming on watch this morning. Two guys in one pickup and one guy in another pickup. I guess impact speed was about one forty or so. I hadn't even had breakfast yet. I still haven't had breakfast and it's two meals later and I'm lookin' at this one—aw shit. What d'you know about her?"

"Nothing. Never saw her. Your guys find any ID?"

"No. Money, car keys. Twenty some bucks and change. But no purse or wallet . . . "

A trooper came up to them and said, "I got a couple next door say they heard a car pull up, car doors open— that's two doors—and shut and then a shout or shouts and then the shot. One shot. Then the car doors slam, the car drives away, 'squealing tires' was, I think, the way they put it."

Patrolman Fischetti from the Rocksburg PD approached them then with his notebook open.

"What d'you got, Rocco?" Balzic said.

"Customers in the bar right there—Caruso's on the other side of the barber shop there?"

"Go ahead."

"Well, four customers plus Mrs. Caruso, the bartender, all heard one very loud gunshot after they heard a car pull up and somebody get out. After that they don't agree. Couple of them say the car stopped, one door opened, then the shot, and the door closes and the car drives off.

Another guy says he heard some loud talking after two
doors opened but did not shut and then a shot and then
two doors slamming shut and the car peeling rubber.
Another guy says one door opened, there were two shots,
then one door shutting with a slam, and then screeching
tires. Mrs. Caruso says they're all drinking, they don't
know what they're talking about, she heard two doors
open, some loud voices, one shot, and two doors being
banged shut and rubber being laid."

"You the first one here, right, Rocco?"

"Yes, sir."

"D'you find anything on her, d'you search her?"

"No, sir. All I did was try to find a pulse in her throat
and when I couldn't find one I knew she was dead—I mean
I knew she was dead from just looking at her head, but,
uh, no, sir, I just called Stramsky and gave him a ten-four
on his call to me and I just kept the area clear until
everybody showed up and then I went into Caruso's there."

"Okay, Rocco, thank you."

"What d'we have here?" Johnson said. "Money but no
wallet, no purse, no ID. No obvious robbery, but a very
obvious gun murder. What the hell is this? Unhappy
husband? Pissed-off boy friend? Rejected lover? Hold on a
second. Hey, Walt, you find the bullet yet or did it
disintegrate?"

"Lieutenant, I found the hole, but it's deeper than my
finger. I think it's probably just a bunch of fragments in
the bricks, but I'll take the bricks out if you want."

"Do the best you can," Johnson said. He turned back to
Balzic. "So? Whatta you think?"

"Well, what I think is this: if she wasn't carrying any
wallet or purse or ID, then what I think's not worth shit.
But if she was carrying ID, and he or they took it, they
took it to make us make a big deal out of finding out who
she is. And the only reason they'd do that—might do

that—is to make us make a lot of noise about her. The more questions we'd have to ask, the more the word would spread. I don't think there's any doubt—especially because that's what we're gonna have to do—she's a message to somebody to do something. What d'you think?"

Johnson nodded. "I agree. But who's it to and what for?"

"Well, what for is pretty clear, I think. Don't you? See things my way or get a big hole in the front and a real big hole in the back? Huh? Don't you think that's it?"

"I think you're right. Christ, look at her. Bet she's not even twenty."

"You look at her."

"Hell, she may not even be eighteen. Hey, Tom! Ho, Tom, get a couple close-ups of her face and don't get this mess of her head in. We're gonna need a lot of copies, okay?"

The photographer acknowledged Johnson's request and went back to work.

"This is kind of a new thing here, huh, Mario?"

"No, it's not new. I mean, it is and it isn't. We just haven't had it for a while, that's all. What's new is killing a woman. That's new. But the method, that's not new. And the place, that's not new either. But one thing I know."

"What's that?"

"My mother's countrymen didn't do it. This they don't do. Except the pimps. Don't let me include the pimps in that. The pimps, they do anything."

"Mario," Johnson said, canting his head, "you know anything about this? Huh? Anything?"

"Not a thing—except I know if I stay around here any longer I'm gonna be sick. Listen, you want more people to interview the citizens? I can get maybe two, three down here—"

"No, I think we got enough. And I also think that what

we heard so far is what we're going to continue to hear. One door slamming, one shot, two doors, two shots, voices, one voice, a man's voice, no voices, tires squealing before the shot, after—I think that's the way it's gonna go. But then, maybe we'll get lucky and find somebody who just happened to be looking out the window at that time. On the other hand, probably not."

Balzic started to walk away but came back. "We had a couple very strange unreported burglaries today. I think you better ask the narcos what they're doing with a dealer named Thurman Burns. At least one of his residences got turned over today after he was escorted someplace in front of a piece. A little while later, another place that looked like the apartment Burns was led out of, that place got turned over, too."

"And?"

"Well, three people escorted Burns away. One was a female. When your photographer gets done, you get a couple views of this girl's face to me and we'll show it to a nurse who lives across the hall from Burns. It's probably not connected, then again, who knows? This place was never a sanctuary for dope dealers either a couple years ago. Now? Shit, anything goes. And anybody. But those narco guys, Walk, no shit, I don't think they can hit themselves in the ass with either hand."

"Hm. That's interesting. This what's-his-face, Burns? He's a dealer?"

"From what I was told. From Pittsburgh. Supposedly moved here less than a year ago. He's been no trouble to me, but then, what the hell do I know? All this dope stuff's new to me. Anyway, what we'll probably have to wait for is good information that wants to trade for some time. I'll see you later. I'm goin' home. I'll check with the coroner tomorrow. Let you know."

Johnson nodded and waved, and Balzic walked to his

cruiser. He drove home in a fury. Not for twenty years had somebody been shot in the street like this girl. For twenty years there had been nothing to compare with it. Twenty years ago a war between Jews and Sicilians over gambling territories had left many casualties, more than a few on the streets.

But there had never been a woman.

On the other hand, until the previous year Balzic had not arrested a female armed robber either. And he'd arrested two of them in the last six months. Just like the fellas they were: small handguns, a small, all-night grocery store, a young clerk working alone, and very convenient parking. Took the money, grabbed a carton of cigarettes, and walked to the car coolly, with a threat tossed over the shoulder. One of them had been nineteen and weighed almost a hundred pounds. The other had been twenty and weighed one thirty. They were both white and blue-eyed. The petite one was the daughter of some kind of evangelical preachers; the other was the daughter of a bank clerk and a substitute teacher. No one posted bond for them, and they were sharing the only cell set aside for women prisoners in the county jail. A month ago they'd asked for a district magistrate; they wanted to be married. When the district magistrate refused without explanation to marry them, they ripped their bedding to shreds and set their mattresses afire.

At their arraignment on charges of prison riot and arson, they attacked a deputy sheriff. The petite one bit his left ear lobe off, and the other one broke the little finger on his right hand. The charges against them increased to include aggravated assault and interference with a police officer in the performance of his duty. Their bond climbed from $10,000 each to $25,000 each. As before, no one came forward to post it. . . .

Balzic stopped at Muscotti's to have a glass of wine. He

heard the roar of the jukebox and the hubbub of dozens of conversations when he was still several steps from the side door. He stuck his head inside the door, and the roar increased threefold. He debated whether to leave at once or to have one drink, and made up his mind to go in when he saw Mo Valcanas at the near end of the bar. Valcanas was talking earnestly to one of the female students from the community college, of whom, male and female, there were twenty-five or thirty in the place. Dom Muscotti was working behind the bar, and he had the expression of a man trying to avoid a communicable disease. Every time he poured a draft or opened a bottle of beer, he served it with only minute variations of, "Why the hell don't you go study or something? I'm gettin' tired. Go on, drink up and get the hell outta here."

Balzic shouldered through the crowd and eased next to Valcanas, who turned briefly to see who he was and then turned back at once to the girl. Balzic tried to eavesdrop, but the crowd noise was too great. He could see only the girl's chin when Valcanas bent his head near to her mouth to hear what she was saying. When Valcanas talked, he hid the girl's face entirely. Balzic felt distinctly unwelcome. He tried motioning to Muscotti to bring him a drink, but Muscotti was too busy pouring drafts and telling people to go home and to quit bothering him to notice Balzic.

Balzic, at last, went to the nearest beer cooler, got out a bottle of Iron City, opened it, and drank from the bottle. The air was blue-brown with cigarette smoke. There were conversations everywhere, the music was loud and not unpleasant, the beer was delicious—even though for this time of year it was much too cold—but Balzic kept feeling more and more like a guest whose chief effect was plainly intrusive.

Valcanas turned away from the girl, whose pretty, plump face Balzic could clearly see now, and looked briefly at

Balzic, who hoisted his beer on high in greeting. Valcanas nodded and licked his lips vacantly and turned back to the girl.

Balzic felt himself sidling over to Valcanas and saying, despite his best intentions not to intrude, "Hey, Mo, whatta you say."

Valcanas never turned around.

"Hey, Mo, what're you up to?" Balzic said loudly.

Valcanas turned obliquely and shot a slightly drunk, slightly mean look at Balzic. "What I'm up to is I'm trying to get lucky. You mind?"

"You're trying to get what?" Balzic said over the din.

"Lucky. You know. As in lucky."

"What? I can't hear you."

"Good," Valcanas said, and turned back to the girl with the plump, pretty face.

"Did you say 'lucky'?"

Valcanas didn't answer, but watched as the girl, holding up her index finger as though to say she'd be right back, hurried off to the lavatory.

"D'you say something, Mario?" Valcanas said.

"Yes. I asked you if you said 'lucky'? D'you say you were trying to get lucky—with that kid?"

"That's what I said. And she's twenty-one."

"You got to be kidding."

"Oh? And just why do I?"

"Why? Christ, man, you're old enough to be her grandfather."

Valcanas turned stiffly to face Balzic. "To the best of my recollection we have known each other since I got out of law school. That was in 1950. Am I correct?"

Balzic nodded, knowing that he was about to hear something unpleasant. Truthful probably, but unpleasant nonetheless.

"In all that time, have I ever asked you about your

sexual behavior, or preferences, or objects?"

"No."

"Then exactly where the hell do you get off questioning me about mine?"

"I was just saying she's a kid, that's all—"

"What you were saying was a jawful of innuendo and implication about my motives. And I don't care how durable or long our friendship is; friendship, by my definition, does not permit your concern or curiosity about whom I try to bed."

Balzic felt himself nodding stupidly. "You're right, you're right. Sorry. I mean it. Won't happen again."

"Good," Valcanas said. "I can count on that, then?"

"Sure. Why not? I just said it."

Balzic drank from the bottle again. The beer suddenly began to have a bitter taste, he was starting to perspire, and the music had increased in volume and tempo so that its overall effect was now distinctly abrasive.

Valcanas said something else to him, but Balzic couldn't hear. Then the girl with the plump, pretty face came back, and Valcanas turned back to her.

Balzic finished his beer and set the bottle on the bar and put two quarters beside it. He pushed and sidled through the crowd and stopped at the top of the steps to see if either Muscotti or Valcanas was taking note of his leaving. Neither was. But the little girl with the plump, pretty face was putting his two quarters into her jeans pocket.

Balzic chewed his lower lip and snorted a small laugh and told himself to go home before he said something else foolish.

Balzic did not get a chance to say hello when he stepped into his living room. His daughter Marie was holding an imaginary phone up to her ear and pointing urgently at him.

"Who is it?" Balzic said, bending down to kiss her cheek.

"It's the mayor. He's only called about a zillion times."

Oh, shit, Balzic thought. What now?

He kissed his daughter Emily in the living room and then his mother in the dining room and finally his wife in the kitchen as she leaned over the sink to finish washing a pan.

"Good luck," Ruth said, sighing disgustedly and shaking her head at the phone.

"How many times has he called?"

"I've answered it twice in the last ten minutes. Marie's answered it twice and so did Emily."

"Oh for crissake," Balzic said, lifting the phone off the back of a kitchen chair. He motioned for Ruth to get the wine out of the refrigerator and said hello into the phone.

"Mario, uh, where have you—I mean, why are, uh, why aren't you at the scene?"

"What scene?"

"Oh my God. You mean you haven't heard?"

"Heard what, Mr. Mayor?"

"The murder! About the murder. The girl. On South Main Street."

"Yes, I've heard. I know about it."

"Well—well, why aren't you there? My God, this is awful!"

Balzic closed his eyes, licked his lips, and went to the cupboard and got a big glass. He motioned for Ruth to fill it. She tried to stop twice, but each time he tapped her on the elbow and motioned with his hand, as though to say, more, more.

"I agree, Mr. Mayor. It is awful. She was a very young girl."

"No, no! That's not what I mean. I mean—uh, I mean, why aren't you there! For God's sake, explain yourself!"

"Mr. Mayor, you're shouting. It's very hard to—"

"Of course I'm shouting. I'm extremely upset! I have not been in office a week and you're, uh—you're—"

"I'm what, sir?"

"My God, Balzic, do I have to spell it out? Why aren't you there? What are you doing at home? Where have you been for the past half-hour?"

"Well, in reverse order, Mr. Mayor, I stopped for a beer on my way home, that's where I've been for the last half hour or so. I'm home because home is where I usually go when I finish work. And I'm not there, again obviously, because I'm here. I mean, I was there and—"

"Well why aren't you still there? I don't understand at all," the mayor very nearly shrieked. "Is the—surely you haven't finished your—your investigation. Have you?"

"Mr. Mayor, except in some instances, homicides in third-class cities are investigated and prosecuted by the state police. All we do is assist them—and that's if they ask for our assistance."

There was silence. Finally the mayor said, "Oh. I didn't— I mean, are you absolutely certain of that? That sounds very strange to me."

"Well, sir, no matter how strange it may seem, it's really just plain old common sense. For example, we've only got one fingerprint kit, and that's always reserved for all breaking-and-entering calls. We've never matched too many sets of prints, so far as I can recall, but it always makes the victims feel like we know what we're doing if we got a man dusting door frames and window sills and so on."

"That sounds very—uh, well, in this case, didn't the state police request your assistance?"

"No, sir."

"Well, why not for God's sake? I don't understand—"

"Mr. Mayor, the officer in charge of the Criminal Investigation Division, that's Lieutenant Walker Johnson, well, sir, he's a very old friend of mine. So, he wouldn't have to request my help. I mean, he knows he's got it. Just as I know that I've got his. And both of us are very familiar with the work of the county coroner. And so there's no problem about cooperation."

Again there was a long period of silence. Finally, the mayor said, "Well, what's being done? What have you learned? How close are you to solving the case?"

Balzic was taking a long drink of wine, three swallows, during the mayor's questions and choked at the third one. Fully thirty seconds passed before Balzic could regain his normal breathing, during which time the mayor asked repeatedly if Balzic was still there.

"Yes, sir, I'm still here. I was taking a bite of a sandwich and I guess some of it got caught in my throat."

"Are you all right?"

"Oh, yes, sir. Fine. Just fine. Where were we?"

"I was asking how close you are—"

"Oh, I remember now. Yes, sir, to solving the case." Balzic chewed his lips and looked at his wife, who had come out of the dining room to see if he was all right when she heard him choking on the wine. Balzic held up his right hand and waved her off.

"Well, sir," Balzic went on, "it's going to—what I mean is, it's not going to be easy to, uh, solve this case, as you put it, sir, because it was a gun murder and there are apparently no witnesses, and also apparently there were no cartridge casings and very likely there won't be any bullet, although I can't say that for sure until tomorrow, and, also, we don't know the identity of the victim, and we have no motive and, uh, all we really know is there's a body and we know the time it happened and that's pretty much it."

"Well what about ballistics?"

"Uh, sir, beg pardon?"

"Ballistics. You know. Identifying the weapon by a comparison of bullets."

Oh Christ, Balzic thought. "Sir, that is only possible if a shell casing is found or if a bullet is found and then later on a weapon is found. I mean, you have to have things to compare. You understand what I mean?"

"Well don't you have a bullet? I mean, how do you know it was a gun murder—isn't that what you called it?"

"Yes, sir. But that was obvious. I mean there was an entry wound in the girl's face and there was an exit wound in the back of her head. The coroner said that. And there was a hole in the bricks behind where the girl had been standing when she was shot. But it was a very large caliber gun, very powerful, and when I left the state police were not very certain at all that they could recover any part of the bullet. They believed at that time that the bullet had probably disintegrated when it entered the bricks. And I can see why they would believe that. I'm not saying they won't be able to recover some parts of that bullet. All I'm saying is that when I left, it seemed that recovery of any part of that bullet was, uh, doubtful, to say the least."

"Oh."

Balzic could have said something else, could have given some assurance that everything that could be done was being done or would be done, but he thought the hell with it. If this clown wants to know, let him ask.

"Mario, uh, Mario," the mayor said after some seconds had passed, "are you still there?"

"Still here, Mr. Mayor."

"Well, uh, isn't there something you can say, I mean, I'm sure the news media will want to know how we're doing on this, don't you agree? I mean, I'll have to have all the information in order to make a statement—if

I'm asked, of course. I will be asked, won't I?"

"Probably not."

"What? Why—why not?"

"Well, there's still only one paper in town, and they get all their information from the desk man in our department or from the state police barracks or from the DA's people. I never knew anybody to ask Angelo—your predecessor— about any police matter unless it had to do with hiring or firing or a budget. But I don't recall anybody asking him about an investigation—"

"Well that's just it, Mario. That's one of the things I campaigned against. I'm absolutely certain that if Angelo Bellotti had opened up the lines of communication as I'm trying to—"

Balzic held the phone away from his head and wondered if he was going to get the minute-long radio ad that Strohn used in his campaign or one of the twenty-second or ten-second ones. He hoped fervently for one of the latter.

"—I want to be open at all times to—"

It sounded like it was going to be the minute job, the one about never closing the door to the mayor's office and opening up council meetings to make them like town meetings and going to the citizens at their jobs on the lunch hour for "brown bag forums" and holding monthly press conferences and—

"—what do you think about that, Mario?"

"Beg your pardon, sir, I had to pick up a piece of my sandwich. Just fell on the floor here. So I didn't hear the—"

"What I said was, what do you think of my idea about calling a press conference first thing tomorrow, say eight or eight-thirty, and you can back me up with the details— what do you think of that? I think it's our only course."

"Oh, well, see there, we won't really know much by that time. The coroner won't have his report by then, and I

won't know what the state guys have by then either, and, if
you don't mind my saying so, I doubt that you're gonna get
anybody from the paper at that time of day."

"There are other news media, Mario. There's the radio
station, there are the Pittsburgh papers and the TV
stations—"

"From Pittsburgh? Pittsburgh TV?"

"Why do you sound so incredulous? Of course the
Pittsburgh television stations. They all covered my election."

"Well, sir, uh, what I think they covered was your win-
ning the election was such a surprise, I mean, they didn't
really cover too much of the, uh, election before you won,
did they? Or maybe they did and maybe, uh, see, I don't
watch too much television."

"They covered my victory, certainly, because it was an
upset, but they were here before, too."

"Yes, sir. Well. But, see, I think this would be a little
different and I don't think—"

"Different how?"

"Mr. Mayor," Balzic said, struggling to control his tone,
"see, this is a murder. Right now there isn't anything really
complicated about it. Uh, and, I mean, what are you
gonna say at this press conference? Besides the fact you
got a dead girl, what's to say? I mean, if you want to use
the news people, if you want to put the girl's picture on the
tube and in the papers, to find out who she is, that's
different, but you don't use those guys like that by getting
'em up at dawn to come to a press conference. Hell, you
make 'em get up that early just 'cause you want to run a
picture and that's the last time you'll ever see 'em. They'll
never forgive you for that. Or me either."

"I didn't say dawn, Mario. I said eight or eight-thirty,"
the mayor said tightly.

"Mr. Mayor, how early you think people get up in this
world to go to work?"

"Eight-thirty is not dawn, Mario."

"All right, sir," Balzic said, suddenly and completely out of patience. "You call up everybody you want to come and you do it. But you count me out. 'Cause I'm not gonna sit there like an asshole for two hours waiting for somebody to show up to ask some dumb-ass question they could've asked over the phone at ten-thirty, which is probably when it'll be before we'll have some information to give 'em—if they want it. 'Cause the truth is, until we hear otherwise from somebody looking for that girl—and this is the plain truth—nobody gives a shit about that girl except us cops and the ambulance attendants and the coroner."

"It seems as though I've been wasting your time," the mayor said. "Perhaps we should discuss this more fully when you can give me all of your attention. I didn't—"

"Mr. Mayor, that's, uh, that's—never mind. You do what you see is your duty, and I'll do what I see is mine."

"All right. Since you put it that way. I'll expect to see you at eight tomorrow morning. We'll meet the press together at eight-thirty. That's my duty as I see it. Now, what is your duty?"

Balzic closed his eyes and let out a long breath through his nose. "Well, I guess I'll see you at eight tomorrow morning."

"Very good, Mario. Very good. Please come informed."

"I'll come with as much information as I can get. Good night." Balzic hung up with a bang. "Asshole," he said, "ignorant, arrogant asshole."

Ruth came quietly around the door frame. "Was that as dumb as I think it was?"

Balzic shook his head. "Can you believe it? That clown actually thinks he's going to have a press conference. He must think that was the president's wife that got killed."

"Who was it?"

"Hell, I don't know. I don't know if we'll ever know. But

he must think this whole end of the state wants to know. He's gonna call the Pittsburgh TV stations."

"Oh no," Ruth said.

"Oh yes. Oh yes," Balzic said and poured himself another glass of wine.

Balzic walked into the duty room at 7:59 A.M. On the way from his house he'd tried to think of the last time he'd been at work before nine. Aside from the times when he'd been too tired to go home the night before and had slept in one of the cells in the lockup downstairs, he could not remember a time since he'd been made chief that he'd ever arrived before nine. But here he was.

Desk Sergeant Joe Royer shook himself at Balzic's appearance and swiveled around to check the wall clock against his wrist watch.

"Don't say a word," Balzic grumbled. "Just tell me one thing. Do I look okay?"

"What d'you mean d'you look okay? How? Okay how?"

"You know, how do I look? My fly ain't open, is it?"

"Are you all drunk or something? You can't look down and see if it's open?"

"Very funny. Where's the asshole?"

"Uh, which asshole is that, Mario?"

"The mayor asshole. Where is he?"

"Oh, that one. He's upstairs in the council meeting room. He's been there since about five after seven. What's going on?"

"A press conference."

"A what. A press conference?"

Balzic scowled at Royer. "Why you keep repeating what I say? Am I mumblin' or something?"

"No, no. I just think that's—a press conference. What the hell for? Which press?"

"Good questions. Very good questions. Now for some sensible questions. Has Johnson called?"

"Nope."

"How about the coroner?"

"Nope."

"Has anybody called about that girl on South Main Street?"

"Nobody's called since I've been here."

Balzic snorted. "Swell." He inhaled deeply and blew it out, pulling his diaphragm up and in to expel the last of the breath, and then inhaling deeply again and repeating the process three more times.

"What's that all about?"

"That's supposed to get the blood flowing. Clear the brain, and all that stuff. Okay. Here I go. Oh, you haven't seen any reporters, have you?"

Royer chuckled silently and shook his head no. "Lotsa luck with, uh, what's-his-face."

"Luck? Shit, I need more than luck with this guy. I need a gypsy with a teapot and a cup."

Balzic took the stairs slowly. When he walked into the council meeting room the mayor was pacing from the long table at the far end of the room to the windows overlooking the parking lot on the south side of the building.

"Morning, Mr. Mayor."

The mayor stopped pacing and made a great show of looking at his watch.

Balzic said nothing.

"Well, Mario. Let's have it."

"Uh, beg pardon?"

"Come on, man. Tell me what you know. The news people will be here in twenty minutes. Fill me in."

"Uh, Mr. Mayor, there's nothing to fill you in on. I

haven't talked to anybody. Johnson from the state CID hasn't called and neither has Coroner Grimes. I don't know any more now than I did last night."

The mayor looked as though he were going to faint. His face grew livid, his eyes fluttered, and his Adam's apple jerked. A full minute passed before the color returned to his face.

"Mario, I'd heard all my life that you were an outstanding policeman. A good administrator, a leader, hard-working, diligent, duty-bound—"

Balzic had had enough of this already. He walked very near to the mayor and said, "I am. All of those things and lots more. But I'll tell you something I am not. I am not gonna stand here and listen to you say all those things and lead up to a 'but.' 'You're duty-bound, Mario, but.' 'You're a good cop, Mario, but.' 'You're hard-working, but.' That I am not. I am not gonna stand here and listen to that.

"I tried to explain to you about this last night, but you didn't want to listen. You didn't want to hear it. Well, Mr. Mayor, I don't know where you get your ideas about how police 'solve' murders, but I'm gonna give you a real fast course in reality. If we don't have a suspect—in custody—before that girl goes in the ground, forget it. The chances that we'll ever have a suspect jump by ten every day after that. Like right now it's five to one against us. Tomorrow it's ten to one. The next day twenty to one. The day after, thirty to one, and so on. In no time flat it's a thousand to one. And the only thing that will make those odds change is an informant, you hear me, Mr. Mayor? A stoolie. A canary. A pigeon. A snitch. A squealer. Remember all those bad names little kids call each other when one of 'em tells on the other one? Remember that?"

The mayor tried to back away from Balzic and nod his head affirmatively and authoritatively at the same time.

It didn't work. He succeeded only in looking extremely nervous.

"We have a real aversion to squealers in our society, Mr. Mayor. Everybody hates 'em. But the everyday goddamn truth, Mr. Mayor, is this: without squealers—or whatever name they go by—without them, police departments fall flat on their asses. We live on informers. We uphold the law on them, we 'solve' cases on them. They're our blood, Mr. Mayor. And you want to know the rotten part of all this—this system of cops and stoolies? Huh? The rotten part is that even cops look down their noses at 'em. Even cops hate 'em. Now that you've heard that, there's only one thing you need to see, Mr. Mayor."

Mayor Strohn was backed against the long table where council sat. "What?"

"What you need to do is go stand next to the coroner while he takes this girl's head apart and weighs her brain to find out how much got blown away last night and also takes it apart to see if there's a piece of a bullet left in there. I believe in my bones that you dearly need to watch that. It'll give you a whole different perspective about this. I think you'll worry a lot less about the crime rate in your administration—which is what you're worried about—and worry a whole lot more about the crazies walking around that no police department in the world can protect you against. That's all, Mr. Mayor."

Balzic turned around to see a woman who looked to be barely out of her teens standing at the door to the council room. Her nose and cheeks were red with cold, and she was standing awkwardly with one foot flat on the floor and the other pointed so that only the ball of her foot touched and her heel wiggled from side to side. "Is there, uh, excuse me, but is this where the press conference is going to be?"

"Ask him," Balzic said, nodding back at the mayor.

Mayor Strohn was around Balzic in what seemed a blur.

He approached the young woman with his hand out. "I'm Ken Strohn and you're, uh, you're?"

"Uh, Judy."

"I know it's Judy. It's your last name I can't remember."

"Meekner."

"Of course, Judy Meekner. And you're from the, uh?"

"*The Rocksburg Gazette.*"

"Of course, of course. I haven't seen you since the election. How've you been?"

"Fine. Well, just okay. I guess."

"That's good. Do you know Chief Balzic?"

"No, I don't think so."

The mayor made a flourish of the introduction. Balzic nodded at the girl and said hello and wondered how many months it had been since her twenty-first birthday.

"Listen, Mario, why don't you make Miss Meeker feel at home here while I go downstairs and check on something. All right then? Fine." That said, the mayor departed the room at a quick pace.

"It's Meek-ner," the girl called shyly after him. She giggled nervously at Balzic and dropped her gaze. "Everybody's always calling it something funny. You could understand it if it was a really hard name, like my roommate's name last year. It was just a bunch of consonants, and people called her everything, but that was only after they saw it written down and tried to pronounce it. It was only four syllables— gee, I don't want to bore you."

"You're not boring me."

"I'm not?" The girl seemed honestly surprised.

"Tell me something. You ever meet him before today?"

"Who?"

"The guy that just left."

"I don't think so. I just started to work last week. I sure never covered any election—was that his election?"

"Yes, it was."

"Well I wonder why he said he knew my first name—oh, maybe I did meet him and was just too nervous to remember."

"No, you didn't meet him. That's a salesman's con for names."

"A what?"

"A—never mind. The guy looks at you like he remembers you and he says you're, uh, you're, only he makes a question out of it and so most people tell him either their first name or their last name—never both unless they know the con—and the guy says, oh, I know it's Meekner, it's your first name I can't remember, get it?"

"Oh. Oh, so that's—I wondered! 'Cause I knew, I mean, I was really sure I'd never seen him before."

"See, what you gotta do whenever you hear that pitch is always give 'em a wrong name. And then when they say, oh sure, I know that name, it's the other name I can't, etc., etc., then you know you're dealing with a hustler."

"Gee. I never would think fast enough I don't think, besides I'm not, well, that would be being really suspicious of people. Well, wouldn't it?" She giggled again.

"Did Tom Murray hire you?"

"Uh-huh. Do you know him?"

Balzic nodded. "You just applied for the job and he interviewed you and he hired you, huh?"

"Yeah. I was really surprised. I had applications everywhere, and nobody even answered them. But he did. Mr. Murray."

"Uh-huh. And did he send you down here this morning, to this press conference?"

The girl bit her upper lip and nodded. "He looked around and I guess everybody was busy or something and he said I'd been doing inside stuff for long enough and I may as well get wet so he was going to throw me in. And here I am." She giggled and shifted her weight from toe to toe. Each time one of her heels came up off the floor it would swivel rapidly from side to side. Balzic remembered seeing his daughters do that when they were in grade school.

The girl looked around at the room, empty except for the two of them. "Where is everybody? I thought I was late but I guess I'm early, or—"

"Go ahead and say it. Or else you're the only one coming."

"Oh you're not serious! What am I going to do? I was just going to let other people ask the ques—oh, what if I'm the only one! Oh. I'm petrified!"

"Hey, Judy, believe me, there's nothing to be scared of. This is no big deal, believe me."

Balzic could see that she did not believe him. He tried to make small talk, asking her about her schooling and her hometown, but she would have none of it.

"What am I going to do!" she cried out in the middle of one of Balzic's questions. "I've never even been in a police station before."

"You're not in a police station. That's downstairs. This is the council meeting room—"

"It's the same thing. It's about a crime. A murder! A girl was murdered and I'm supposed to ask questions and if I'm the only one here I'll probably go blank. It happens all the time. It can't happen, it can't happen, it can't happen. . . ." The girl's voice got quieter and quieter.

"Hey, I got an idea," Balzic said. "Practice on me."

"Oh I couldn't. I'm so embarrassed. What am I going to tell Mr. Murray. What—"

"Forget about Murray. Forget about the mayor. Look at it this way. It's a job. You do it, you get paid. You don't do it, somebody else will—"

"Boy, you're really helpful. I mean, really."

"Listen, little girl, I'm not gonna sit here and throw

roses at you. You wanna ask me the questions, go ahead. I'm offering to be practice. But I'm not gonna coax you."

The mayor came into the room then, practically bouncing with anxiety. "Uh, well, I see you're still here, Miss Meeker."

"It's Meek-ner," the girl said just above a whisper. "And I never met you before. And the reason I'm sure of that is because I never covered anybody's election. I didn't even start this job until last week."

"Well, uh, obviously, Miss Meeker—Miss Meekner, I've made a mistake. It happens. I meet many people, and quite often I go up to total strangers and think I've met them, and it's—uh, Mario, I think you can handle any questions Miss Meekner has about the murder last night. I've just learned that I've got something pressing to do, and it can't be put off. So, Mario, if you will, please? Thank you."

Balzic wouldn't have traded that moment for a month's pay. The look on Strohn's face was worth at least that.

Balzic scratched his scalp behind his ear and watched over the rims of his glasses as the mayor withdrew to that pressing something—whatever it was.

"Now what?" Judy Meekner said. "I don't understand—"

"Well, I'm not sure I do either. What time is it?"

The girl held up her wristwatch so Balzic could see. "I can't see it without my glasses," she said.

It was nearly a quarter after nine. And what Balzic guessed was that the mayor had gone downstairs to make some phone calls and discovered that in order for there to be a press conference, there had to be a press, and that if that essential part was going to be missing then there wasn't much point in his hanging around to look foolish for one very inexperienced girl reporter and one very smug old cop.

"Now what? Do I have to ask you questions?"

"Certainly. Go right ahead. Practice. It won't hurt a bit."

"But he said—him. You know, the mayor. He said you'd handle any questions. So this isn't going to be practice. This'll be real."

"So? I don't have anything to do. You ask, I'll answer."

"Well wait a minute till I get my notebook and stuff." The girl took off her gloves and coat and scarf but left her knit cap on and rooted through her shoulder bag for a pen. When she finally found one, it wouldn't write.

Balzic gave her one of his.

"Boy, wait'll I tell my folks about this."

"Forget about them. They can't help you now."

"Oh—where do—okay. Okay. So why did you call this press conference?"

"I didn't. The mayor did."

"Well why did *he* call it?"

"Miss Meekner, here's your first lesson in asking questions. Don't ever ask a person why his boss did something. The only way you'll get a straight answer—the only way you might get a straight answer—would be if it's off the record. So, knowing that, any other answer is gonna be bull."

"Oh. I never thought about—well, okay. So what happened last night? Did something happen last night? I mean, was there somebody murdered last night?"

"Yes, there was." And Balzic went on to explain all that he knew, while admitting at length that what he knew was not much at all. He finished by saying, "Listen, if you could help us out, I'd really appreciate it."

"You want me to help you? How am I—I mean, what could I do?"

"You go to the state police barracks and you ask for Walker Johnson—he's the officer in charge of the Criminal Investigation Division—and you tell him I sent you and he's to give you a photograph of the girl. Then you get your boss to put it on page two at least, no farther back than that, and put something in there asking if anybody knows this girl to get in touch with me or with Johnson. See? That's all there is to it. And you'd really be doing us a big favor.

" 'Cause the truth is," Balzic said, "we really have no idea who this girl is. We can't notify her family, we can't even start to work on finding out who did this to her. I mean, that girl wasn't any older than you are."

"I don't know. I don't know if I can," Judy Meekner said. "If there's one thing Mr. Murray hates, it's for somebody to get free advertising in a news story. That's all he's been telling me all week about all this stuff I've been rewriting. No advertising. No puff stuff. And this would be like—I don't know—don't you think it would? I don't know. Maybe not. I guess not."

"Look," Balzic said, "you just get the picture from Lieutenant Johnson and give it to your boss and tell him I said to run it on page two at least. Better yet on page one, but no farther back than two, okay? And if he says anything, you tell him to call me. Now what could be easier than that?"

"I don't know," the girl said, almost singsong fashion. "But, okay. I'll tell him to call you. Only you have to help me, too."

"Sure. Name it."

"You have to tell me where the state police barracks is."

Christ, Balzic thought, Murray must've been desperate to hire this one—or drunk. Not, in Murray's case, that the two conditions were mutually exclusive. Balzic put aside his thoughts about Murray's present state of mind and drew a crude map for the girl and explained to her at length about how easily she would find her way to Troop A headquarters.

"I don't know," the girl said. "I get lost all the time."

"Uh-huh. Well. All you gotta do, if you get lost, is get to a phone and call 911 or the operator. Either one, they'll help you out. But I guarantee, you follow my map, you won't get lost."

Balzic walked her down to her car and practically led her out to Main Street out of the parking lot to make sure she got started in the right direction. He shook his head in wonder and disbelief as she drove off, and then he went inside City Hall to the duty room to await some word from either Coroner Grimes or Walker Johnson.

Balzic nosed around for some minutes in the log on Royer's desk and tossed it down with a sigh.

"How'd it go?" Royer said, fighting to contain a grin.

"How'd what go?"

"You know. The, uh, the—upstairs." Royer jerked his thumb toward the ceiling.

"Now how the hell do you think it went? I mean, there were about a thousand news guys who did not show up. His Excellency, the King of Fitness, he is what you call pissed. He just found out he's about as interesting as snow in the wintertime. He found out he's news when he wins an election, but that's the end of it. So he's pissed. There isn't anything, usually, can piss you off faster than reality, Joseph, me boy."

"You mean," said Royer, "that that little air-head girl was the only one showed up?"

"Where were you? They had to walk past you to get upstairs. How many came past you?"

"I was in the can for a little while. I thought maybe somebody else showed up."

Balzic was going to make a crack about Royer's absence, but the phone rang. Royer answered it and told Balzic to pick up an extension.

"Grimes," Royer said.

"Yes, Doc. Balzic. Whatta you got?"

"Not much more than my first observations at the scene last evening, Mario. Massive loss of brain matter as a result of gunshot, massive hemorrhaging, massive damage to brain, entry wound approximately the size of a .38 caliber, but all other indications are that it was a hollow point .357 Magnum bullet. And I say that because the loss of the occipital bone was extensive. I can give you exact dimensions if you like—"

"No, that's okay. Didn't find any fragments of the bullet, then?"

"No. I didn't think I would last night, and I didn't. That cartridge is simply too powerful and too fast."

"Anything else about the girl?"

"Nothing unusual. You saw what she was. Not much dental work if identification becomes a problem. And she had had no surgery. She was an extremely heavy smoker. Other than that, there were no physical problems. That's about it."

"She didn't put up a beef, huh? Didn't grab any—"

"Oh no. She was shot from at least two to three feet away. She never touched anybody in duress. Sorry."

"Okay, Doc. D'you call Johnson up the State CID?"

"Just this moment before I called you."

"Uh, Doc, in case their pictures didn't turn out, did you photograph her face?"

"Of course, Mario. I always do."

"No, what I mean is, d'you get a picture in such a way that we could show it to people and put it in the paper even, and they wouldn't get sick?"

"Oh yes. A full frontal of the face would show only the black circle of the entry wound. No, it wouldn't be offensive. So if you need one, you can make copies of mine."

"I don't think we will, but I just wanted to make sure. Okay, Doc. Thanks very much."

Balzic depressed the receiver buttons and then dialed

the state police and asked for Walker Johnson.

"What's the good news, Walk?"

"I could take early retirement in two years, how's that?"

"Oh that's sweet. And then whatta you do? Get a job in front of some mill checking ID's at the gate?"

"There are worse ways to go, Mario."

"Yeah? For instance?"

"Oh, I've always had this terrible, terrible fear that the day before I was supposed to start drawing my pension I'd get called out to some damn, dumb domestic bullshit and catch one in the neck and spend the rest of my days in a rehab center trying to learn to write with a pencil in my teeth."

"Jesus Christ, you've got some top-shelf fears there. Hell, I was only kidding."

"You never think about shit like that?"

"Not when I'm sober."

"What's that mean?"

"It means what it sounds like. When I'm sober I don't let myself think about shit like that. When I get drunk, now that's different."

"Well come on, tell me what you're scared of. I told you, goddammit. I want to hear yours."

"What the hell is this, Walk? We don't have anything better to do? Kee-rist. What's new on that girl?"

"Ha. Everything we find out'll be new. We don't know anything, and I do mean anything. We talked to everybody for two blocks up and down and sideways and all we got was more of the stuff we were getting last night: one shot, two shots, somebody yelling, nobody yelling, one car door, two cars, two car doors. Shit. Soon as one of my people gets back with her clothes, we'll start checking labels, but that, hell, you know what our chances are there."

"Uh, what about the bullet?"

"Oh shit, that just disintegrated into the bricks and

blocks. That had to be a .357 at least. Maybe bigger. But it was damn sure nothing smaller. It went through, oh, I'm guessing, but I'd say probably one brick and two cinder blocks. The hole in there was at least sixteen inches deep. We'd have to tear that whole wall down and there's still no guarantee we'd find anything but lead and copper powder."

"I thought I heard one of your guys say he could stick his finger in the hole last night."

"That's what he said. I was standing right beside you when he said it. But he didn't say he could touch anything but the sides."

"Well, so much for that," Balzic said. "We're not doing too good. Oh, by the way, I just sent a young kid reporter up to see you to get a mug shot of that girl, and we'll see if we can't get it on page two of the paper. Way it stands right now, that's about it."

"I think we got one maybe isn't bad, but there was a lot of blood, Mario. I think your reporter'd do better with one from Grimes. He had to wash that blood off before he took his pictures. I think we'd do better if we got one from him and let the paper have it, don't you?"

"Yeah, I guess—"

"Well, I'm gonna call Grimes and tell him to give a picture to my man going for her clothes. Say. I want to ask you about something."

"What's that?"

"Those burglaries you were talking about yesterday right before you left. What the hell was that all about?"

"I don't know anymore than I told you. Some dope dealer got his apartment knocked over by two guys after two other guys and a woman led him away in front of a piece. Then about an hour later, I got a call that another apartment, decorated just like the first one, it got knocked over too. Both cases, the complaint came from a neighbor.

"So then," Balzic went on, "while I go check this first

one out with one of my detectives, we get a bunch of bullshit from a state narc named Gensheimer about how he went to lunch or supper or whatever meal break he was on while he had this place staked out."

"And that's it?"

"That's all I have now. I haven't heard anything from my detective yet."

"Well why d'you even mention all this last night? I really don't understand that."

"I don't understand it either. But it was the only weird thing that happened yesterday before that girl bought it, and I just thought I'd mention it to you. You want to check it out, why don't you call that asshole in charge of this region for the state narcs and find out what he knows."

"Why don't you call him?"

" 'Cause I don't want to talk to the sonofabitch, that's why. He's a fucking asshole and I've already had trouble with him and I don't ever want to even see him again, let alone have to talk to him."

"My, you're touchy about this. You mean Rilkin?"

"That's him. That's the asshole."

"Well, Mario, you gotta understand these drug guys. They're always on the make without a complaint. So they're all a little nuts, you know? They all got cricks in their necks from looking behind them and peeking around corners and shaking down dealers and figuring out which of their buddies they can trust and which'll blow their brains away for a pound of white powder. You know? You just gotta know how to treat paranoid people, that's all. Wups, here's your little girl reporter. I'll talk to you, Mario."

Balzic nodded at the click and hung the phone up. He sat for a long moment staring at it, as though that act would help him generate a coherent thought about the events of the past several days. He was just starting to stand up when he remembered Carlucci and Fischetti and the two apartments, and wondered why he had not heard from them.

"Hey, Joe," Balzic said, standing and going over to the duty rosters posted on the bulletin board. "Fischetti still working three to eleven? What about Carlucci?" He flipped through the roster but couldn't find what he was looking for and turned away from it, because he thought Royer would recall the information more quickly than it could be found. He was right.

"This is Fischetti's day off. Carlucci'll be working his usual stuff. He called while you were talking on the phone."

"What'd he say?"

"He said he was still looking and still couldn't find anything, but he wanted me to be sure and tell you he was still looking. He said something like, oh, something about he finds this Burns guy fascinating. Yeah. Whatever the hell that means."

"I know what it means." Balzic looked at Royer for a moment and then said, "Hey, whatta you know about this goddamn mayor? You know anything about him?"

"I don't know any more than anybody else. Probably a lot less. Why?"

"What I mean, do you know what he does? I mean, I don't know anything about this guy except that he's a runner and he doesn't know shit about anything."

"All I know is he's in business for himself. Must do all right at it." Royer shrugged. "He really busted his hump campaigning, I know that."

Balzic stuck his hands in his pockets and rocked from his toes to his heels and back. "I wonder if he learned anything from that fiasco this morning."

Royer laughed silently, his shoulders and head bobbing. "I bet it'll be a while before he calls another press conference. But what do I know? I mean, why the hell would anybody bust his ass to get a job that only paid a buck a year? That's all ego, if you ask me."

"You really think that's what it is with this guy—ego?"

Royer shrugged again. "Hell, the only mayor I ever knew was Bellotti. And he had the most serious case of ego I ever saw. That man just loved for people to say, 'Good morning, Mister Mayor.' 'Hiya doin', Mister Mayor.' He just sucked it up. But I don't know about this guy. He hasn't said two words to me."

"Wish the hell I could say that," Balzic grumbled. "Ah piss on it. I'm going to find Carlucci. Did he say which one of those two apartments he was gonna be at?"

"Yeah. I wrote it down here. The one, uh, the one by the hospital."

"Good enough," Balzic said, heading toward the door. "If His Honor wants me, I'm lost."

Balzic fairly sprinted to his cruiser to get away without encountering the mayor. Once in the car and moving, he knew that he was acting foolishly; the truth was that at that moment he had no idea where the mayor was. For all he knew, Mayor Kenny Strohn may have gone into hiding in embarrassment over the fact that only one reporter showed up for his first press conference. But that aside, most certainly the mayor was not going to spend his days in his public office in a job that paid a dollar a year—no matter how big his ego. Each hour spent in his public office was one less spent in his own, and no man could indulge his ego that much.

Balzic made a note to do some checking on this mayor— if for no other reason than to know where Strohn was if Balzic needed him. That settled in his mind, Balzic forgot about it. He had something else he wanted to check, if only to dismiss it as one thing less to be concerned about later on. He drove to Conemaugh General Hospital's parking lot for doctors only, parked on a yellow line, and hurried in to see the coroner. Grimes wasn't in, but one of the interns assigned to him was, and Balzic asked to see the pictures Grimes had taken of the girl shot on South Main. Balzic found one of the girl taken full-face, and another of her profile. He pocketed them, thanked the intern, headed for his car, and then drove on to the apartment where yesterday he'd first heard of Thurman Burns, the apartment with the mirrors and the stainless steel and the burgundy velour drapes and the burgundy and black upholstered furniture.

Balzic parked across the street and tried to locate an unmarked four-door sedan that would have indicated the state Bureau of Drug Enforcement was still interested. He couldn't find one.

He hurried across the street—the wind had picked up, and was gusting and swirling and stinging cold—and into the foyer of the old, gray-stone house. Just inside he found Carlucci talking to a young woman, who was looking around her door, exposing only her face.

"Oh, uh, Chief, this is, uh, this is Miss Raymond. The nurse? Remember?"

"Yeah, yeah, I remember. The one who saw all these strange happenings yesterday."

"Am I going to have to tell everything to you too?" Miss Raymond said, none too pleasantly. "I really have to get some sleep. I mean, I—"

"I'm sure you do, Miss Raymond. But I want you to tell me what you saw yesterday—"

"But I told him three times already!"

"Yes, I know, but I'd like you to tell me."

"Oh come on! I told him three times today and twice yesterday. What do you want from me?"

"Miss Raymond, all I want from you is for you to tell me what you told Detective Carlucci here, nothing more, nothing less, okay?"

Miss Raymond sighed noisily. "Okay. All right. But this is it. I mean it. After this, forget it. I have got to get some sleep, okay? Okay?"

"Okay, okay. So the sooner you tell me, the sooner you get to sleep. So tell me."

"Okay. They woke me up with their knocking—"

"They? Which they?"

"Two guys and a girl."

"After you woke up you came to the door and looked through your peep hole, right?"

"Right. Yes. I thought, uh, the knocking was so loud, I thought it was on my door. So I got out of bed and I put on my robe and I came and looked out the peephole. And, uh . . ."

"And that's when you saw the gun? That's what kept you there at your peephole looking, right? You saw the—"

"The gun, yes. That's exactly what I did."

"And then what?"

"And then the door opened a little bit, just a crack, and the girl started talking about a wreck. She said she hit his car with her car, or what kind of car did he have, or something like that, 'cause she hit somebody's car and she just couldn't run away without finding out whose car it was."

"Where was the gun? Who was holding it, and where was he standing?"

"Uh, on the other side of the door."

"You saw the gun clearly? No mistake in your mind, it was a gun?"

"Oh no. No mistake. Absolutely not."

"You familiar with guns, Miss Raymond?"

"Familiar? Did I ever shoot one or hold one? Like that familiar?"

Balzic nodded slowly.

"No. But it was very big and very shiny, very metallic—it was not a toy—and the one holding it was very nervous, his fingers were going up and down on the handle and he was licking his lips and I think shivering a little bit."

"What was the other fellow doing?"

"Nothing. He was just standing there. He had his back to me."

"Where were his hands?"

"In his pockets."

"Coat pockets, pants pockets?"

"What difference does that make?"

"Just tell me if you remember, that's all."

"Coat pockets."

"You sure?"

"Yes. I am. But I don't see what dif—"

"Then what happened?"

"Huh? Oh. Well, for a long time he didn't want to open the door. He was very suspicious. Very suspicious."

"But he did finally."

"Yes. And the second he did, the one with the gun put it right against his face and said something to him, I don't remember what. I just remember at that time I was thinking, my God, they're going to shoot him right here, right in front of me, what am I going to do. And so I started looking very carefully at their faces."

"Carlucci tells me you're an art student, is that right? You're taking an art class or something?"

"Yes. A portrait class and a life study class. And I'm telling myself at the time to study them like I would a model."

"And you did?"

"Yes, that's what I'm telling you."

Balzic reached into his pocket for the photos he'd taken from the coroner's office. "Was this the girl?"

"Oh . . . oh wow. She looks, uh, she looks—is she?"

"Yes, she's dead. These pictures were taken by the coroner last night. Is that the girl?"

Miss Raymond nodded slowly. "Yes, it is. She's really got a great face. But boy that black spot sure looks ugly."

Balzic had truly not expected that answer. He had brought along the pictures to separate this gunshot victim from these two burglaries. He didn't know what to say for a long moment.

Finally he said, "It's not as ugly as the other side, but it's ugly enough. Miss Raymond, before you go to sleep, tell me again. Is this the girl you saw in this foyer yesterday?"

"That's her. Definitely."

"And you'd say that in front of a magistrate, if you had to?"

"Sure, why not?"

"Okay, we'll probably be talking to you again. And thank you very much."

"You're welcome—I hope." Miss Raymond pulled her face from view and closed her door.

Carlucci looked at Balzic and said, "What the hell's going on? How'd you think of this?"

"I didn't think of anything. I just thought I wanted to make sure these things were not connected. Honest to Christ, I said to myself, get these mug shots up here so this nurse can say she never saw this girl, so we could forget about tying these things together—no shit, Rugs. I'm not joking. That's the last thing I thought I was gonna hear. Ha boy, now I don't know what to think."

Balzic turned away from Carlucci and stared out the front door glass at the street. He turned back to Carlucci and nodded toward the door to Thurman Burns's apartment.

Without prompting, Carlucci found a key in his pocket and unlocked the door. They went in and Balzic dropped onto one of the black leather couches. "So tell me about this guy. What'd you tell Royer—he was 'fascinating'? Is that what you said?"

"Yeah. He is. Pittsburgh vice guys got a small book on

this guy. A thousand rumors, a hundred leads, a dozen tips, and a couple of arrests. But no convictions. And they admit they had nothing on this guy when they arrested him. They were trying to shake him up."

"And he doesn't shake."

"Nope. He knows the law and he knows himself. He doesn't smoke, he doesn't drink, he doesn't inhale anything, he doesn't swallow anything, he doesn't stick any needles in himself. Everytime they picked him up, they gave him a physical, they tested his urine, they tested his blood, you know what he told 'em? This'll kill you. I mean, it really shows what kind of mind he got. He told them, something like, 'Go ahead and take my liquids, but someday this'll go to the Supreme Court and you guys will get the bad news that taking my urine violates my right not to incriminate myself under the Fifth Amendment.' How do you like that? Huh? That guy's got a hell of a mind."

"Hey, I don't want you getting too impressed with this guy, Rugsy."

"Mario, you told me a long time ago: you got to admire some of these guys. Their skill, their intelligence, their—"

"I know, I know," Balzic said. "But not so you lose your perspective, all right? So tell me about this guy. What's his hustle?"

"Apparently, a little of everything. Street dealer, shipper, wholesaler, importer, the whole number. Spends a lot of time in Florida and a lot of time in Pittsburgh hanging out at airports, Greater Pitt and Miami. Hangs around with pilots and flight attendants. He has himself undergone six complete body searches at Greater Pitt, and nobody has ever turned up so much as an aspirin. And he never complains. And he never says he's gonna write a letter to his congressman or call his lawyer. He just submits to the search, gets dressed, and goes on his way. What the Pittsburgh vice guys think is he's got the flight attendants bringing it up for him. But they don't know. They can't prove it one way or another. They just keep watching him."

"I assume you're talking about cocaine now. You wouldn't be talking about marijuana, am I right?"

Carlucci nodded. "Oh sure."

"Well, either his flight attendant friends are carrying for him, or else the whole business with hanging around airports and pilots is a front. Why don't the drug guys go after one of the flight crews?"

"I don't know," Carlucci said.

"Well, shit, they're all just blowing smoke then. So what else?"

"He's got a lot of money. Pays cash for everything and he likes a lot of different things. All expensive. Plus the obvious fact that he doesn't have a job. Plus the even more obvious fact that he pays a whole lot of income taxes. Guess what he says his employment is?"

"Go ahead. I see you're impressed."

"No shit, listen to this. This is balls, man. It really is. He says he's a self-employed consultant on wholesaling and retailing. How's that for jackin' everybody off, huh?"

"Jesus Christ, Rugsy, maybe you should have a couple thousand eight-by-ten glossies made up of this guy. He can autograph 'em and you can sell 'em."

"Come on, Mario. You know what I'm saying."

"Yeah? What are you saying? You admire this guy? Huh? Well, knock it off. Or else do it on your own time." Balzic looked around the apartment. "Hey, Rugs, what'd you find out about the narcos on this one?"

Carlucci shrugged. "Not much. I haven't really been getting too much cooperation. The three guys working hardest on Burns are, uh, one William Cortese, one Michael Franks, and one Frank Gensheimer—him, you met. They got a lot in common. They're all pretty young, under thirty, all college educated, all eager as hell, not too much experience. Gensheimer not even six months. Cortese less than a year. Franks is the veteran. He's got two years. He's also the oldest. He's twenty-eight. They're also all from Pittsburgh."

"Anything smell?"

Carlucci shook his head no. "If there is, nobody I know has smelled it. Nah, these guys may not be too bright, but they're not on the make either—at least not so anybody's noticed."

"Are you getting this from your Pittsburgh friends or what?"

"No. I haven't even talked to them yet. This is all local news so far. Most of it I got from your buddy Russell."

Balzic nodded.

"The only thing Russell said was that professionally he didn't have anything against these guys, but personally he didn't really, I mean, he couldn't really say what he thought of them. He said he thought they were all a little too young for their own good. But I figured that's just Russell's way of talking. I don't think he meant anything by it."

"Rugsy," Balzic said, squinting at Carlucci, "you're holding out on me."

"What? C'mon. What're you talking about?" Carlucci laughed.

"Cut the bullshit. What else you know about these guys? And where'd you get it from?"

Carlucci scratched his scalp and then rubbed the bridge of his nose and stared at the floor. "Hey. This is strictly early information, okay? Not to be held against me later on, all right?"

"Will you cut it out! Who's listening here but me? C'mon, man, if you've heard something, let's have it."

"Okay, okay. The early word on this Michael Franks is not good. His evidence comes up a little short on weight.

And sometimes it comes up a lot short. Remember what I said, now. This is the early word."

"How good is it?"

"Generally, very good. And in two instances, the voice is only two removed from the guys who got grabbed with the weight."

"How much weight? Rugsy, you got to spell this stuff out for me," Balzic protested. "I don't know from yesterday about this drug stuff."

"Well, okay. The one bust occurred three months ago. There was a hundred pounds of grass involved. Franks was the arresting agent, but at the magistrate's hearing only twenty pounds was introduced."

"So?" Balzic said. "Maybe he didn't feel like carrying one hundred pounds around."

"No, no, you don't understand. It was broken down into bricks—you know what a brick is?"

"No."

"That's a kilogram. Two-point-three-two pounds."

"So?"

"So when the, uh, bust was made, nothing had been packaged. It was in a bale. This guy Franks, or somebody he knew, was breaking it down into bricks, and that's what he showed up at the hearing with. And the testimony at the hearing was that only twenty pounds had been confiscated. Now you see?"

Balzic ran his tongue over his front teeth and nodded. "The other information the same?"

"Yes. The numbers change. The disparity is even bigger. That happened last month."

"This information is not from Russell?"

"No, no. This is from my guys."

"D'you check it out against the testimony in the hearings?"

"Not yet, but I'm working on it."

"Uh-huh. So. So tell me, Rugsy, whatta you think?"

"Right now I don't think anything. I'm still asking questions. But one thing I think is, it was really convenient for Gensheimer to go buy supper when he did. And before you say anything, I'm telling you right now, this is all the speculating I'm gonna do."

"Okay, Rugs, okay. You know what you're doing. What do you want from me? Anything?"

"Yeah. Give me the pictures of that girl. I want to show them to somebody."

"Done," Balzic said, handling both photos over. "Anything else?"

Carlucci's eyebrows went up, and he shrugged. "Lean on your buddy Russell. I think he wants to say something, but he thinks he can't say it to me."

"Okay, that's no problem. What else?"

Carlucci shook his head. "That's it. Just gonna confirm the early word or not. Either way it's gonna be a million phone calls and a lotta riding around. Oh, one thing you can do. Call my mother and tell her that it's your fault I'm working so many hours, and that's why I haven't been over to see her for the last couple days."

"Come on, Rugs, for crissake. Take a break. Give yourself an hour off and go see her. I don't want to call her up and give her that baloney. Go see her."

"Well, to tell the truth, I don't want to go see her. When I haven't seen her for a couple days, boy, she really gets on my ass about it. And the older she gets, the worse it gets. No, really. Call her, please? I'd owe you one."

"All right. I'll call her. Hey, I gotta go. Let me hear from you, all right?"

Carlucci left first, going wherever it was he was going, and Balzic followed, stopping first at a drugstore pay phone to call Carlucci's mother to tell her not to worry, her son was fine, but he had important work to do. The nicest thing Mrs. Carlucci called him was "slavedriver"; some of the other things she said were not things Balzic would have guessed she had even heard, let alone used. "Prick" was one of them. Coming from a seventyish-year-old woman, the word took on a different tone, one Balzic believed he could have lived just as nicely without ever having heard.

Then he called Lieutenant Walker Johnson to ask about progress on that end. Johnson's vocabulary was more polite than Mrs. Carlucci's, but his tone was about the same. He had been getting what he thought was a monumental snow job from AIC Rilkin of the Bureau of Drug Enforcement. Johnson was debating—while talking to Balzic—how far over Rilkin's head to go to get the information he wanted, and the idea of going over Rilkin's head was sufficient to make Johnson aggressive, sullen, and short with Balzic.

Balzic knew better than to push. He hung up with as many wishes for good fortune as he could muster without making himself sound simple.

He went to a clerk who was chewing bubble gum and buffing her fingernails, and asked her for change for a dollar bill. She acted as though she could tolerate his imposition, but only barely. She placed the change on the counter without a word, and went back to her nails.

Balzic was tempted to respond to her rudeness, but thought better of it. He scooped up his change without so much as a glance in the clerk's direction.

He checked his address and phone book for the number of the Bureau of Drug Enforcement, dialed it, asked for Agent Russell, and was told that Russell was out of the office and wasn't expected back until five or so. The speaker asked if there was a message.

Balzic said there was not, and hung up. He rubbed his

chin and then his lips and then his forehead. He could have rubbed his entire body, for all that it mattered; he didn't have the faintest idea what to do next. And when he didn't know what to do, he headed for the place where not knowing what to do was best done, and that was Muscotti's Bar and Grille.

It was the slow time of the day: the lunch crowd had left, and it would be hours before anybody stopping after work showed up. Worse, something had gone wrong with Muscotti's boiler, and the people Balzic thought at first were bar customers were not; they were tenants from apartments on the second and third floors, and they were crankily awaiting Dom Muscotti's arrival.

Vinnie the bartender was being as reasonable and sympathetic as he could be in the circumstances; he was wearing his outer coat and had his hands jammed deep into the pockets. His breath was visible.

"Why the fuck don't youns all go back upstairs? It ain't any warmer down here. And youns ain't gonna get Dom to get the plumbers here any faster than I'm gonna get them, so what d'youse want from me?

"Mario! Whatta you want? You want something? Huh?"

"Jesus Christ, try it a little quieter, you know? I just got here."

"Hey, I'm freezing my ass off here and I got this citizens' committee, this tenants' rights group, they're pissed off at me, like I went and broke the boiler myself, see, 'cause I don't get cold like them, oh no, I like it this fuckin' temperature, so that's how's come I put the boiler on the fritz, and now here you are, and I guess you're gonna want something to drink, huh? Only you can't make up your mind what, so I gotta stand here and get my chain pulled—"

"Hey! Stop! Jesus Christ, I came in here to find a little peace and quiet—"

"Go to church. You'll find a whole building full of peace and quiet."

"—and you give me a whole goddamn opera here about your life today. Jesus, all I want's a little wine, you know? If you didn't break the boiler, Christ knows I didn't either, okay?"

"Yeah, yeah. What kind you want. Red? White? What?"

Balzic sighed noisily. "White. Jesus."

Vinnie brought a glass back and filled it to the edge with a mountain white from California. "Your boss called you little while ago. I told him I ain't seen you for a week. He didn't know what to say. I mean, there was a long, long, long pause, get it? I mean, I'm lying and he knows and he knows I know he knows, get it?"

"So?"

"He said he'd call back."

"That's all?"

"Hey, what more you want? I pulled his chain, he got the message, he said he'd call back. I figure you owe me."

"Terrific. A simple thank-you won't do?"

"Nope. My sister-in-law got a ticket—"

"Aw bullshit. I told you twenty years ago don't ever ask me to fix a ticket—"

"My sister-in-law is—"

"Sister-in-law, mother-in-law, mother—I don't care and you know I don't care—"

"—she's got a half-share in a lot I'm looking at—"

"—I don't care if she got a half-share of the numbers, I don't fix tickets, not twenty years ago, not today, not twenty years from now if I'm so lucky I'm still alive—"

"—but it's a twenty-five dollar ticket for crissake!"

"Pay it! Make yourself look good! Take her the receipt with your name on it—what could be better?"

"Aw, Mario, Jesus Christ—"

"I told you a hundred times—because for some reason

you never believe me and I have to keep telling you—I
don't fix tickets! The trouble is three times more than not
fixing them. It's as simple as that. And before you say it,
the next time the mayor calls, don't exaggerate. A simple
lie will be enough."

"You're a beauty, you are," Vinnie said. "Where's the
bread for the wine?"

"Bread! Wine! The holy marriage," came the voice of
Iron City Steve. "Take eat, this is my bread, my pasta, my
wheat, my flour. Take drink, this is my wine, my blood, my
sweat, my tears, take this bread, this wine—"

"Aw shut the fuck up and take your ass over in the
corner and be still."

"—these are all holy marriages. Liver and onions,
cucumbers and sour cream, chicken and dumplings, muscatel and beer—"

"Don't even look like you want a drink, you—you two-
bit hustler. . . . Look at him, he takes his check to the bank
and blows half of it in some other joints and he comes
back here tapped out and it's three weeks plus until his
next check. Jesus. Go sit down."

Iron City Steve swayed to an inner breeze. His arms
flapped, his fingers sawed the air. "Did you ever think," he
whispered hoarsely to Balzic, "what the world would be if
the Last Supper was hot dogs and beer?"

"They didn't even have hot dogs back then, for crissake.
Whatta you talking about?" Vinnie shouted.

"But what if they did? Or what if it was prunes? Prunes
and muscatel?"

"Oh, shit, go sit down, will ya? Prunes and muscatel, I'm
telling ya. You hear this, Mario? Huh? I gotta listen to this
guy all day long—except when he goes and cashes his
check someplace else, and then I don't see him, no sir!"

"I thought it was gonna be quiet in here," Balzic said. "I
really don't care whether it's cold. But I did think it was

gonna be quiet, so I could maybe do a little thinking."

"It could've been anything," Iron City Steve said. "It could've been potatoes and buttermilk. It wouldn't've made no difference which two he picked—"

"Which two who picked?" Vinnie roared.

"Who was I talkin' about? Jesus. He could've picked anything. He could've picked fish and honey, I mean, who told him to pick bread and wine? And if he'd've picked fish and honey, or potatoes and buttermilk, or, or—"

One of the tenants from upstairs, a very old, very frail, very angry man, stood up at the far end of the bar. In a quaking voice, he did his best to snarl: "Quit that blasphemy, you drunk bastard before I hit you with something!"

"Ha-ha!" Vinnie roared approvingly. "There. Another tenant heard from."

Iron City Steve's head spun. "Oh. It's just him. I thought it was somebody with a brain."

"You got a lotta balls talking about somebody else's brains," Vinnie said. "How much you got left up there?"

"I got this much left," Steve said. "I know what I get for my money. I get drunk. That guy gives all his money to television preachers. Bunch of tent-show hustlers. He thinks they're gonna save his soul. But look at him. The temperature drops twenty degrees, and he's as scared as everybody else he's gonna freeze. You tell me who spends his money better. And he's down there calling me names and making threats, just 'cause I let my mind go and it don't suit him. He's waiting for one of those TV preachers to come out of the set and make him young again and make his arthritis go away and make his blood pressure go down. And he calls me a drunk."

"Which is what you are," Vinnie said.

"I never said I wasn't," Steve said, his elbows flapping, his head going from side to side. "I don't pretend to be

nothing I ain't. I ain't scared to tell the world I'm scared—
like that guy down there. You ask him if he's scared—go
'head, ask him—and he'll tell you some bull about Jesus is
looking out for him so he don't have to be scared. And
watch him puff out his chest and throw back his shoulders
and say he got Jesus on his side and all I got on mine is
what's in a glass. But go tell him Easter is canceled this
year and watch his face. Tell him Easter's a bunch of bull
and watch his eyes and take a deep sniff. What you smell'll
be his pants getting full. That's what kind of brain he got.
And he calls me a drunk!"

"So you ain't a Christian," Vinnie said. "So you're a
drunk. So what else is new?"

"You tell 'em, Vinnie," came the voice from the far end
of the bar.

Iron City Steve's shoulders hitched and jerked, and his
lips and hands quivered. "I ask you a simple question.
What do you think of a father who lets his son be tortured
to prove a point? And if you can explain the crucifixion to
me any other way, I'll shut my mouth forever."

"Somebody better come up with something—fast!" said
Vinnie. "For my sake! C'mon, Mario, come up with
something!"

Balzic shrugged. "Whatta you want me to say? That's
bothered me for a long time. It never bothered me until I
had kids. Then, every Easter, I'd go to church and hear
that business about God giving his only begotten son for
our sins—boy, I'll tell you, that's hard to figure. I mean,
you put it in those terms, I don't have any idea what could
make me want to sacrifice one of my girls for."

"See there?" Iron City Steve said. "See there? There's a
father talking! And a whole religion's been built on that
kind of torture. And guys standing down there, not twenty
feet away, they give their last dimes to them TV tent
preachers, and they call me names. And here's a father

right here—and a good man too, don't forget that—he's no
damn crook. He's a cop. An honest man. No damn liar just
cause it makes him feel good."

"At ease, at ease, for crissake," Vinnie said. "It's starting
to sound like Channel 13 in here. Bunch of got-damn
intellectuals, that's what it's starting to sound like in here."

"Give us a drink," Balzic said.

"Us?" Vinnie said. "Is that you and me? Or is that you
and your buddy, the drunk non-believer there?"

"That's all three," Balzic said, pointing to himself, Steve,
and Vinnie. "And why don't you ask the tenants' rights
group if they'll have something too?"

"Shit, forget them," Vinnie said, dismissing the tenants
with a wave of his hand. "They don't go for nothing. It's
us here." He poured for himself, Balzic, and Iron City
Steve.

Steve raised his muscatel high. "If any of us gets cruci-
fied, I pray there's a friend nearby with a shotgun."

"Amen," said Balzic, nodding his head and hoisting his
glass. "Better yet, let's pray there's a friend around with a
bag of money before anybody starts hammering."

"Now you're talking," Vinnie said, raising his glass high.
"Bribery. That's the answer."

"A wise and practical prayer," Steve said, nodding and
taking a long drink of his thick wine. "Wise and practical.
Yessir. Yessiree. The best kind."

   Balzic was brought up short out of his
slightly drunken reverie by Vinnie's words that the phone
call was for him.

"Huh? What?"

"The phone. You know? The black thing you talk into?
Under the bar? It's for you."

"It isn't, uh—"

"No, it ain't him. I think it's Rugsy."

Balzic did his best to hurry to the end of the bar, and reached for the phone. "Rugsy? This you?"

"Yeah. The pictures are a zero. I knew it was a long shot. But my guys are definite. They never saw her."

"Aw, that's too bad, Rugs. I'm sorry."

"Hey, don't apologize. It's not your—"

"What about Franks? Anything new on him?"

"Nothing hard. But nobody likes him. There is definitely something unlikeable about him. But I still haven't talked to my guys in Pittsburgh."

"Well, keep pitching."

"You talk to Russell yet?"

"Not yet. But I will. If not today, then tomorrow. I'll try him again before five."

"Hey, Mario, I don't want to say anything out of line, but it was five o'clock five minutes ago."

"What? Oh Christ. Talk to you later." Balzic hung up and tried to think what he'd been doing since he'd come into Muscotti's. All he could remember was a conversation with Iron City Steve about something religious. Christ, how much have I drunk, he asked himself. He wasn't even feeling very cold—and, given the hunched-over, huddled-up appearance of the few people at the bar, not feeling cold was not a good sign.

He found his address book, got the number of the Bureau of Drug Enforcement, and dialed it before Vinnie had a chance to complain about him not using the pay phone.

Balzic got a message that Russell had left for the day; what was worse, he also learned that Russell's home phone number was not his for the asking.

"Goddammit, this is official," Balzic said. "I'm the chief of Rocksburg PD, and I got to talk to him. If you won't give me his number then, goddammit, you give him my number and you tell him to call me. It's urgent. You got that?"

"Hey, buddy. I don't care who you're chief of. Go fuck yourself."

Balzic looked stupidly at the phone for several seconds before he hung it up. "Days like this," he said to himself, "used to not happen as often. I really think they didn't. But I'm probably not right about that either."

He went back to his seat at the bar, and looked at his glass. It was almost empty. He motioned to Vinnie to come over and he asked him, "How many of these have I had?"

Vinnie shrugged. "I don't know. A couple. Why?"

"I just lost some time there. I don't know where it went."

"Oh, you were sitting there staring for a while. But you wasn't drinking nothing. You were just staring. I figured I'd let you alone."

Balzic chewed the inside of his cheek and nodded. "Uh-huh. Well, give me another one. Maybe I'll remember what I was trying to forget."

"Don't bet on it," Vinnie said, filling Balzic's glass. "Sometimes I get like that after a couple drinks myself. Not every time, you understand, but every once in a while. It's like I been asleep or something. Sometimes I think I had one of those little strokes they show you in those TV commercials. Yeah. No shit. You're laughing."

"No, I'm not laughing. But it's just, uh, that's the way it felt to me. Like I was—like I had a stroke and couldn't remember what the hell I'd done for the last hour or so. Jesus Christ, this is scary, you know? Who'd I talk to besides Steve—anybody?"

"Nah, nobody."

Balzic screwed up his face and whistled softly. "Jesus, I'm supposed to be finding a murderer, and running a police department, and I can't even remember what the hell I was doing for the last hour. How long d'you think I'd keep this job if this got out?"

"Hold the job? Shit," Vinnie said, snorting. "You let that stuff out, you won't have to worry about your job. You'll be worrying about whether they're ever gonna take the straitjacket off."

Balzic was at home when Russell of the Bureau of Drug Enforcement called. It was almost seven, and Balzic was just finishing his rigatoni.

"Hey, Russell, I didn't think I'd hear from you for, oh—"

"I heard about your little thing with the guy from my office. He's okay. Just got no patience, no manners. So whatta you want?"

"You been talking to my guy Carlucci, right?"

"Yeah. He's called me a couple times. Why?"

"He thinks you're holding out on him."

"What? Ah c'mon. About what?"

"About your guy Franks. Carlucci's no dummy, you know? He thinks you want to say something, but it sounds to him like you don't want to say it to him. Does that sound right?"

There was no answer.

"Hey, Russell, if you want to say something about the guy, go ahead and say it. I mean, Carlucci got enough on him already about evidence coming up way short of weight in front of several different magistrates, you know? Carlucci's out checking testimony now. But he tells me that the message on Franks on the street is he's not to be trusted—by anybody."

Again, there was no answer.

"Hey, Russell, you still there?"

"Yeah, yeah, I'm still here."

"So say something!"

"Whatta you want me to say?"

"I don't care if you say it not for the record. Just for me. I don't care—"

"The fuck you don't, Mario. Anything I say you're gonna use. Not officially, but you'll find some way to use it. You're too old to change now."

"That's some opinion you got of me."

"Mario, knock it off. Come on. What can I tell you? This guy, this Franks, uh, he, uh, he's got some noses open."

"How's that?"

"You said it yourself. He turns up at hearings with, uh, maybe ten percent of what he confiscates. He's got a fierce arrest record. I mean, he busts 'em, boy. All over the place. But his conviction rate, well, that's a different matter. Always something seems to go wrong with either his warrants or with the improper searches. I can't say this officially—because I really haven't checked the numbers myself—but his prosecution-to-arrest record is about one to thirty. I mean, he's not even trying to be subtle."

"So whose noses are open?" Balzic said.

"I don't want to say."

"Aw come on. You've told me—"

"I haven't told you anything you couldn't have guessed, I mean, considering what you already know from your Carlucci. But I'm not gonna give you any—"

"Is he under active investigation? Just tell me that."

"Yes."

"Does Rilkin know about it?"

"I don't know."

"Who does know about it?"

"I don't—I can't say. But people are looking at him."

"How close are they looking? Is he being watched?"

"Yes."

"Since when?"

"Since today. Word came down today. Twenty-four-hour surveillance."

"But not before today?"

"No. Definitely not."

"Why today? What happened today?"

"What do I know today? Who said something had to happen today? Christ, if anybody knows how decisions are made, you ought to. We got the word today for something that could've got started six months ago."

"That sounds like a bullshit answer to me."

"Come on, Mario, huh? Fuck you. I shouldn't even be telling you any of this and I swear to Christ you tell anybody I told you and I tell the whole world—I'll look your mother right in her eyes with my hand on a Bible and I'll tell her you're lying. I mean it. Friendship can only go so—"

"Yeah, yeah, take it easy. Just remember, I'm the guy with a dead girl on his hands, you know? I won't screw you. But I want to know what you can tell me. And, uh, that brings me to Franks's partners lately. Cortese, I believe, and Gensheimer. What about them?"

All Balzic heard was a long, muffled sigh.

"Well?"

"Well what?"

"What about 'em, huh? C'mon, for crissake, Russell. Tell me something. Knowledge is what I don't have. I need it."

"Them, too."

"Since today?"

"Same order."

"Uh, who signed that order?"

"Some deputy attorney general in Harrisburg, I don't know. It doesn't make any difference. It wasn't a local order. Is that all? Huh? Can I take a break now?"

"Who's gonna get a sore ass all from this? Your guys?"

"C'mon. Are you kiddin' me? They're sending guys in from Scranton or Philadelphia or someplace. There are only four people—five including you—who know about this here. Rilkin, me, and two guys you don't know."

"Uh, I'm curious. How's that asshole Rilkin taking all this?"

"Don't even talk about it. Franks was one of his boys. Now he's got to act like everything's cool at the same time he knows he's responsible for Franks. You know how that's gonna go. All I know is, if it turns out that Franks and Cortese and that other guy are dealing, Rilkin is not gonna be easy to live with. Mario, I'm done talking. Enough's enough."

"Okay, okay. Hey, I thank you. I mean it."

"Yeah, sure. Just keep it between us, huh? That's all I ask."

Balzic gave his word and hung up. Before his hand left the phone, it was ringing. He hoped it was somebody calling for one of his daughters. It wasn't.

"Mario, Carlucci. What're you doing? Never mind. You got to come meet me. I got somebody you need to talk to."

"Aw, Rugs. Right now?"

"This man waits for no man. Not even you. And you, he's scared of."

"Rugs, Jesus Christ, what's this—never mind. Where?"

"A little black joint down the river about six miles. You know who I mean?"

Balzic grumbled and sighed. "Yes I know. Rufee's. But I'll tell you right now, I don't look forward to this."

"Hey, Mario, you wanna know about wine, you go to the vintner. You wanna know about dope, you go to the dopers. And, uh, try to make it fast, okay? I don't feature sitting in there by myself, you know? Even if I am sitting with the main man. There are some guys in there coked up to their molars, and they're drinking rum right behind it. So hurry up, okay?"

"Be there in twelve, fifteen minutes. I got to change clothes."

Balzic apologized to his family, and went into the bedroom and changed back into his working clothes: a suit, white shirt, dark tie, raincoat, fedora, and thick-soled, plain-toed, black shoes. Once out of the house and calling over his shoulder that no one should wait up for him, he quickly got into his cruiser and drove off, stopping as soon as he was out of sight of his house.

He put on the parking brake and went back to the trunk, opened it, and took out his three-foot-long riot baton. He closed and locked the trunk, tossed the baton on the front seat, and drove off. From that moment it took him ten minutes to drive into one of the three or four parking lots surrounding Rufee's.

Rufee's was a nondescript three-story brick house that was situated near the Conemaugh River in an incorporated village known to mapmakers and whites as Frick Mine Four. To the residents, half of whom were black, and to the tourists, nearly all of whom were black, Frick Mine Four was known as Buzzardtown.

Rufee's had no signs announcing its existence. One either knew where one was going and so went there, or one was taken there by somebody who knew where to go.

Rufee's only concession to white society was its liquor license. Aside from that, it did not exist. Its liquor license listed the address merely as Frick Mine Four, Conemaugh County, and the owner as Robert Feeler, a cousin of Rufee's who had been in and out of mental hospitals for half his life. Since no Liquor Control Board agent had ever cited Rufee's for a violation, and since any business Rufee had with the Liquor Control Board was carried out in Harrisburg by Rufee's attorneys, no mail was ever delivered. Since Rufee had not believed in telephones ever since somebody had shown him that one of his was tapped, there were no phones in the place. There was, instead, a pay booth in the parking lot farthest from the house. If you wanted to make a phone call, that was where you went to make it. If you wanted to call somebody in Rufee's, you found out the number of that pay phone and called it. The phone would be answered by one of three old men who took eight-hour turns sitting in a heated shack nearby, and who were paid to answer it. They were also paid never to deliver messages to anyone but Rufee. If you had a message for someone in Rufee's, you had to deliver it yourself, and you had to deliver it quietly. Raising a voice meant instant eviction. That rule was inviolable. Not only had no one ever been murdered in Rufee's, no one had ever been assaulted—except by Rufee's bouncers, about whom it was said by policemen of several departments that they could spot impending violence faster than any Secret Serviceman assigned to protect a president.

Rufee's was the center of black night music in Buzzard-town as well as many surrounding municipalities, including Rocksburg. It was not the center of black music rehashed by white imitators who then sold it back to blacks; it was a sanctuary for black musicians who played the blues for free after they tired of playing other things for money. Big Maybelle sang "You Ain't Nothin' But a Hound Dawg" in Rufee's years before anybody heard Elvis Presley sing his up-tempo version of it. When Elvis sang it, it was a novelty. When Big Maybelle sang it, it was a lament, one that moved her so, she finished it in tears—or at least she had the time Balzic heard her sing it. It was in 1950, and it was the first time Balzic had been summoned to Rufee's. Balzic had just been promoted to sergeant from patrolman, and Rufee's call had come through Dom Muscotti. Balzic walked into Rufee's expecting he knew not what, but stopped in his tracks at the sound of that short, fat, black woman's voice that sounded like worn-out luggage being dragged along a road. His skin had reacted and was standing up gooseflesh on both arms, and then he kept trying to swallow because his mouth had gone dry, and he kept looking at Big Maybelle's massive, sweating face, and wondering why he was so affected. "Stand there long enough," Rufee had said (though Balzic hadn't known it was Rufee), "and she'll sing you out of your shoes." Balzic didn't know what that meant, exactly, but it sounded like something she could have done. . . .

Balzic went inside with one end of the riot baton in his right hand and the other end laid back on his right shoulder. He wanted there to be no mistaken identity. He wanted there to be no doubt that he had mistaken his destination. He knew that the doorman and the bouncers would know; he worried about someone else, someone with perhaps a drink too much, or a memory too vivid, or a resentment too strong.

The doorman pointed to the center stairway. "Up the stairs, Balzic," the doorman said. "The man's waitin'."

The man, Balzic snorted under his breath. The Reverend Rutherford Feeler. Balzic snorted again as he started up the steps. The snort was something Balzic did when he felt contempt. It was also something he did when he felt a half-dozen emotions that did not sit well with each other or with the even more contradictory thoughts he had. Contempt or confusion, the snort sounded the same. . . .

The Reverend Feeler preached in black clothes on Sunday at his taxi garage cum Tabernacle of the Black Word. Monday through Saturday he wore white—from tie to shoes, and spread the word of dice and cards, homemade whiskey and heroin, the latest line on the games in all the different time zones, and everything that fell between the cracks. If the Reverend Feeler didn't know the answer to what was asked, he knew who did and where they were

and how long it would take to see them. The Reverend
Feeler fed and clothed uncountable children and old people
for free, and fed those in between whatever they could pay
for, strictly cash. Rufee had his principle: he didn't lend
money. It was the part of him that was Moslem, he said.
All the rest he had learned from Arabs, Jews, and Italians—
with a few courses from Gorgeous George the wrestler
and Billy Graham the evangelist. . . .

Balzic got to the top of the stairs having been touched by
no one, not so much as by one indiscreet elbow. The climb
had been brief, but his senses were overloaded. The music
was loud and thumpingly sensuous. The smell of marijuana
was everywhere. And the clothes were a sequined rainbow.
A young man, head to toe in orange and charcoal browns,
stood one step above a woman whose sheath dress was a
dazzling yellow and whose eye shadow matched it, and
told her something " . . . cost too much to sell to her
for. . . . " Balzic was past them, and didn't hear the rest. He
was at the top of the stairs anyway, and felt himself gaping
and chuckling increduously at Rufee, straight ahead of
him, on a great, white, peacock chair, jeweled rings on
every finger, and a white fur collar on his white tuxedo.

Rufee saw Balzic at once, and pointed at him with
his gold-knobbed, white walking stick made from the tusk
of an elephant Rufee reputedly killed on safari in Kenya
as a guest of Jomo Kenyatta. Behind Rufee, on the wall
on the right of his chair, was a large black-and-white
photo of Kenyatta and Rufee embracing, and on the left
was a black satin flag, with a coiled golden rattlesnake
in its middle poised above the words: "Don't Get Over
On Me."

Standing to Rufee's right was the pale, slouching figure
of Ruggiero Carlucci. A black woman, easily six feet tall,
with hair dyed in two blonde stripes and one red, was
refreshing Carlucci's drink. Her breasts were nearly com-

ing out of her dress, and Carlucci could not take his eyes off her or them.

Balzic took three steps into the room and was still five steps or so away from Rufee. Rufee tapped the tall woman gently on the leg with his ivory walking stick and said to her and to Balzic, "I believe it's wine, is it not, Chief Balzic? Would a claret do you? Medoc? Alicia, bring me a Medoc nicely chilled, but not too much, eh, Balzic? Also close the doors, please. I don't want to be interrupted."

Alicia, giving what might be construed as a bow, said, "Yes, sir, Reverend," and left the room with a pleasant rustle of skirt, and a fine scent trailing after.

Balzic didn't have to look hard to see that there was only one chair in the room, and it was occupied. The Reverend Feeler observed Balzic looking around for chairs, and promptly stood and came close to Balzic with his right hand extended.

Balzic, after shifting his riot baton to his left hand, shook hands in what had been a conventional way twenty years before.

"Balzic," Rufee said, "thank God you haven't taken to shakin' hands like some nigger basketball player on TV."

"Reverend, how are you?"

"Can't you tell? Sheee-it, I am so well and healthy and prosperous, praise the Lord and the numbers zero through nine and all the things that grow, don't you know—Balzic, can't you tell I am well?" Rufee spoke-sang, and shook with laughter.

"I just bet you are," Balzic said.

Rufee howled with confident laughter that somehow avoided being condescending. Rufee also made a point of not going back to his chair. He stepped around Balzic, putting Balzic between the chair and himself.

Up close, Rufee looked an ordinary man. He was short, no more than five feet seven, he was slightly on the portly side, and, except for his numerous gold fillings, he had no distinguishing features. He could have been forty, he could have been sixty. He seemed always on the verge of laughter. His eyes were bright. He looked people in the eye, especially white people, and he was looking at Balzic in the eye now, but his laughter was fading.

"Ah, your man Carlucci, my old friend, tells me you have a problem. He tells me that my help would be remembered. Is that true?"

"I've never forgotten your help before," Balzic said.

"Ah, yes, but this time, I think you've got a serious problem, and I think you've got a dead girl, and I think you've got some hostile narcotics officers to deal with, and isn't that what you want to know about?"

Balzic nodded.

The door opened and the six-foot girl with the striped hair came in with a tray, on which were a bottle of Medoc and three glasses. She went behind the white peacock chair, and bent over. In moments, she was working a corkscrew into the cork of the bottle and then bringing the cork out to Balzic to smell and feel. Balzic was impressed—with the girl and with the wine. The girl seemed to float, and in a second she was back with glasses for all three and was pouring a splash into Balzic's glass.

He took it in his mouth, sloshed it around, and swallowed it. The aftertaste was clear and crisp. "Good stuff," he said.

The girl poured all their glasses half-full and disappeared into the far corner of the room.

"The Pennsylvania Liquor Control Board is shit," Rufee said. "It's worse than shit. I have to send people clear to Ligonier to get stuff even this good. But in Ligonier, all those rich, white Protestants, they make bloody fuckin' certain that the wine they want is there." Rufee's voice changed accents as easily as he breathed. Now, he was talking like a black from the West Indies, with a strong British clip to his words. Then, as he rolled a swallow of wine in his mouth and let it down his throat, his words came out northeastern American black. "Now that's some fine shit, Balzic. I mean, my daddy woulda drunk a whole lotta this shit and got so tore up—um-uh! Whoo-eee! . . . Where were we?"

"Several places," Balzic said. "Hostile state narcs was one place. A dead girl was another. Wine in the Ligonier State Store."

"Ahhh, those shits in Ligonier. Those goddamn Presbyterians. This year I think I'll buy two or three hundred tickets to those steeplechase races they have, and I'll hire some buses and just go through the Hill District and Homewood-Brushton and East Liberty and load up every wino and smack addict and all the fine whores, and take 'em out there and turn 'em loose and tell 'em no matter what they do, they DO NOT look at the races! Can you dig it, Balzic? A hundred juiceheads and a hundred skag addicts and fifty foxy whores all standin' by the rail at the finish line looking back at the white folks watchin' the ponies! I mean, can you dig it?" Rufee howled with spiteful joy at the thought. "Then, then, on the other hand, I may just send Alicia there in a yellow Rolls—with a gray chauffeur of course—she should be stepping out wearing red vinyl shorts—the kind that show the bottom of the cheeks?—and a crocheted blouse and suede boots that come halfway up her thigh. Alicia! Alicia, would you like that? Hey! Alicia, are you payin' attention? What do you say, young heart? Don't you think you should be carrying ten thousand in cash to give to their favorite charity? Mary, mother of God, Balzic, can you dig it?"

Balzic had to admit to himself that he would like to see it. Alicia, with striped hair, in the outfit Rufee had just described, getting out of a yellow Rolls-Royce driven by a

white chauffeur at those steeplechase races in Ligonier—
there was no telling how many fixed ideas would come
unfixed.

"Now, about your man Michael Franks," Rufee said,
startling Balzic. Rufee stepped around Balzic and quickly
occupied the seat in the peacock chair. Rufee settled back
and crossed his legs. "You do have a problem here, don't
you?" Rufee smiled hugely.

"I don't know," Balzic said. "You tell me."

"Oh you know, Balzic. Your man Roger here"—Rufee
motioned with his glass toward Carlucci—"he's been doing
his homework, and you know he has. I mean, here you
are, aren't you?" Rufee was now back speaking in the West
Indies accent.

"We're here, all right," Balzic said. "But my man Roger
didn't tell me anything except to come here. I knew he was
doing his homework, but I don't know the results."

"She-it, Balzic. You know that fuckin' Jew been short-
weighin' evidence. Maybe you can't quote edition, chapter,
and verse, but you know you got a Jew in the woodpile.
And I knows you knows it. I knows his own knows it. They
on his case, man! Now ain't that right?"

"Just how do you know that?" Balzic said.

"Ha! No spades in the Bureau of Drug Enforcement,
right? No niggers in there? So I'm not 'sposed to know
what you just found out! The equality of man spreads
before us. The age of human understanding beckons.
Brotherhood welcomes us all unto its everlasting bosom.
HA! How do I know? I pay to know! I pay for it! You think
white cops don't take nigger money? They take dago money!
It's green. It's same as Jew money, same as Irish money,
same as Methodist, same as Black Muslim, she-it, Balzic,
money speaketh the same language everywhere. When
Caesar must be rendered unto, then by the Great God
above us all, gray and shine alike, we may render unto

Caesar as we are able, Brother Balzic. Praise the Lord and pass the loot—what I need to get is a license from the Federal Communications Commission, I'm sick of lookin' at those Tom motherfuckers sellin' their ass for white Jesus—from Virginia! The state that has a goddamn city named Lynchburg in it. From Virginia, Balzic! I mean, Jesus Christ, Balzic, even a lukewarm Christmas-Easter believer like yourself has got to be outraged by the sight of those niggers on that praise-the-lord train out of Virginia—got-damn!"

Balzic drank his wine, and shook his head.

"Alicia! Alicia, young heart," Rufee called out. "Come wipe my face, child. I'm perspirin' like a nigger in a steel mill. Injustice and—hurry, child, I'm 'bout to stain my fur here."

Balzic watched as the six-foot Alicia with the striped hair floated out of the darkness with a golden towel, upon which was coiled a black rattlesnake, and began to pat dry Rufee's sweating face.

"When you finish, good heart, my guests have empty glasses, and you know how a guest with an empty glass shames me."

Alicia gave a few last pats and then floated about, filling first Balzic's and then Carlucci's glass. Then she floated back into the darkness of a far corner. Carlucci looked admiringly after her.

Balzic sipped the Medoc and let it work its way. Then he said, "I'm curious, Reverend. Why do you want to turn Franks over?"

"Turn him over! Turn him over! Now what kind of bullshit is that, Balzic? Who said one motherfuckin' word 'bout turnin' anybody over—"

"Aw cut it out, will you? Huh?" Balzic said. "Who you talking to here? Somebody from the Welfare Department? Huh? You're turning him over cause he screwed you. I'm just curious, that's all. What kind of number did he pull?"

Rufee's eyes became slits for the briefest moment. Then his face softened. He stood and held out his glass of wine. In a soft flash, Alicia was there to capture the glass and retreat. Rufee approached Balzic.

"It is not merely a matter of pulling a number, my friend. If it was only a number—ONE number—or even two or five, I would take care of it myself. No, no. This was not a number. This was not fast hands and slow eyes and why not cheat friends, friends are trusting, simple motherfuckers who wouldn't think of looking for the Jew in the woodpile. Oh, no. Not this Jew. No. I said to him, almost a year ago, don't get greedy, don't get too much ambition, and I will send you an opportunist at every opportunity.

"Now that's fair, Balzic. There's nothing unfair about that. I get a member of my staff who finds himself lusting after the temptations of Satan, and there's no harm in helping a lawman's career, now is there?"

Rufee waited momentarily for Balzic to answer. When he didn't, Rufee continued. "There are men, Balzic, and you know this, so don't get holy with me, who are bribed by the committers of felonies even more easily than they are by dollars. Your man Franks looked for a while like he was one of those. So I threw him some wayward hearts. But then, then, your man Franks developed hungers that names in his arrest record could not satisfy. Your man Franks began to want other things."

"Such as what?" Balzic said.

"Can't you guess? I mean, don't you know? Your man Franks has emotional appetites that even I did not consider. Your man Franks like to beat on bodies. Especially female bodies. Especially young female bodies. And I could have handed you any piece of bullshit I wanted to hand you. But I'm telling you, and—hear me carefully now—I want

that motherfucker in Western Penitentiary. I want him in
the Wall. I have several associates there who will deliver
him into the hands of the righteous."

"I want to know what he did," Balzic said evenly.

"You want to know, I will tell you. We had an associate
who owed me a great deal more respect than he was
paying me. I turned him over to Franks, as I had turned
several others. Mea culpa. This nigger stands naked before you in all his guilt. But I did not know—I swear to
whatever is still holy—I did not know that the dealer had
two daughters. One eleven, one nine. Consequently, I did
not have reason to think that the dealer would sell his
daughters to Franks for his out. I did not know until their
mother came and told me that the girls had been seriously
fucked with. The younger has only a broken nose. The
older one has more serious damage. He bit the end of her
tongue off. She has lost her speech.

"Now," Rufee went on, "I could catch me that Jew and
burn his tongue out of his throat with lye. But that's not
enough. I want that Jew cop, that narc, in Western Pen.
I want him down there with those twelve hundred wild
men who know that he's coming and who know what he
did. I want his whole history to precede him. I want him
there for at least three years. I want that Jew motherfucker
to know what it's like to be weak and friendless and with
no voice. Now, Balzic, I ask you. Am I not right in my wish
for this justice?"

Balzic took another sip of wine. "Was biting off the girl's
tongue only the start?"

"Only," Rufee said. "Just the start. She has no nipples
either. She is only eleven, Balzic. You have daughters.
Imagine it. This motherfucker is an agent of the state.
This motherfucker was not satisfied with a good arrest
record and all the dope he could steal. Oh no. This
motherfucker is a Jew with the soul of a Nazi. And I

hereby turn him over to you. I have a list of dates, arrests, arraignments, amounts confiscated, and amounts turned in as evidence. I appeal to your sense of the rightness of things, Balzic."

"I have some questions," Balzic said.

"Ask your questions. If they pertain to Franks, ask them."

"What d'you want for this?"

"Come on, Balzic. Pay attention, mon. I have told you. I want the bastard in the Wall, against the wall, friendless and weak and without a voice."

"That's it?"

"Balzic. You speak as though 'it' was a thing easily done. How can I accomplish this without your assistance? The law's assistance? White law has to do this. Powerful as I am, and I have great power, I have no illusion about my power. My power is still nigger power, because I do not deliver votes. I merely have lots of money, and I know that those who wish to be bribed seek me out. That is no small knowledge, Balzic, but it cannot do what it cannot do."

Balzic took another sip of wine and scratched his eyebrows. He swallowed again and licked his lips. "What about my problem? I have a dead girl with no name."

"Balzic, my friends tell me that your dead girl is a mystery. Nobody knows her. She is not from here."

"That's it?" Balzic said, growing suddenly angry.

"I did not say that was it. What I said—"

"I know what you said."

"—so you know. Good. So the other part is that she was a recruit of our bottomless Mr. Franks."

Balzic, lips parted, glowered over the rims of his glasses.

"The scenario must have gone something like this," Rufee said. "Franks wants to score off Red Dog Burns. But Burns is a sly one. Franks recruits the female to entice Burns away from his residence so that it and his other

residence may be searched. The first apartment gives up
nothing. Franks and his associate then go to the second
apartment. The result is the same. Franks then believes
that his recruit has scored for herself and her two companions and has cut him, Franks, adrift. Franks responds as
only he can."

Balzic held up his hand. "Wait a minute. This is a nice
theory. But where's the facts I take to the DA?"

"Balzic, Jesus Christ, man, how much work am I 'sposed
to do for y'all?"

"Hey, Rufee," Balzic said. "So far you've given me the
reason why you want Franks in Western Pen. That's one.
Then you've given me the theory behind why this girl
might've been shot. But so far these are just nice stories.
Stories don't impress the guys in the DA's office. They
want something they can tell a jury."

"I've already told you I'll make you a present of Frank's
story. Dates, weights—what the fuck you want, man?"

"Rufee, are you—you, yourself—are you gonna testify?"

"Come on, man," Rufee said, snorting.

"Then who is gonna present this evidence?"

"Hey man, that's your problem. Jesus Christ, you have
to do some work, you know?"

It was Balzic's turn to snort. "Shit, this is a waste of
time. You're not gonna testify, who is?"

Rufee turned his back to Balzic, and waved to Alicia to
refill his glass and to bring it to him. "Balzic, got-damn.
Use your imagination. There were two dudes with the girl.
There was Franks's partner. And there is Burns. And if
you can't come up with heavy evidence out of that group,
then she-it, you ought to be workin' in the mill. Doin'
dumb shit."

"Call me whatever," Balzic said. "The fact remains, all
you're givin' me is stories. I can't convict—convict, shit. I
wouldn't get out of the magistrate's office with this stuff.

Christ, you haven't even told me who is the father of those two girls who sold them to Franks."

"Never mind about him," Rufee said sharply.

"Never mind! Christ, the next thing you'll tell me is you can't remember the girls' names either!"

"I can't—as a matter of fact."

"Aw fuck you, Rufee. Whatta you think you're doing here, for crissake? Huh? You want the law's help, Christ, man, you got to help the law."

"I can't tell you more than I've told you. If you can't use it, then I'll go to the state police. Or the state narcs—"

"But, Rufee, the goddamn problem will be the same. They'll want to know the same things I want to know. You want Franks done up right, then, shit, man, you got to come up with something. The little girls' father would be something. A start."

"Impossible." Rufee said it without emotion.

"Why?"

"Because the man is no longer with the living."

"Then what about the mother?"

"She doesn't know any of the facts. All she knows is the results."

Balzic shook his head strenuously. "Then what the hell am I supposed to do?"

"Balzic, do you mean to stand there, with all your experience and with all your connections, and tell me that with the information I have to give you, you could not present enough evidence to the DA to get Franks convicted, is that what you mean to tell me?"

"Rufee, in the first place, without even looking at the information, I have to say no. For two very simple reasons. These are drug things, and that's the state BDE. And the other is, I doubt if any of them, except for the thing connected with the girl, happened inside my territory. Now before you start hollering and shouting, I have to pretty much account for my time. Didn't use to have to, but I got a new mayor to deal with and now I have to account for—"

"You got a murder in your territory, man! All the rest is, is confiscated pot. The people who it was confiscated from are doing their time. They can be got to testify. You don't have to do this yourself, man! You can make some honky pal of yours a hero. They are already on his case. But it'll take those dudes weeks, months. With what I give you, you could turn Franks around, inside out in a week!" That said, Rufee wheeled about and went back to his white peacock chair. "Got-damn, I don't believe I'm stand- ing here tellin' a honky cop how to make his case. She-it!"

Balzic waited his moment until Rufee closed his eyes and rolled his head from side to side, and then Balzic winked quickly at Carlucci.

"Uh, Rufee," Balzic said, "you sure you don't know about the two guys who were with that girl?"

"I'm working on it! Got-damn!" Rufee exploded. "I don't know everymotherfuckinthing! Some things take an hour or two, she-it."

"Just one of them would be enough."

"I know that, Balzic, got-damn, man, don't you think I know that? But in the meantime, why can't you get started on the end I already got you started on?"

"Fair enough," Balzic said, approaching Rufee with his right hand extended. "I want to thank you, Reverend. You've been very helpful."

"Don't you come at me with helpful jive. And get your hand outta my face."

Balzic shrugged. "Okay, let's quit the jive. Let's start by recognizing that you don't have the first idea who was with the girl. You don't have to say a word. I know you don't know. And because you don't know that, you really don't have the first idea that Franks had anything to do with her.

All you been doing is sitting here on your throne waiting for something to happen that looked like it might have been Franks, and figuring which honky you'd get to do your number for you. And a girl gets it in the head in my town and I'm the elected honky, isn't that right?"

Rufee had been gazing intently at Balzic, but he began to smile and then to laugh and sputter and speak. Perspiration and spittle flew off his face as his body shook with laughter. "Oh-ho, oh, Balzic, oh you're still the boss honky, yes sir, you de boss honky, awwright."

"Rufee," Balzic said after Rufee's hilarity had subsided, "Whatta you really got? And leave out all the advertising this time."

"Balzic, I got what I said. I got a list of transactions. All the information is there. All you got to do is feed it to somebody you want to get promoted. Now, here's the part I left out before. While some of the state narcs are checking out this information, the rest of those narco clowns are gonna be steppin' like a city nigger runnin' through a pigpen—you know, holdin' his nose with one hand and tryin' to hold up his pants with the other hand, and finding out he can't do both. Either he's gonna get his pants in it or else he's gonna have to smell it, and what he wants to do is get the hell outta there.

"Which is what them narcs gonna do—get the hell out the way. And if they get out the way, then I can find whoever was with that girl. Cause I don't want Franks goin' away for just three years. Oh no. I want that scumbag goin' away for fifteen to life."

"Why didn't you say this all before, for crissake?" Balzic groused.

"Oh, Balzic, some day you'll understand. I could tell you that I enjoy playing with white people, but it'll take you years to understand. 'Cause you don't wanna bee—lieve that a man would take his fun makin' another man wait. You think that's too petty, too mean, too chicken-shitty. And you won't believe it even though I come right out and tell you. I love to get over on you white mother-fuckers. I mean it is one of those few things in life I can never get enough of. It's like pussy. Or cocaine! The more you gets, the more you wants. I was jus' playin', Balzic, tha's all, jus' playin'."

"You done playing?"

Rufee smiled a great smile. "I am now," he said. "And so, I bid you both good night. Alicia, child, come collect these glasses."

Alicia floated out of her dark corner and took the glasses first from Balzic and then from Carlucci.

"What about the list?" Balzic said.

"It will be yours before you depart the premises. Good night."

"Good night, Rufee. It's been interesting." Balzic turned and led Carlucci out of the room and down the stairs. Just as they were approaching the door, the doorman presented Balzic with a white business envelope. Balzic took it, put it in his pocket, and walked through the door held open for him.

They were fifty yards from the house, halfway to their cars before either spoke. The wind stung their faces and made their eyes water.

"That guy's a trip," Carlucci said, shaking his head in wonder.

Balzic grunted, then stopped, catching Carlucci by the sleeve. "What part of that didn't you believe?"

"Huh?"

"What part of that didn't you believe?"

Carlucci shrugged and looked away for a moment. "I don't know. Till I check it out, you know, I don't believe anything."

"Yeah, I know that, but beyond that," Balzic said, still

holding Carlucci by the sleeve, "uh, what part didn't you really go for?"

"I don't know," Carlucci said, shrugging. "I don't know what answer you want me to give you."

"C'mon, huh? What answer to give me, ha? Just give me an answer, okay?"

"Okay. Okay. Uh, the thing about the little girls sounds a little shaky."

"Yeah? Why?"

" 'Cause how we gonna check it?"

"You noticed that, huh? No names? No names of nobody there, no girls, no momma, no poppa, no address, no nothing."

"Yeah, but, you know, uh, who's gonna talk about that? I don't know about you, Mario, but I go asking questions about that, hey, that's a tough one. There's nobody gonna talk to me about that one."

Balzic wiped his nose with the back of his hand. He nodded strenuously several times. "That's what I was thinking. That nobody's gonna talk to me about it either. It's too fuckin' embarrassing, for one. For two, no spooks are gonna talk to white cops about what a crazy white cop did to two spook girls, 'cause they know nobody's gonna believe it."

Carlucci shrugged again. "It's a hell of a story."

"Hey," Balzic said, shaking Carlucci's sleeve. "It's more than that. It's the best kind of story there is. It's either true, or it's the best lie Rufee ever told. But what makes it even better is Rufee knows there's no way we can know. 'Cause for sure nobody's gonna talk to us about it."

"I could check the emergency room records. Wouldn't take too long. I just eliminate everybody who isn't black, female, and over, say, fourteen or fifteen."

"Hey, you're a good man, Rugs," Balzic said, taking the envelope out of his pocket and tapping Carlucci on

the chest with it. "Check this stuff out, and feed it to
Russellini. And let me know what's happening. Let's get
outta here."

    Balzic awoke next morning to see that a
fine, powdery snow that had fallen during the night was
being whipped about by a wind that seemed to be blowing
in a different direction every other second. He shivered at
the thought of going out in it.

He poured himself a glass of orange juice and looked
wistfully at the clock. The new mayor had caused Balzic
to upend his morning routine. He had to get up late
enough to be sure that his daughters were out of the
bathroom, but too early to have more than passing conversation with his wife or his mother. By the time Balzic was
out of the bathroom, his daughters were on their way to
school, his mother was going back to bed for the sixth or
seventh time since she first tried to get to sleep, and his
wife was waiting for him to eat so she could use the
bathroom herself.

"This is lousy. I really miss seeing the kids in the morning."

"He called already this morning."

Balzic put down his coffee. "I don't believe it."

"Well, believe it. Emily answered. I wasn't even up yet."

"It ain't gonna do any good, but I gotta talk to him. This
is crazy."

Balzic finished eating—he left most of his breakfast on
the dish—and said good-bye to Ruth as he headed for the
front door and she headed to the bathroom. They touched
lips on the oblique.

The wind was dry and still blowing in every way, sending the snow in wicked swirls. Balzic's irritation with the
mayor calling so early and with the weather was com-
pounded by traffic. He heard himself saying, "Where the

hell do all these people work? Do they all have to get there at eight? Why don't people start at five-minute intervals— somebody must've thought of that. . . . " He parked in his slot and got out in a morbid funk over the thought that he had nearly four years to go with this mayor.

Going up the steps of City Hall he found the one patch of ice on the steps and went down on his left knee, barking the kneecap and managing not to go down completely only by catching hold of the handrail. He got up slowly and looked down at his knee to see that his trousers were torn and that there was the barest hint of red. His morbid funk began to spread and settled over both shoulders. He looked up as he started back up the steps and saw Mayor Ken Strohn's confused face, caught somewhere between suspicion at Balzic's tardiness and sympathy for Balzic's fall. The combination gave Strohn the look of a very small terrier about to yip in alarm and protest.

"Are you all right?" the mayor said as Balzic entered.

"No, I'm not all right. I just ripped my pants, I just scraped the skin off my knee, and I'm sore as hell about you calling my house this morning."

"Oh. Well, wait now, I can explain that," Strohn said, hurrying after Balzic as he limped along to get a first-aid kit.

"I wish you would," Balzic said, rooting through the kit to find the peroxide. He pulled up his pant leg and then poured some peroxide on a ball of cotton and dabbed it against the abrasion.

"Mario, you have to understand that if I'm to do any good here at all, I have to be here by five-thirty at the latest. I've got to get to my business by eight-thirty. That leaves me about two hours and forty-five minutes to work on city business. Then—"

Balzic looked up from his ministrations to his knee and said coldly, "Why do I have to understand that?"

"Well, because, of course, if you understand how early I get here, then it follows you'll understand why I call you so early."

"It's five after eight," Balzic said, nodding to the wall clock.

"Well, of course. That's my point. I'm down here with lots of things to attend to and I want to know how you're coming along with—"

"You can't call me from your place of business at nine o'clock? While I'm here?"

"Well, perhaps I could in ordinary circumstances. But this is hardly ordinary. There is that girl's murder."

"I can't work on a murder when I'm asleep, except maybe in my subconscious—but my family is damn sure not working on any murder, whether they're awake, asleep, or in the shower. My family, they all take a lot of crap because of me. There's no telling how much shit my daughters have taken because I'm what I am. My wife considers herself lucky if she gets through one day without being reminded of who she's married to—"

"I understand all that, Mario, but—"

"You don't understand anything yet. You haven't been mayor long enough. People will find out your phone number soon enough and then you're gonna know what I'm talking about. My numbers get changed like every three or four months. But people find 'em. Don't ask me how, I don't know, but they do. That's just one of the things that goes with the job. You'll have to ask my wife how many times she's been called and told that I'm dead—which is one of the milder lies they tell her about me.

"Then we change the number and get about ten weeks of peace and then it starts in again. So what I'm trying to tell you is, my family doesn't need any more phone calls. So what I want you to do is sit down and reconsider your priorities with me. 'Cause right now it's almost a quarter after eight and I don't know a whole hell of a lot more today than I did yesterday about that murder. Is that what you wanted to know?"

The mayor nodded slowly and then shrugged as though to apologize.

Balzic was pushing it, he knew, but he wanted this thing settled if nothing else ever got settled. "I haven't talked to the state police, I haven't heard anything new from my own men, and I already told you that each day that passes is just making the odds higher. We still don't know who the girl is and—and this is my point—this is what I would've told you if my daughter had waked me up to take your call."

"I think you've made your point," the mayor said.

"I wonder," Balzic said, nodding his head rapidly and wondering whether more conversation was futile.

"Well, what's next?" Strohn said, abruptly changing the subject.

"What's next about what?" Balzic affixed a square adhesive bandage to his knee, disposed of the wrapper and backing, and rolled down his pant leg.

"About the girl?"

"Mr. Mayor, I told you before, we're working on some informants and we're waiting to see if anybody has information to sell or trade. Until that happens, we pretty much count thumbs or pick lint out of bellybuttons."

"Uh, that's very, uh, that's very colorful, but it's not very helpful."

"Well, I'm sorry, Mr. Mayor, but that's the way it is."

"What did you learn last night in Rufee's?"

Balzic had been shifting from foot to foot, testing his skinned knee, and stopped in mid-shift. "Nothing, uh, nothing much. It was about something else. I wouldn't've thought you'd know anything about Rufee's, Mr. Mayor."

"Not firsthand I don't, but I've heard about it, like a lot

of people." Strohn looked not quite smug, but certainly confident. "And I haven't talked to your Detective, uh, Carlucci?"

"I'm sure you haven't," Balzic said, not at all sure of that, and not knowing whether to laugh or curse. Power-happy people, he thought, whether white or black, whether Strohn or Rufee, had more things in common than they'd ever think of admitting, and playing with other people, toying with them, was just one of their commonalities, one of their less injurious ones.

"Well? What did Rufee tell you?"

Balzic sighed slowly, puzzled about this man, this Republican marathoner with the heart that beat fifty times a minute at rest, who now suddenly was acknowledging a different side of himself. Then again, Balzic thought, it probably wasn't another side at all; it just looked like another side because Strohn didn't seem the type to have a connection even remotely near Rufee's. But he had somebody. To run as an Independent when everyone knew he was a Republican in this town, that must've taken a lot of somebodies. Balzic shook his head to try to clear his mind of all this thinking about who Strohn knew, or was connected to, or had in his employ.

Strohn took Balzic's head shaking to mean something else. "You're not going to tell me?"

"No—I mean, that's not it. I'll tell you. Why not? Rufee's offered to trade information in return for the guaranteed conviction of a state narc."

Strohn's face went slack with surprise. "Why—why, my God. That's incredible. A state narcotics agent? But, how does Rufee know?"

"Mr. Mayor, where Rufee's concerned, what he doesn't know hurts him. So he tries to know everything. He doesn't, but he comes close. Besides, in this instance, I think he's just covering his ass. The state guys already began an investigation—yesterday, as a matter of fact. Rufee knew that too. The timing's a little too close. I doubt that it was a coincidence."

"So then Rufee was involved with this corrupt agent? Did Rufee corrupt him? Is that how he knew?"

Balzic couldn't help himself; he didn't even try to suppress his laughter. "Mr. Mayor, bad guys don't corrupt good guys. Good guys see bad guys making it and they go tell the bad guys that if they want to keep on making it, they're going to have to set a little something aside for the good guy fund. And if the bad guys do, there's no problem. But if they don't, there's problems for everybody, but especially for the bad guys. Usually, when bad guys go out of business, it's because they forgot to take care of the good guys."

"That is the most cynical description of corruption I've ever heard," Strohn said.

"Call it anything you like. The only people who go to cops to get certain things done are small-timers. Big money bad guys wouldn't have big money if they were so goddamn anxious to give it away to cops just for the privilege of making more so they could keep giving it to cops. I don't care what you've grown up believing, Mr. Mayor, or how cynical you think I am. Nobody goes to a cop to corrupt him. That's like saying shoplifters take most of the profit from retailers. That's pure bullshit. If a retailer is getting creamed by theft, it's by his own employees. Or by the security people he hires to stop the employees."

"How long have you been a police officer?" the mayor said weakly.

"Long time. A long time."

"And this is what you've learned?"

Balzic shrugged. "I'll tell you what, Mr. Mayor. You may as well know this for a fact. You've probably heard it as a rumor. I made a deal a long time ago. I traded

gambling against prostitution and drugs. It so happened
that the guy I traded with didn't like the whores or dope
any better than I did, so it was an easy trade. But he's
never offered me a penny, and I've never asked him for
one. From my point of view, that trade was the most
practical thing I could do. Nobody is ever going to enforce
the gambling laws in this town. The people here are too
sports-happy. Plus a lot of other reasons. But what're you
supposed to do about something that can't be enforced?
You control it the best way you can and try to make sure
nobody gets burned too bad. And that's what I've done."

"My God! Who—who else knows about this?" Strohn
was so shaken by what he'd heard that he was sagging.
He looked as though he was going to collapse. Suddenly,
he shot a look at Sergeant Vic Stramsky yawning into
the microphone by the radio console, and he said to
Balzic through barely parted lips, "We've got to talk
about this."

"We are talking about it."

"I mean we've got to talk!"

"Well I don't know what you call what we're doing, but I
call it talking."

"I mean not here." Strohn fired another glance at
Stramsky.

Balzic nodded and sighed, exasperated. He went back
to his office, went in and held the door till the mayor was
in, and then closed it.

Strohn wheeled about at the click of the latch and tried
hard not to shout. "For Christ sake, Balzic, what have you
got me into?" For a moment he looked as though he might
burst into tears.

"What has—what have I got you—I got you into? Is that
what you're asking me?"

"Yes!" the mayor shouted. "Explain yourself!"

"Mr. Mayor, I think you better get yourself together,

'cause you're not talking much sense here. I did not get you into anything."

"Bullshit!" the mayor screeched.

Balzic blinked slowly and let his gaze circle the room, pausing finally on Strohn's flushed face.

"Mr. Mayor, I'll say it again. It won't come out any different. But here goes. I . . . did not . . . get you . . . into any . . . thing, got that? You got yourself elected all by yourself without so much as one vote from me. I did—"

"Oh stop that! You know perfectly well what I'm saying. I want to know who else knows about this deal. This god-damnable deal you've made!" The mayor was finding it impossible to open his mouth when he spoke. His teeth seemed locked together, and his face was growing more flushed by the minute.

"Mr. Mayor, I'm—"

"Answer me!"

"I'm trying to, goddamnit! But you've got yourself out of joint practically from your nose to your toes. Hell, man, there isn't anybody I know who doesn't know about it. What d'you think people are? Stupid? Hell, people read the papers. They see who gets arrested. They know who the arresting officers are and what the charges are. Pretty soon they figure it out. It's no big goddamn mystery. You gonna stand there and try to tell me you don't bet on football games, college and pro? Huh?"

The mayor's face was now crimson. "I never bet more than ten dollars," he said feebly.

"Eleven to make ten," Balzic snapped. "Per game. And I suppose you're gonna stand there and tell me that until this fuckin' moment you didn't know that was illegal? Don't! I mean, just don't. That is the one thing I do not want to hear."

"But I was not a public official when I made those bets and—"

Balzic brushed past the mayor, none too softly, and sat at his desk. He waited for fully ten seconds to pass. Then he said, "Mr. Mayor, Strohn, do you have any idea how simple you look now? Do you have any idea how stupid you sound? I mean, are you actually going to stand there and try to con me that you didn't know gambling on sports was illegal when you were placing those bets? Are you gonna try to tell me that a ten dollar bet was a 'little' bet, so it was only a 'little' illegal? Who the hell'd you think you were betting with—the Sisters of Charity? And what were they gonna do with all those 'little' bets? Run an orphanage on the vigorish?

"Mr. Mayor, I got to tell you something. I believe you thought you were sneaking into the cookie jar. But now all of a sudden, you find out how it was possible for you to sneak and you see the trouble that could go with it and now, now the guy who made it possible for you to sneak and have fun being sneaky, now that guy—me—has got you into something!

"Mr. Mayor, you got a serious psychological problem. You not only want to *be* good, you want to *look* good. But the problem is, you've been bad. And now, there's only one way out. And that's to blame it on somebody else. If they had not created the possibility for you to be bad, why, of course, you'd still be as good as you want to look. Which is very good. Naturally. Some psychologists call that transference. Some call it projection. Judges and prosecutors call it copping a plea. Cops call it rolling over. In other words, Mr. Mayor, you have just demonstrated the basic behavior, the fundamental attitude, the starter set, for your low-grade, bottom-shelf informant. Stoolie. Squealer. Snitch. Those people you said you can't tolerate. I think you said all those words had such an 'odious' ring. Isn't that what you said?"

The mayor's mouth seemed frozen shut. Except for a

small rippling of his cheeks near and below his ears, he appeared mesmerized.

"Relax, Mr. Mayor. Go to your business. Just keep in mind that gambling is like the weather. Everybody talks about it and so forth. Get it? Only very rarely does somebody do anything about it. And it has about the same effect as doing something about the weather. Which is nothing. Some guys get fined. But not much. And some people even go to jail. But not for long. And afterwards, everybody smiles and gets their bets down, just like you did. You never asked Dom Scalzo how many times he's been arrested?"

"Wha-what?"

"Dom. Scalzo. 'Soup.' Didn't you bet with him?"

"Yes. Yes."

"And you never once asked him about all the times he'd been arrested and fined and, once, I think he even went to the joint for a month or so. You never discussed it with him?"

The mayor did not reply.

Balzic shook his head. "Strohn, you got a problem. I think you better get some professional help. But Christ, don't let that get out. Boy, that'd be a hundred times worse than what you think I got you into. Which, once again, for the record, I didn't. I should tell you, Strohn. I have never voted once since I became chief. I never wanted to walk into a council meeting and know that I had voted for or against anybody in that room. It would make my life just too damn complicated."

Strohn seemed unable to say anything. All he could do was look at Balzic, and alternately frown and look puzzled. After some seconds of this, he went to the door, opened it, and left without bothering to close it.

Balzic shook his head and scratched the end of his nose and wondered why some people who more or less had lives of their own choosing became so distressed when they were confronted by small trouble. You'd think, Balzic mused, that because they'd had it all their own way for so long, they'd be a bottomless pit of optimism. But that was not the case at all. Most people who had never really had any trouble in their lives reacted to trouble when it happened as though it were overpowering, final even. They'd never learned all the ways there were to fail, so they thought that their first failure was the only one and they took it like Strohn did. The silly bastards, Balzic thought. What right do they have to their successes?

January ended. Then February. Then came the first week of March, and the second, and the third. Temperatures seldom rose above forty-five and rarely went below twenty. There was rain and sleet one day and damp winds the next and snow flurries mixed with driving rains the day after that. One day utility companies were re-stringing power and phone lines; the next, volunteer fire companies were pumping out basements. It seemed to Balzic that it had been months since he'd seen sunlight; always there was a bleakness in the weather that seemed to reflect Balzic's temper and mood about the girl on South Main Street.

Ten weeks after her murder, not only were the state police or the Rocksburg PD no closer to the answer of who had killed her, they had yet to learn who she was. All that was known about her had been known in the first forty-eight hours, and that was that she had been the person who knocked on Thurman Burns's door and talked him out of his apartment. She had no numbers by which she might be traced, no licenses, no Social Security card, no insurance cards, none of the pieces of paper by which one establishes or hides an identity. Her clothing had all come from major discount houses; thousands of garments like hers had been sold in a half-dozen Northeastern states. Her fingerprints, sent to the FBI's National Crime Information Computer, matched none of their records. Her physical measurements corresponded to nothing on any list of missing persons. Her photograph, published not only in *The Rocksburg Gazette* but in nearly a dozen Tri-State newspapers, brought not one response. Her body continued to occupy a drawer in the storage section of the pathology department of Conemaugh General Hospital.

The contents of Thurman Burns's apartments—and because the decor in both was so much alike, no one argued when the assumption was made that both apartments were rented to Burns, even though the names on the leases were Ted Brown and Thurman Brown—were put in a storage room in the basement of Conemaugh Manor, the county home for the elderly and infirm. The apartments were subsequently leased in no time at all; it took about two months for the furniture, stored at city expense, to be pilfered. By the time only two heavy glass and chrome tables remained, the county had sued the city to collect storage charges and the city had counter-sued to claim damages for property stolen.

The internal investigation of Michael Franks by the Bureau of Drug Enforcement seemed to go in circles of its own. Agents brought in from the eastern part of the state refused to accept any information from Agent Russell, which information had been researched by Carlucci. It was good information. Testimony of magistrates' hearings involving Franks in four separate arrests revealed certain amounts of confiscated marijuana and money. Interviews with the incarcerated defendants all revealed large discrepancies between the amounts they said they were holding at the time of their arrests and the amounts testified to and produced by Franks at the magistrates' hearings.

This information—all of it obtained and corroborated within a week, as the Reverend Rutherford Feeler had claimed—refused to move the agents brought from the eastern half of the state to investigate Franks. Carlucci was wild with frustration.

"The bastards think we're using a bunch of low-life niggers to railroad one of their own," Carlucci said. "They say the niggers got nothing to lose by nailing an agent, but they do have lots of good time to gain. And if Franks did hold out all this pot, they want to know what he did with it. Who'd he sell it to? How come we don't have one person who'll come forward and swear he bought dope from Franks? They want to know how come the only guys talking are niggers that Franks put in the joint. Don't I know any white people, one of them says to me. Shit, I wanted to spit on him."

So they went to Rufee's, not once but many times. Carlucci alone. And Carlucci and Balzic. Balzic alone. Balzic with Walker Johnson. Balzic with Russell. All conversations were reduced to certain essentials.

"I done told you and told you and told you, Balzic. I give Franks every one of those niggers and I know he wound up with the dope."

"But you won't tell me how you gave them to him, you just keep on saying you yourself never talked to Franks. And you still haven't come up with either one of the guys who went up to the door with that girl to Burns's apartment. And what's more, you been saying for the last month you know where Burns is, and every address you've given us has been bullshit. You got a hell of a thing going here, Rufee."

"All I got is a headache and upset stomach 'cause you honkies can't make a case 'gainst one stupid Jew."

The last time Balzic talked to Rufee was on a Friday. It was late afternoon, and Rufee's was almost deserted. Aside from a doorman, a couple of waitresses, and a bartender, there were only a handful of customers. Rufee was upstairs, pacing back and forth and talking none too softly to himself. Balzic was in the room for almost a minute before he realized that Rufee was rehearsing a sermon. Rufee's eyes were partly closed as the words tumbled out.

" . . . the Lord does not want any man to be poor, nor woman, nor child. For the Lord has told us all to go forth and flourish! Uh, to go forth and flourish—aw she-it, Balzic, what'd you all want now? Got-damn! Everytime I turn around there's your face next to my face. Whatta you all want?"

"What I want is pretty much what you want. But you and I are gonna have to find another way to get it."

"What's that mean?"

"One thing it means is that the state narcs gave Franks a clean bill. They turned in their report last Wednesday. I just heard about it today. Their conclusion is that, for reasons they can't determine, Franks has been the object of a campaign to 'impugn his integrity,' was the way they put it, to 'dishonor the bureau,' and so forth and so on."

"I should've known," Rufee said softly. "Ain't nothing changed. Alicia told me I was jivin' myself, but I didn't pay the girl no mind. I say to myself, she jus' a chile, what she know? But that chile know more than me."

"It ain't over," Balzic said. "We just got to go at him from a different direction, that's—"

"We!" Rufee exploded. "We! Where you get this 'we' shit? When did you and me turn into 'we'? You and me ain't 'we,' Balzic. You is you and me is me. You and me may talk in the same language, you and me may inhabit the same planet, you and me may even want the same thing, but you and me is not 'we.' "

"Yeah, yeah," Balzic grumbled. "So whatta you know about Burns? Whatta you know about those two guys?"

"Why do I have to know everything? Why do I have to have the answers? Whatta you know about who was in the car with Franks that day?"

"How do you know that anybody was?"

"I know the man's number. He never did nothing without another pair of hands. You know how that goes, Balzic. Another pair of hands to help, another pair of shoulders to accept the blame when the shit goes wrong. Franks never hustled alone. He always had another body there. Always a body to trade come trading time. The man was always looking out for his future."

"Always?"

"Always."

"Then who was with him when he did his thing on the eleven-year-old girl?"

"Oh. In that I'm wrong. No, when he made a mute, when he bit off that girl's tongue, he did that alone."

"Then, Rufee, you better come up with Burns, or with those two who were with that girl."

"I better come up with this, I better come up with that—why is it always me who has to come up with this, that, or whatever? Why can't you pick up Franks and throw him in a cell with no lights and no food for a couple days, why can't you do that? Put a phone book on his head and beat on it, why don't you? Put a pistol beside his ear and fire it!"

"You want me in the joint too now, huh?"

"She-it, mon, somebody besides ole Rufee gots to do his share, mon. Sweat the sonofabitch! How many people has he sweated? People better than him by a damn distance."

"That won't make it, Rufee. We—you and I—need the other players in the game."

"Burns is so far underground, he must be living in a sewer. Either that or he's in Colombia. But he's not around here. Not above ground."

"The other two?"

Rufee dropped his gaze and shook his head. "My fear is that they have joined your lady in the morgue. That's my most considered opinion, Balzic. Only he didn't leave them lying around. He made his point with the girl. I'm telling you, you better get one of his protégés. That Cortese and that Gensheimer. One of them had to be in the car with him that day. . . . "

Balzic returned home by way of Muscotti's, where he drank wine for what seemed hours with Mo Valcanas. Valcanas was alternately querulous and whimsical. Balzic let him go on, knowing that sooner or later Valcanas would get bored with arguing and with himself for being peevish, and would become the intelligent and sensible friend he always could be.

"Still running in the mayor's conditioning runs?" Valcanas said.

"Haven't made a one," Balzic said.

"How're you getting out of them? I mean, I thought he was hot on this conditioning crap, and on you for being a piss-poor leader of men."

"He was."

"Well how're you getting out of it? C'mon, I want to hear. I want to know how one goes about snowing the bright young leader."

"I don't do anything. I just haven't gone to one of them."

"You just don't show up? And he doesn't say anything?"

"He hasn't so far."

"I'm curious. What're you going to say when he does?"

"I'm curious, too," Balzic said. "You can be sure I'll be paying attention, whatever I say. I won't forget a word of it."

"You really don't have anything planned?"

"Oh, I've planned few things, but they're all stupid. Just get me into a real jackpot if I said 'em."

"And you just haven't showed up and he hasn't said anything," Valcanas said. "That's funny as hell."

"There's nothing funny about it. It's sensible. It's two guys not wanting to stare each other down. And that's sensible as hell. Almost makes me think he's got some brains."

"That's evasion, that's all it is."

"Well, shit, it's not having an argument. And you like arguments. All lawyers do. If you didn't like arguments, you'd be something else. Fuckin' undertaker or something."

Valcanas licked his lips and tossed off the last quarter-ounce of his gin. "Can you—I mean, do you really see me as an undertaker? I don't believe it."

"Well what else the hell d'you think you can do?" Balzic said. He was feeling seriously drunk.

Valcanas looked at Balzic sideways, with his chin down and his eyes turned as far as they would go in their sockets.

"I'll admit," Valcanas said after a long moment, "that I do enjoy an argument for its own sake. I always have. But I'll be goddamned if I'd be an undertaker if I wasn't a lawyer."

"Shit," Balzic said, banging the bar with the side of his fist. "You tell me another job, another profession that wears three-piece suits in the summertime—lawyers, preachers, and undertakers. Nobody else. And you guys could all do each other's jobs. You could preach. You could console widows. I've seen you do it. Shit, you're good at consoling widows."

"Only the ones who got a lot of money coming. I don't do too good with the ones whose old man left it all to the chippie the widow didn't know existed."

"That's what I mean," Balzic said, signaling for another drink. He was most seriously drunk now. He knew it beyond any doubt. And when he reached the point of drunkenness where he now was, he said weightily and often, "That's what I mean," as though those words explained what he meant with a clarity and precision that no other words could express.

"That's what I mean."

"You don't know what the hell you mean," Valcanas said.

"Fuckin' lawyers. Huh? Goddamn right. That's what I mean. . . ."

Balzic awoke to the telephone jangling his ears and the alcohol jangling his nerves. He had fallen asleep, fully clothed, in the recliner in the living room. He didn't know what time he'd come home, or how. From about eight p.m. last night until he found himself fighting to blot out the sounds of the phone, there was a vacant, winey space. Balzic drank nearly every day of his life. Some days he drank too much, but only a little too much. Then there were the times, like Friday after talking to Rufee, that Balzic got seriously drunk. He didn't do it often, not more than two or three times a year, and for many years it never bothered him. It was his frustration drunk; he used to tell himself—and others, particularly his wife and mother—that he had to do it every so often because the frustrations got too much to deal with and so he obliterated them and gave himself at least six or eight or ten hours of freedom from their pursuit.

This last time it was frustration over the girl, over the state narcotics agent, Franks, over the other state narcotics agents' whitewash of Franks, over Rufee, over all of them. He had been monumentally frustrated; he got monumentally drunk. His nerves, his muscles, his eyes, his head all paid homage to the twin monuments of frustration and alcoholic freedom from it.

He struggled to get to the phone, not knowing what

time it was but thinking it was early, and wanting to spare his family the disturbance.

The phone quit ringing when he was about to turn the corner into the kitchen and jerk it off its cradle. He swore under his breath and then heard his wife say to hold on, that she'd get him. She handed the phone around to him and walked by him, on her way back to the bedroom, holding her nose. "You smell like Muscotti's," she said, and kept on walking.

Balzic's eyes closed, and he caught himself weaving. He leaned against the door frame and mumbled a hello into the phone.

"Chief Balzic? Is that you?"

"Uh-huh. Yeah."

"Okay. Sorry to call you so early but I got a prisoner here who—"

"Who is this?"

"Oh, sorry. Deputy Warden Canestrale. Down at Southern Regional."

"Oh."

"You remember me. I met you a couple times. Oh, maybe three years ago, I think it was an FOP picnic."

"Yeah. Uh-huh. So?"

"So, uh, look I'm sorry to bother you, no kidding I am—"

"Hey, I'm sure you are. So what's it about?"

"Oh. I got a prisoner here who says he got to talk to you. He's in fear for his life. He says you're the only one who can help him. So I figure maybe you'd want to know about it."

"Uh-huh. Well. Uh, who is it? What's his name?"

"Randolph Kolesar. He says you are the only man he will talk to, he don't want to talk to no lawyer, and there's nobody here that will believe him, but you will."

"Uh. What's he—what's he in on?"

"He was transferred from Allegheny County Jail. He's

awaiting trial on seventy-five thousand dollars bond. All dope charges, maybe some, uh, conspiracy and bribery stuff, also, but mostly dope. You know, marijuana and things like that. So what d'you wanna do? You wanna come talk with him, or you want me to place him in isolation? I mean that's the only choices I got."

"I never heard of him. He says he's in fear for his life, huh?"

"Yes, sir, that's what he says. I mean, I throw him in the ice cell, he's got no worries there. But he practically begged me to call you."

"Well, look. You better put him, uh, separate him, 'cause I won't make it down there for at least four, five hours."

"Whatsamatter, Chief, bad night, huh? Boy, you sure sound like you partied it up, you know? What'd you have, a wedding or something?"

"No, no, nothing like that. Just drank too much, that's all. Look, do what I said. Separate him and I'll be down four, five hours, okay?"

"Okay. And I'll tell the warden, too, so he'll know what you're here for. Okay, Chief, nice talking to you again. Say hello to your mother for me. She knows my Aunt Rena and my Aunt Louise."

"Yeah, yeah, I'll do that. Bye."

Four hours later turned out to be eleven a.m., and Balzic was waiting in the warden's office for the prisoner, Randolph Kolesar, to be brought to him. The warden had sent for Kolesar and then had left with the guard, who was to have brought him about ten minutes later. Ten minutes after that, the warden was back, saying, "He won't leave his cell. He's scared. I asked who he's scared of, he won't say. He says you got to go to him. It's up to you."

"You got any idea what it's about?"

The warden shook his head no.

"Ever had him before?"

"No."

"Well, I'm here. May as well go see what he wants to sell."

"You're not carrying anything, are you? Oh. You're the one who doesn't carry—you that one?"

"That's me. I'm the one."

The warden shrugged, and nodded to the guard who had accompanied him. "Filkosky'll take you. And he'll be right outside if anything happens."

Balzic nodded and followed the guard. Filkosky was short, wide, and thick. There were two wrinkles in the back of his neck—which was almost no neck at all—and his gait was fast and heavy. His breathing, through a nose broken more than once, was noisy. His eyes were brown and dull and in the ten minutes it took to get from the warden's office to the isolation cellblock, Filkosky said only one thing.

"The warden asked me, I'd've brung the son of a bitch. I'd've brung him, one fuckin' hand I'd've brung him."

When they reached the isolation cellblock, Filkosky stopped and unlocked the plain, white metal door without a word. Then he let Balzic in and pointed to the end of the corridor some twenty feet away. "I'll be right there you need me. Holler when you're done."

Southern Regional was a minimum-security prison. Most of the residents lived in dormitories. The few who had broken the rules or who were afraid were sent to the isolation cellblock. Isolation was another word for solitary confinement; it depended upon one's viewpoint. No matter the viewpoint, the cells were tiny, barren, and cold. There was a metal rack that served as a bed built into one wall. At the end of the cell opposite the door was a stainless steel unit that was a sink above and a toilet below. There was one clotheshook in the wall opposite the steel

rack. The clotheshook was designed to break under fifteen pounds of pressure, to preclude suicide by hanging.
There was a window in the door, but it could only be
opened from the outside. Fluorescent lights were built
into the ceiling. There was no mirror.

What there was in the cell was a tall, board-thin man
with long brown hair, brown eyes, and a face that was
twitching in two places—to the right of and just under his
lower lip, and in the eyelid of his right eye. He was
wearing very expensive blue jeans, a white silk shirt, a
short, purplish leather jacket, and blue shoes made of
some reptile skin. He wore no socks, and no jewelry. He
had pressed himself against the wall between the steel
rack and the sink-toilet, and looked close to panic.

"You Balzic? Huh? You Balzic?"

"Yeah. That's me. Who're you?"

"Kolesar. Randy, Randolph John Kolesar."

Balzic nodded several times and sat down on the steel
rack. "What d'you want?"

"You kiddin' me? Whatta you think I want?"

Balzic nodded. "Yeah, yeah. So does everybody. How
do you propose to get what you want?"

"Listen, man, uh, Chief Balzic. Listen, man, I heard you
were number one fuckin' straight dude, man. I mean, I
heard that, I been hearing that from a whole pile of cats,
you know?"

"Yeah? So?"

"So I heard that a dude wanted to trade with you, I
mean, like what I heard was, you'd really go to bat for the
dude."

"I'm listening, Randolph—that's your name, right?"

"Yes, sir. That's it. Randolph John Kolesar."

"I never saw you before, Randolph, so why me?"

"Hey, why me? I mean, why the both of us? You know?
But I mean, here I am, you know? And there you were and

we both got like, uh, big problems. And then, you know, why not you? Why not me? Get it? Why should we not get to know each other?" All the while Kolesar spoke, his shoulders remained against the wall and his hands remained clasped over his crotch. When he spoke, he moved nothing but his face.

"What kind of big problems do we have, Randy? Is that what they call you—Randy?"

"No. They don't. They call me a whole lot of things, none of which I care to repeat right now, at this moment."

"What would you like me to call you?"

"Whatever you want to call me, hey, Chief, that's okay with me."

"Well, which is it? Randy or Randolph?"

"Okay. Uh, you can, uh, you can call me Randolph."

"All right, Randolph. Now what's our problem—uh, why don't you sit down?"

"I'll stand, that's okay. I'm okay right where I'm at, okay?"

"If you want to stand there, that's fine with me. Whatever makes you comfortable."

"Comfortable—ho, man, is that . . . comfortable. I mean, if there's one thing I'm not at this moment it's comfortable."

"No, listen, Randolph, all I'm talking about is where you're standing right now. If that makes you feel better—I mean under the circumstances—why you just stay right there."

"Okay, okay. This is where I want to stay."

"Good. Now what's our big problem?"

"Uh, right. Our big problem is this. Mine. I mean, my big problem is I'm—I'm, uh," Kolesar licked his lips twice and could get no saliva. He quickly brought up his left hand and pinched at the corners of his mouth.

"Why don't you get a drink there?" Balzic said. "Go ahead. Run a little water and get a drink. You can turn your back, Randolph. I'm what you heard. I will not move toward you. On that you have my word."

"For sure?" The twitching under Kolesar's lip stopped, but the twitching in his eyelid seemed to double its pace.

"For sure. Go ahead. Get some water."

Kolesar slipped around the sink without turning his back to Balzic. Then he bent over and pushed a button and held it and drank out of his cupped hand. He stopped several times to look up at Balzic. Finally, after he satisfied his thirst, he splashed some on his face and then straightened up.

"Randolph, where'd you come from? Was it Allegheny County? Were you in the county jail down there?"

Kolesar could not speak. There had not been much healthy color in his face; at Balzic's last question, that color took on a bluish cast. After some moments, he nodded. It was the briefest of nods, done so quickly that Balzic had to ask himself if that slight, almost spastic downward movement of Kolesar's head could be called a nod.

"How long were you there?"

"Seven days! Jesus. Forever . . . I can't remember when I wasn't there." He lurched downward and drank from his cupped hand again. When he straightened, his eyes were red and raw. "I been in different lockups. I ain't no cherry. But they ain't none of them like that. None of them. . . . " He began to sob. The emotion seemed to catch him by surprise; he did not turn away from Balzic as the tears poured forth and as a large bubble of mucus puffed from his left nostril and then broke with a soft pop. He sucked in his breath and looked alternately wide-eyed and then squinty as the fits of emotion shook him.

"Take your time."

Kolesar giggled at the thought. "Take my time! Christ, would I like to. But time ain't mine to take." He giggled nervously again, and then sobbed. "You got to keep me here. I mean, I ain't goin' back there. I'll kill myself before I go back there."

"That's what you want—to stay here? That's what you want from me? That's it?"

Kolesar nodded frantically. "My bond's seventy-five grand. Shit. There's no way I can make seventy-five-hundred cash, no fuckin' way."

"That's a lot of bond, Randolph. What are the charges?"

"All the usual. Dope. You know, conspiracy, all the shit."

"Must've been a lot of dope."

"Three hundred pounds. That's what they say."

"Who's they?"

"The narcs. The state BDE guys."

"They got you with three hundred pounds of marijuana?"

"That's what they say."

"Whatta you say?"

"I say I . . . I say, uh. I say if somebody don't help me a little bit—and Jesus Christ I'm not asking for much, hear? I mean if you don't come through, man, and I go back there, they're gonna take me apart." Kolesar began to shiver and his teeth to chatter.

"Do you need something?"

Kolesar shook his head no. "This is—this is just fear, man. Just fear. I don't use nothing but a little pot now and then. I don't even smoke it. It's bad for your lungs. I eat it."

"I'm learning something new every day," Balzic said. "You eat it?"

Kolesar nodded. "I just, just throw some in the ground meat and have a hamburger, th-that's all."

"Whatever you say. Well. What's the trade? You want to stay here—what's the trade?"

Kolesar swallowed several times and fought to control his fear. "That, uh, that girl?"

"What girl?"

"You know the one. The one that got her lunch on your beat."

"What about her?"

"I was one of the guys with her."

"With her when?"

"When, uh, when we got what's-his-face out of his pad. She talked him out and then we took him the rest of the way."

Balzic nodded slowly. "Go on."

"Go on how—how d'you mean?"

"Randolph, you want me to do a thing for you, then you have to do a thing for me. What you've said so far is interesting. But that's all it is. I have to know a whole lot more and I have to be able to check it out. I mean, for example, I don't understand how you even got here in the first place. That's not part of your trade, but it's part of you and I'm really curious about you. How'd you get here from the Allegheny County Jail?"

"I got here real easy. I said to the turnkeys down there that if I didn't get some protection I was gonna make trouble for everybody."

"And just like that they transferred you? On that?"

"Come on, man. I had to tell the warden something and when I told him something he made up a number and moved me. But don't ask me what I told him. 'Cause you're gonna get a call from him tonight and you can tell him whether I came through for you or not."

"I'm going to get a call from the warden of the Allegheny County Jail tonight and I'm going to tell him you came through for me, is that what you said?"

Kolesar nodded.

"And if I tell him that you didn't, are you going back there?"

"That's the deal. Only I ain't. Either you put the word in

to keep me here or I kiss off. Those are my outs. Just the two. One or the other. No other out. Just them two."

Balzic sighed and chewed his upper lip. "Okay. Okay, Randolph. We'll go your way for a while. Tell me what you're gonna tell me. From the beginning."

"No. Can't do it that way, man. I mean I heard you were straight and I like what I see so far, but you got to understand what's happening here. Where I'm coming from. I got to have almost, like, uh, like a blood oath, you know? I mean, this is serious. Mr. Balzic, my whole everything is right here on it. I mean, if you don't do this thing for me, you're gonna hear about me goin' right in the shit-can. Right down there in the garbage, man. Those niggers in Pittsburgh are never gettin' me again, I promise you. I swear. And you got to swear. You got to promise on something. I know you won't write it down, but you got to—"

"Randolph, listen a minute," Balzic said. "You may as well know this right now. I will not swear to anything until I hear what I'm swearing to and that's it. I will promise you now only one thing. And that is that I will listen. But right now, that is all—the only promise I will make. Is that understood? I mean, at this point, that is not up for arguing about. Are we clear?"

"Oh, man, oh . . . oh man. This makes it tough, this—"

"Randolph, understand this part. I walk out that door anytime I holler for the guard to come open it. You don't. It's that simple. Now, I've already promised you that I'm goin' to listen. But I've also promised you not one thing else. No other thing. Clear? Huh?"

"Shit, man—"

"Shit man nothin'!" Balzic roared. "Your position here, shit, you practically got no position. So don't shit-man me nothin'. I told you I'd listen. So go ahead and give me something to listen to. From the beginning. And don't leave anything out. Start by giving me the name of the other male who was with you."

Kolesar looked at the floor and edged away from the sink, moved back between the sink and the rack, put his shoulders against the wall, and folded his hands protectively over his crotch. His gaze danced from the floor to Balzic's eyes to the walls to the floor and back to Balzic's eyes.

"Uh, you're a hard man—"

"Harder than you know," Balzic said sharply.

"Well, uh, Jesus—"

Balzic stood up and stepped to the door and raised his hand as though to slap it.

"Wait! Wait a—please! Oh, please, man, I'll tell you. Right from the—his name is Skowronek. Eddie. He's from the South Side. But that's it, man. I don't know too much about him. He was with the girl."

"Okay, that's a start," Balzic said, sitting back down. "Go on."

"Uh, he—he was—"

"Whose idea was it?"

"Huh? Was what?"

"Whose idea was it to go to Thurman Burns's apartment? You didn't suddenly out of the goddamn blue just decide to go to this guy's apartment because you wanted to scare the shit out of him. Why him? Whose idea?"

"Uh, that was his. Eddie's."

"What for?"

"To score some coke, man. Eddie said this cat had two places, and we were supposed to get him out of one and take him to his other one, and we were supposed to score all this coke, man. Like real weight. Two or three keys."

"How did you two get acquainted, you and Eddie?"

"Oh, you know, we were in the life, you know. We were in the business. I seen him around, he seen me around."

"You see the girl around?"

"No, man. Not until that day. No, the night before, I saw her. First time."

"Where?"

"Some bar in the South Side, man. I don't think I could find it if I tried."

"Were you doing some business?"

"No, I was just boogeyin' around, you know."

"And you ran into Eddie and this girl?"

"Yeah. And he said was I doing anything the next day. And I told him—"

"This guy who you say you know only casually 'cause you're both in the business, all of a sudden he comes up to you and asks you what you're doing the next day?"

"Yeah. Right."

"And the upshot of this is you're going to score two or three keys—that's kilos, and that's what? Two point something pounds of cocaine?" Balzic stood up and started for the door again.

"Hey! Where you—wait a second! Wait a second, shit, where you goin'?"

"You think I'm gonna sit here and listen to you tell me about some guy, who is practically a stranger to you, tell you about say it's two kilos, that's almost four and a half pounds of something that sells for almost twelve or thirteen hundred dollars an ounce! This casual acquaintance is going to cut you in on this deal just because—because why? You tell me, for crissake! Because you're both in the business and he happens to run into you in a bar! That's bullshit!"

"No, man, no. Oh please sit down, please! Honest, I'm telling you. Hey, listen, please sit down, I can explain that to you."

Balzic took a step backward but did not sit down.

"Hey, come on, please? Sit down, okay? This is not bullshit I'm giving you, I promise. Why should I give you bullshit? I'm in a bad place here, and, uh—"

"All you have to do, Randolph, if you want me to do something for you—you hear me? All you have to do is for once in your young life quit trying to con somebody. You been doing it so long, you can't help yourself anymore. You start talking to a cop—even when you say your life is on the table here—and here you are trying to bullshit me. So just knock it off and tell me what happened, 'cause if you throw one more piece of bullshit at me, I'm gone."

"Okay okay okay okay okay," Kolesar said, rattling the words together into a chant. Still, he moved only his face; the rest of his body remained fixed in relation to its parts and to the wall, the sink, and the rack.

"Once again, how'd you get tied up with Skowronek?"

"We made some business together two, three times."

"What kind of business?"

"All pot. Nothing else. We were what they call brick dealers or pound dealers. A brick is a key, a kilo. A pound is—you know what a pound is. Smaller than that I did not deal. Sometimes I get short, I'd go see Eddie. He'd hold me for a while. And the other way around, too."

"For how long?"

"Two, three years. I don't know. Maybe longer, maybe not. I don't know."

"But suddenly he comes to you with a deal about cocaine, is that right?"

"Right."

"Something you have never dealt in before."

"Right. Ex-actly."

"Why not?"

" 'Cause, man. Coke is something you just don't move into like with pot. Pot's everywhere. Everybody's doin' it. There's this guy bringing a truck up or an RV—"

"A what?"

"RV. You know. Recreational vehicle. A motor home. A Winnebago."

"Okay."

"Man, U.S. 1 from Miami is the Marijuana Trail. Mommas and poppas doin' it. School teachers. Doctors, lawyers, and yeah, got to say it, man, po-lice chiefs. Man, I'm gonna tell you, nobody deals more dope than some narcs I know."

"This is interesting background, but that's all it is. Come on back to the question."

"It is the question, Chief. You asked me how come I never did the coke business. I'm trying to tell you. With pot, shit, you never know who's holding if you ain't. Anybody can be holding. And if you ain't holding, how can you do business? I mean, I go to my main men and if they ain't holding, then I go to somebody else. And nobody gets uptight. You work the best way you can. Don't screw nobody, don't bullshit, don't pay with nothing but cash, and you'll make a living. 'Cause—and this is the main point—you deal in weight with pot, you can't step on it with anything. You can't cut it.

"Some smart-asses, kids, when they're dealing in ounces, they try oregano and parsley and all that cute shit. But once the word goes out, you stop making a living.

"But coke, Chief," Kolesar said, "that's a whole different trip. They can fuck with that stuff so many ways, you can't believe it. 'Cause you just don't make a living with coke, man. With coke, you get rich. Fast. I've known guys, man, went from Chevy Monte Carlos to Learjets in three years and paid for 'em in cash, man. You know how much a Learjet costs, man? And these guys bought one apiece!"

"So," Balzic said, "what's your point?"

"The point? Chief, my point is, unless you're a heavyweight, either 'cause you know the chemicals, or 'cause you got the paper, or 'cause you know somebody who has the paper and you got the balls, I mean if you don't have two of those three in that combination, you don't mess with coke except maybe like an ounce dealer. To deal weight, you're talking about heavy-duty people. I know some of 'em, man. They're crazy."

"How?" said Balzic. "Why? In what way? And what's this got to do with anything?"

"It has everything to do with it. I'm trying to tell you. It's this way. I'm a heavyweight pot dealer. Good week, I clear five hundred a week. Coke dealers, man, clear five-thousand! When you're talking those kind of numbers, you got to have a bunch of up front money—or a bunch of balls—or the brains. Just wanting to go to the big leagues, man, that don't make it. Unless, unless you fall into something. You luck into a happy scene. Somebody thinks you're their connection and hands you a suitcase by his dumb mistake, and you open it up and see all these bags of white crystals and rocks, man. Or unless somebody is pissed-off at somebody, and sets that somebody up for a little armed robbery, you know?"

"And that's how we get to Thurman Burns?"

"Ex-actly. Thurman Burns pissed somebody off. A lot. I mean a real lot."

"Skowronek heard about it, is that it?" Balzic said.

Kolesar nodded. "All we needed was a broad. 'Cause that was supposed to be Burns's main problem. He'd forget business to be with a broad."

"Skowronek provided her too?"

"Yes, sir, he did."

"Did you see her before that night?"

"Couple times. She was coming down off something, I don't know what. Something you use needles for, and I can't stand to be around them needle freaks, man. They're all fuckin' crazy and it don't matter what they put in them needles."

"Was she close to Eddie? She his friend or did he just use her?"

"He used her—I guess. I don't know. It don't make no difference anyway. They're both stone dead." Kolesar giggled and his teeth chattered and he belched as spasms of fear shook him. "They're both—both of them gone."

"Tell me what happened. Skowronek came to you about Burns. When? How long before you went to Burns's apartment? The day before? A week? When?"

"The day before. He came up to me in this hunky club in the South Side. He says what am I doing, do I got some plans for tomorrow and shit like that. I tell him I'm loose. Not doin' nothin', what's he got in mind. And he takes me outside and in the middle of the sidewalk he tells me he fell into something, we could both really score, all we needed to do was a simple robbery. He had the guns and the way to get the guy to forget to look out for himself and once we got him out of his place all we had to do was get him to take us to his other place and there was gonna be the start of a whole new career."

"Was the girl with him then?"

"No. Not on the street. No, she was inside the club."

"She was with him when he approached you?"

Kolesar nodded.

"Okay. Go ahead."

"Hey, so, uh. So, uh, I listened to him and I thought about the certain guys I knew who graduated to coke and I thought, fuck, you know, why not? I wasn't too happy about the guns, but if that's the way we had to go, then shit, you know, I was willin'."

"So you did it and you got Burns out of his apartment and to his other apartment and you turned the place upside down and you didn't score, right?"

Kolesar shook his head emphatically no. "Nah-uh, no. We didn't turn his place anything. We didn't touch it."

Balzic stared hard into Kolesar's eyes. "Why not?"

" 'Cause there was no point. 'Cause on the way that

dude, uh, that Red Dog, he told us we been conned. I mean, he didn't say nothing until we said for him to tell us where to go to his other place. And he said, 'You clowns been had.' And naturally we said what was he talking about and he said one of us been talking to a narc and we both said bullshit, it wasn't me, and he just smiled and said, 'You can say it wasn't you,' but there was no way anybody else was gonna rob him 'cause nobody else knew where he was but the narcs. He said a couple narcs been watching him and hassling him for months and he was moving so often in Pittsburgh nobody knew where he was and he said nobody. And then he moved out to this little town down the road from here and he thought he had it made for a while and then one day he said he was coming out of the supermarket and walked smack into this narc who tried to fake like he didn't know who he was but he said he knew he'd have to move fast or they'd be on his ass again."

"Did he say who the narc was? State? Federal, which?"

"State. His name was Cortese. Soon as he said the name me and Eddie knew he wasn't lying. We knew we'd been set up. 'Cause we'd both had shit from that motherfucker."

"What did you do then?"

"We just went on to the dude's place—"

"Burns's?"

"—yeah. And he told us straight out, man we were walking into a first-class fuckin'. The narcs needed somebody to stage a robbery to get him out of his office so they could tear it up and find his stash. He told us what his setup was. He always rented at least three pads. One out by the airport and two in Pittsburgh—until they started to hassle him. But he always kept like four or five cars parked around and he was always watching the mirrors when he drove, so he knew in a minute when somebody was on his ass. And since Cortese and his buddies been on his ass he didn't keep nothin' on him. Nowhere. All three of his pads were fronts. He had his stash with some stewardess out by the airport."

"And you believed him?" Balzic said.

"Hey, man, what was there not to believe? He took us in his pad, he said, 'Go to it. Look. I'll show you all the places you can store coke,' and he told us how coke, you know, like if you put it at the wrong temperature, it just turns into glop. And so he gave us a tour of his place. He didn't have nothin' there. Not even a fuckin' aspirin. He showed us the wallpaper and the floor, the carpets, the tile, the crapper, the pipes in the shower, everything. He was cool. He just kept shakin' his head and sayin' how they was back in his other place just wreckin' it, destroyin' all that great fuckin' furniture. And then, and then, he said, if we didn't get the fuck out of there, we'd be lookin' at them comin' in the windows and tearin' up that joint, and that was it, man. We split. And, wait! I almost forgot. He reached in his underwear and pulled out this stack of bills, man, and he said, 'You cats split this,' like, it was for us, uh, for us believing him. Man, there was, like, over two thousand bills there. And Eddie and me split it and we took off."

"And was that the last you saw of Eddie and the girl?"

"Uh-uh. No. That was the last I saw the girl, right. But I seen Eddie a lot up until about two weeks ago."

"When did you hear about the girl?"

"Huh? Oh, the girl. The next day it was in the papers, on the TV, everywhere."

"Were you alone when you heard about it?"

"No, I was with Eddie."

"What did you do?"

"Hey, man, I started moving. I almost shit to get out of Pittsburgh. I told Eddie to get me that piece back, and he did, and I went and got all my cheese and split. I drove to Charleston, and I left the car in the parking lot, and I caught a plane south, man, to Myrtle Beach, South Carolina. I laid around on the beach down there for two or three days and then I took a bus to Atlanta, and then I took a plane to Tampa and I stayed right in the hotel in the airport."

"Why'd you do all that?"

"Why? You kiddin' me? I never been that scared—wrong, that's the second scaredest I been in my life. 'Cause when I read about that girl, that's when I knew Burns didn't bullshit us."

"So Eddie told you that a state narc was the one who set Burns up?"

"Oh yeah! Are you kiddin'? Absolutely. I told him, I said, hey, man, you got to tell me what's happenin', 'cause our ass is on the table here, and that's when he told me how he made the connection."

"Okay, now just wait a minute. I'm gonna go call the DA and see if he can get a stenographer down here, and you can tell them."

"I got more to tell, man. I mean, how I landed in the Allegheny slam, that's important. I mean, I'm really on a fuckin' rail, man, and these narcs are getting ready to ride me right outta life into death. I'm on a one-way ticket, man. They're tryin' to kill me, man. They almost made it in Allegheny. But I got to the warden. And you got to hear the rest, otherwise when the warden calls you tonight you ain't gonna be able to tell him what I did for you, you know?"

"Listen, Randolph, I appreciate what you're telling me, but I never did have the greatest memory, and I learned long ago to have a good stenographer be my memory as soon as I decided I needed to remember something. Your story will be heard, I promise. But there's no point in telling the whole thing twice. I've heard enough to believe you. I'm just curious about one thing."

"What?"

"What the hell did you tell that warden to get him to transfer you?"

"Oh, that. That motherfucker. He didn't believe me till them niggers . . . Never mind. But he believed me then. I got a cousin, she works for a newspaper. It's just a jerk newspaper and she's only a society reporter, you know, weddings and garden clubs and shit like that, but she's a reporter, and I told him she was looking to win some award for her career. And he thought I was bullshittin' for the first two days, but after the niggers got me, and I told him again, he checked it out."

"Is it true?"

"Fuckin'-A it's the truth. You think I'd make something like that up? Christ, I almost got killed in there. I was *supposed* to get killed in there! That's how come I got locked up in there! I only had one play, man, and it couldn't be bullshit. For all I knew it was the fuckin' warden who was supposed to off my ass, I didn't know. But I wanted him to know I had something goin' for me."

"Okay," Balzic said. "Okay. I'll be right back. Is there anything I can get you?"

"You serious? Hey, I'd sure like to have a cheeseburger, man, and a chocolate shake."

"Is that all?"

Kolesar nodded. "Yeah, and I'd also like to have a doctor look at me. Not some fuckin' prison bones, man, but a good doctor. I patched myself up, but it's infected."

"What happened, what's wrong?"

Kolesar began to shiver and belch with fear again. "Oh, them niggers that was 'sposed to do me, man, they thought they'd have a little fun first. So they tried to cut my balls off. Only thing was there just happened to be a straight

guard on duty and he heard me hollerin', man. And he
stopped 'em. . . . If there's a heaven . . . and he don't go, man,
I don't want to. . . . " Kolesar broke down completely then.
His sobbing seemed to take the strength out of his knees,
and he slowly began to crumple until he was on the floor.

Balzic bent down and put his hand on Kolesar's neck
and rubbed it. "There," he said, "there, you go 'head. Just
go 'head."

Outside the cell, in a corridor barely three
feet wide, Balzic spoke as softly and as emphatically as he
could to the guard, Filkosky.

"That person is an important witness, Filkosky, do you
understand me?"

"You have to talk up. I can't hear you. I'm a little deaf. I
was in the mortars in Korea."

Balzic stopped at the end of the corridor and confronted
the guard. "Listen harder. This is important. That prisoner,
that Kolesar back there I was talkin' to? You know the one?"

"Yeah. I know the one."

"He's a witness to a murder case I'm workin' on. Do you
know who I am?"

"You a cop?"

"Hell yeah I'm a cop—who'd you think I was?"

"What do I know? I thought you was his lawyer or
somethin'. I didn't even know you was a cop."

"I'm the chief of police in Rocksburg. You're in my
jurisdiction in this lockup, in case nobody told you. Never
mind. That prisoner there, I'm making you responsible for
him. Now pay attention. You payin' attention?"

"Yeah. Right. Sure I'm payin' attention."

"My name is Balzic. That prisoner, Kolesar, is my
prisioner. He was transferred here from Allegheny County
Jail on my say-so. I don't want anybody fuckin' with him,

you understand me? Nobody. He's a witness to a murder that happened three months ago. Lots of people are after him, including state narcotics officers. Right now, I'm going to get a stenographer and an assistant DA. I don't know how long it's gonna take me to get them, but I want that prisoner here—alive—in good health—when I get back. You understand?"

"Yeah, sure."

"You was in the mortars, huh? What mortars?"

"Heavy Weapons Company, First Battalion, First Marine Brigade."

"I thought so," Balzic said, clapping the guard lightly on the shoulder. "I knew you was a Marine. I could just tell, just from looking at you."

"You could? Huh? You could tell that, that I was in the Marines? No shit. Hey, was you in the Crotch, too?"

"Fuckin'-A," Balzic said. "In World War Two. Fifth Division."

"They only had three divisions when I was in. First, Second, and Third. Did they have five divisions in World War Two?"

"More than that. They had six."

"I'll be a son of a bitch, how 'bout that. Six divisions. Hey, the Corps. The Corps was something," Filkosky said, grinning almost as wide as his neck, which was very wide. "Hey, eat the apple and fuck the Corps, right?"

"Right," Balzic said, grinning back. "Eat the apple—"

"And fuck the Corps!" Filkosky bellowed, giving Balzic a thunderous slap on the shoulder.

Balzic was nearly knocked off balance by the blow. He said quickly, "Remember, now. One Marine to another, you take care of my prisoner. I don't care who wants him, you don't let nobody in there to see him until I get back, okay?"

"Okay, you got it. Hey, semper fi, right? Huh? Always faithful, right?"

"Right," Balzic said. "Semper fidelis. Always faithful."

"Fuckin'-A," said Filkosky, opening the door at the end of the corridor and leading Balzic part of the way back to the warden's office. "Not even the fuckin' warden'll see your prisoner. You can bet your ass on that. Hey, 'cause if it wasn't for youse guys winnin' World War Two, I wouldn't've had no chance to kill no gooks in Korea, you know? I mean, I'm grateful to youse guys for the opportunity, you know?"

"Hey, you're welcome," Balzic said. "My pleasure. See you in a little while."

Balzic bounded away. He went through the warden's office only slowly enough to say how much he valued the prisoner Kolesar, and then made a dash for the outside and the air and sky and the sight of trees and grass and of traffic on the highway half a mile away, below the main gate. He sometimes forgot about the Filkoskys of the world, of the brutes who were lucky enough to be allowed their savagery in the name of patriotism, and who could still find socially acceptable employment.

Balzic stood by his cruiser for some moments thinking about Filkosky, about what he'd be doing if he hadn't found this job. Probably not much that was good or kind or beautiful, Balzic thought sourly, and there was no telling how many heads he put lumps on just for the mean hell of it. But when you needed a Filkosky, you needed him, and that was that.

Balzic slid behind the wheel and called the DA's office on his radio. He got a secretary who told him that all the assistants were in court or in conference and that it would be late in the day before any of them could be reached. The DA himself was out of town, and there wasn't one stenographer left in the office—she didn't know where they'd all gone.

Balzic thanked her and then called his station.

"Hey, Mario," Sergeant Stramsky said, "where the hell

are you? The mayor's been looking for you all day."

"What's he want?"

"He wants to talk to you, what do I know? He says he hasn't seen you for over a month. I couldn't tell him nothing. I looked pretty stupid, Mario."

"Forget about it. Is the mayor there?"

"He was five seconds ago."

"Well, find him. Tell him to hire a stenographer from one of those temporary help agencies, one that takes good shorthand, and bring her out here to Southern Regional. Tell him we finally got a break. Tell him he can see for himself how us great detectives solve crimes. And you tell him I absolutely have to have that stenographer."

"Okay, okay," Stramsky said.

Balzic clicked off the radio and got out and walked around for five minutes or so, just stretching his legs, his mind bounding and rebounding from thoughts of Kolesar to Filkosky to Deputy Warden Canestrale to Bureau of Drug Enforcement Agent Michael Franks. And then he thought of Mayor Kenny Strohn and his block parents and crime prevention and ten thousand-meter conditioning runs.... Christ, how would Strohn react to these four people, respond to them, analyze them? Where would they fit in his social scheme?

Balzic got back in the car and called Stramsky again. "Tell Strohn to stop at a hamburger joint and get a cheeseburger and a chocolate shake. Tell him I got to have those two things. Also, call the hospital. See if they got a spare emergency-room doctor who wants to make a house call. If they do, send him out here. If not, tell them I'm gonna bring a prisoner to them and I don't want to wait around for service...."

Almost an hour and a half had passed before Mayor Kenny Strohn and the stenographer arrived in the deputy warden's office, and Strohn was full of excuses about why it had taken so long.

Balzic didn't want to hear any of them. "Where's the milk shake and the cheeseburger?"

Strohn snapped his fingers and made a great show of having forgotten. "Why'd you want them anyway? Can't you get anything to eat here?"

"They were not for me, Mr. Mayor. They were for the person who's 'solving' our murder for us."

"What? You mean this is not a confession?"

Christ, Balzic thought, where'd he get that idea? "No, no. Never mind. Introduce me to the lady."

"Oh. Excuse me," Strohn said. "Forgetting my manners here. Chief Balzic, this is Mary Ilberti. She's been with me for, oh, five years now."

"How do you do, Mary?" Balzic said, trying not to look at the woman's badly deformed right leg. She wore a shoe that had a sole at least eight inches thick. Balzic could not help himself; he always felt extremely awkward when confronted by someone's deformity, no matter the cause.

"Hello," said Mary. She had a deep, powerful voice which sounded almost ludicrous in relation to everything else about her, which seemed frail in the extreme.

"Mary, have you done this before?"

"What? Taken dictation in a prison?"

"From a prisoner?"

"No. Is it different?" She smiled a little too confidently.

"Uh, Mary, let's put it this way. The fellow we're gonna be talking to has very nearly been killed for what he's trying to tell me. I haven't confirmed that yet, but I don't doubt it. And, uh, the language he uses may upset you or disturb you, but whatever your feelings are, they can't interfere in this, in what you're doing. I want his words down there on your notebook and I don't want you picking and choosing which words. Do you understand?"

"I think I'm professional enough to do that," Mary said. "Mr. Strohn has never complained about my professionalism."

"Absolutely!" said Strohn. "She's the best. That's why I brought her. I couldn't go get some temporary help as you suggested."

"Okay. Let's go. Oh, hey, Canestrale—"

"Yes, sir," the deputy warden said. He'd been hanging back, out of the conversation. "What can I do for you?"

"Call the state police. Get Lieutenant Walker Johnson, tell him to get one of his people to get a cheeseburger and a chocolate shake and don't ask no questions, it's a favor to me, and to bring it here and give it to you, okay? You wanna do that for me?"

"Nothing to it. It's done," Canestrale said happily, reaching for the phone.

"Okay," Balzic said, "let's go."

They had to wait for the guard, Filkosky, to come back from the lavatory to let them into the cellblock where the isolation cells were. Filkosky opened the door to the narrow hall and locked it after they had passed through. Then they pressed against the wall to let Filkosky by, and he led the way to Kolesar's cell.

"Oh shit," Balzic said as soon as Filkosky opened the door. "Oh shit!" He was going to tell Filkosky to call for an ambulance, but as soon as he touched Kolesar's carotid arteries he knew there was no use in that. Kolesar had sliced his radial arteries from the base of each thumb up his wrists for at least two inches. He had done it with the sharpened edge of a Medic-Alert necklace that proclaimed an allergy to penicillin. On the floor, in his blood, he had written: "Balzic your all alike."

Mary Ilberti passed out at the same time Filkosky began

to protest that it had not been his fault, that he had sat right outside Kolesar's cell the whole time, except for the last ten minutes.

"I had to take a crap. I held it long as I could. I didn't know when youns was comin' back. I had to go. Hell, you can't blame me for that!"

"Nobody's blamin' you for anything," Balzic said.

"Oh my God," Mayor Strohn said. His mouth was open and his jaw and mouth were jerking downward in tiny, bubbly spasms.

"Oh shut the fuck up," Balzic said, turning at once to Strohn's secretary, who had slid down the wall in an almost leisurely manner and now was slouched on the floor in Kolesar's blood, her good leg bent awkwardly under her bad one. "For crissake, Strohn, let's get her up and out of here. Shit. Look here, she's got blood all over her skirt, Christ almighty."

"What?" said Strohn, his jaw working in those odd little bubbly spasms. "What?"

"Get in here and help me, goddammit!"

"Oh. Oh, yes. Sure." That said, Strohn dropped straight to the floor, as faint as his secretary.

" . . . I only went to take a crap. I didn't even go. It was just gas. You can't blame me for that—"

"Nobody's blamin' you for anything, Filkosky. You take him and I'll take her. We gotta get 'em out of here. They wake up and see what they're layin' in, they're gonna either faint again or get hysterical. Now you take him and go, and I'll take her and be right behind you."

"It was just gas or something—"

"Pick him up goddammit! I don't care what it was. Get him out of here."

Filkosky hoisted Mayor Strohn as though he were a small, rumpled pillow. He started to go rapidly down the corridor.

Balzic, the stenographer in his arms, bellowed at Filkosky to stop. "Come back here and lock this goddamn door! Put him down and come back here!"

"Oh yeah. Okay. Oh yeah." Filkosky said, nearly dropping Strohn in his haste to comply with Balzic's order.

Balzic had to back up to let Filkosky get to the door to close it and lock it. As he did, he could feel Mary Ilberti stirring. Balzic let her down slowly, letting her get her feet under her. "You okay now? Huh? You all right?"

"No," she said. "No, I'm not. I think I'm going to be sick."

"Well, if you have to, you have to, but I'd appreciate it a lot if you weren't. Your boss is passed out up there and I got enough other things to do, so—"

"I'll try not to," she said. "It's not something I want to do." She put her hand over her mouth to cover her small belches.

"Come on," Balzic said, taking her by the arm and leading her down the narrow corridor toward Filkosky and a now-awakening Mayor Strohn.

"My goodness," Strohn said, "did I pass out?"

"Just like that," Filkosky said, snapping his fingers. "Both of youse."

"You get up?" Balzic asked Strohn.

"I don't—I don't know."

"Well how 'bout trying, huh? There's a lot to do. . . . "

Strohn struggled clumsily to stand. He grimaced several times, looking at the blood on his secretary and on himself.

Filkosky opened the isolation-block door, finally, and stood aside as Balzic led the way out and to the deputy warden's office. Balzic asked Canestrale to do what he could to help Strohn and Mary Ilberti, and then went to the phone and dialed the state police CID.

"CID, Lieutenant Johnson speaking."

"Walker, this is Balzic. Don't ask me no questions and I'll explain everything later. Right now I want you to pick up and hold separately the following Bureau of Drug Enforcement agents: Michael Franks, William Cortese, and Frank Gensheimer. Under no circumstance are they to be permitted to talk to one another."

"Uh, no questions, huh? Just go pick them up, is that it?"

"Yes, sir, Walker, if you would, please. I will appreciate it and so will you."

"Is that all?"

"Boy do I wish it was. But no, it isn't. Get your people together and call the coroner. We got a suicide—"

"Where the hell are you?"

"Southern Regional."

"Uh-huh. Who's the suicide?"

"A dope dealer named Kolesar. He made Cortese for us. Cortese and Franks. And then I don't know what happened. I left him alone too long, I didn't reassure him enough, I don't know what, but the skinny bastard really tried to lay it all on me."

"What? Laid what on you?"

"Skip it, I'll tell you later. Hey, listen, I really want this sonofabitch Franks. I mean, this bastard, uh, I really don't care how we do it, but I'm gonna put this guy's ass on a wall one way or another—"

"Hey, Mario, old friend, slow down. Just take it easy. If he can be got, we'll get him, but—"

"Walker, but me no buts, quote me no laws, ethics, common sense, nothin'. This piece of shit makes us all look like assholes—"

"Hey, Mario—"

"—I mean, a kid writes in his own blood that we're all alike, goddammit, because of this scumbag, uh-uh, Walker, goddammit, that's not right, that's not right."

"Mario, you hang on, I'll be down there, you hear me? I'm on my way, you hear me?"

"I hear you," Balzic said. "I hear. . . . "

Balzic was outside, standing in the sun, feeling the sun on his face, when he heard someone approach on the gravel in the parking lot outside the administration building.

"How you feelin', Mayor? You doing okay?"

"Okay?" Strohn said. "No, not at all. I'm not doing anywhere near that good. . . . May I ask you some questions?"

Balzic nodded. "Sure. But on one condition. You don't argue with my answers."

"No, no, nothing like that. I just want information."

"If I have it, you can have it. If I don't, we'll go to the next question."

"All right," said Strohn. "Who is—who was that person?"

"His name was Randolph Kolesar. He was a drug dealer. And he knew who killed the girl on South Main. He wanted to trade."

"Did he take his own life?"

"I'm sure he did, yes."

"Do you know why?"

"No, I don't."

"Can't you speculate?"

"I won't."

"Did you really have no case before this?"

"No."

"Was he, uh, did he really have information that would make a case?"

"Yes."

"Cannot the, uh, cannot the case go forward without him?"

"Oh, it not only can, it will. It'll just have to go in a different direction, that's all."

"So you know, now, who killed that girl?"

"No."

"But I thought you just said—"

"I said he knew. I didn't say I knew. I went to get a stenographer to get what he knew in writing. There's a big difference between what he knew and what I can surmise from what he knew. And a really big difference between what he told me and what I can corroborate."

"I don't understand," the mayor said. "Do you have a case or not?"

"We've been making a case, Mr. Mayor. What we needed was somebody who knew the answers to questions we could only speculate about. And I had him, and I didn't take him—I didn't take as good care of him as I should've. I got too goddamn anxious to make my case and, uh, I forgot, uh, I forgot what was right in front of me."

"What was that? In front of you, I mean."

"A very scared guy. Very scared. You can't get any more scared than he was. . . ."

Balzic walked heavily into Troop A headquarters. His legs felt thick and stiff, and his shoulders ached, and there was a cramp in the left side of his neck. He was hot and sweaty and parched. Folded in his coat pocket was a statement he had dictated to Mary Ilberti at Southern Regional, in Deputy Warden Canestrale's office, and to which he had signed Randolph Kolesar's name.

Balzic asked the desk man where Lieutenant Walker Johnson was, and followed the directions to a holding cell in the rear of the building. Walker Johnson was just turning away from the cell door as Balzic approached.

"Who's in there?"

"Cortese," Johnson said. "We don't know where the other two are."

"Beautiful," Balzic said, nodding his head. "Couldn't've worked out better. C'mon, we're gonna Mutt and Jeff this clown right into—"

"Hold it, Mario. Easy," Johnson said, leading Balzic a short distance away from the door of the cell. "What the hell's goin' on?"

Balzic took the papers out of his coat pocket and held them out in front of him, waggling them from side to side. "I got a statement—I'll admit it's second-hand and after the fact—"

"After what fact? A suicide?"

Balzic nodded. "Yes, but—"

"Aw, Mario, for crissake, we—"

"Now, listen, Walk, this is not an ordinary thing here. We got—"

"We got crap and you know it, and you walk in with a phony statement from a suicide. Mario, Jesus Christ, what the hell am I supposed to do with that?"

Balzic took a step backward. "Hey, Walker, is this you here? And me? Or did I get in the wrong building? C'mon, Walk, we can wave this—no, not we. Me. I can wave this at Cortese and tell him enough shit and you can tell him enough roses and together, between your roses and my shit, we can do real business with this guy. I know it."

"Mario, listen to me for a second, will you please? This guy is a kid, true. But he's already called a lawyer. He knows all about Mutt and Jeff, hell, he's worked it plenty of times himself. We can't—"

"Walker, goddamnit, that's exactly why we can! He won't know what we're doing. He won't believe it. He won't be able to let himself believe it."

"Aw, Mario."

"Walker, Jesus Christ, we got to try. I mean, I got two dead people on my head. The last one wrote in his goddamn blood that I was no different from the rest, and the rest he meant was shit like is in that cell there. And, Walker, I am different from the rest. And so are you. And if we don't try to get to that prick before his lawyer shows up, then we can just dump it right now. We got nothin'. What we need is a witness with immunity."

"I know we do."

"Then let's get him!"

Johnson shook his head morosely and jammed his hands into his pockets and puffed out his cheeks, blowing out a heavy sigh. He looked at the floor for what seemed to Balzic a minute. Finally, Johnson shrugged and said, "What the hell."

"Good man," Balzic said, cuffing Johnson lightly on the shoulder. "Let me get in there and ugly this clown to death."

Balzic stepped quickly into the holding cell and blocked Cortese's view of the door until Johnson could close it and step away from the small window.

"Cortese? You are William Cortese, are you not?"

Cortese, a tall, wide-shouldered young man, sat with his chin in his very long hands. He didn't bother to look up. "I've already called my lawyer. And I've told a lot of people their rights, so I know what mine are. And among my rights is to remain silent until my attorney is present to counsel me about what I should or should not say. So you can just—"

"Hey, you punk. You stuff your rights up your ass. I got two dead people on my hands, one of them your buddy shot in the face and the other one cut his wrists with a blade you may as well've put in his hand."

"What are you talking about?" Cortese said, sneering.

"You know goddamn well what I'm talking about. Randy Kolesar's dead, his blood spilled all over a cell 'cause of the harrassment you and Franks and Gensheimer put him through. Eddie Skowronek is dead, his girlfriend is dead—"

"Eddie who? What girlfriend?"

"The girlfriend Franks shot in the face on South Main Street in Rocksburg three months ago. That girlfriend."

Cortese rubbed his forehead and peered up under his hand at Balzic. "I don't have to say anything, and on the advice of my counsel I'm not going to."

"Okay, fine. That's just peachy fuckin' keen with me. Don't say anything. Just listen. I'll do all the talkin'. Any time you feel like it, you just jump in."

Cortese continued to rub his forehead and to look up at Balzic under and around his hand. He said nothing.

"You listenin', huh? You payin' careful attention?" Balzic shouted. "Here goes. All of this stuff is provable and admissible, you got that part so far, huh? Provable and admissible. Ready?"

Cortese seemed to slump ever so slightly.

"Your superior officer and compadre, one Michael Franks, has been short-weighin' evidence in preliminary hearings for two years. He scores a pound, he turns up in front of the magistrate with an ounce. Two pounds, two ounces. Thirty pounds, three pounds. Three hundred pounds, thirty pounds. He's famous for it. We got magistrates' records, and we got defendants' testimony, bang, bang, bang, right down the line. Your name, William Joseph Cortese, agent, Pennsylvania Justice Department, Bureau of Drug Enforcement, your name, clown! You hear? Your name appears on several—that's more than one—of those preliminary hearing records. That's conspiracy to obstruct justice—and that is just the fuck-ing-god-damn-be-gin-ning, clown."

Cortese seemed to be breathing faster, and he seemed to be rubbing his forehead just a bit harder. But he said nothing.

"Question," thundered Balzic. "What happened to all the dope that was confiscated and never got submitted as evidence? Huh? Answer! It turned up for sale among known drug dealers—three, count 'em, that's one, two, three, known and notorious marijuana dealers who will testify, in return for certain favors in their upcoming trials, that—guess who?—sold 'em the dope. If your answer is Franks, Gensheimer, or Cortese, you win a violation of the Drug and Device Act, you win a violation for possession and another one for sale, and you also win a conspiracy to possess and to sell—you still with me, clown?"

Cortese's nostrils were flaring slightly. He was rubbing his forehead with such force that his flesh was starting to get red.

"But we're just now gonna get to the good stuff," Balzic snarled. "What we're gonna talk about now, prick, you hear me? You payin' attention down there? Rubbing on your forehead like that, you look like you're gonna rub the skin off. Well, you rub all you want, but you keep listening, 'cause here comes the heavy-duty stuff.

"Yessir, here comes the shit that sends you away for so long your family forgets about you. Yessir, that's a long time, when even a good Italian mother forgets what her son looks like. And it takes a long time for a mother to forget that. But she will, 'cause what we think about now is the harassment of Thurman Burns, notorious dealer in controlled drugs, namely marijuana and cocaine. Sound familiar there, Cortese? Huh?"

Cortese suddenly stood up and pulled off his jacket and

stripped off his tie. He sat back down abruptly and re-
sumed rubbing his forehead.

"What'sa matter, prick? Getting hot in here, huh? You
think it's hot now, wait'll you hear this. Thurman Burns,
A.K.A. Red Dog Burns, notorious dealer in marijuana and
cocaine, friend of flight crews traveling from Miami to
Pittsburgh and back, finds himself harassed by agents
Franks, Gensheimer, and Cortese of the BDE for a period
of many months.

"Question: is this harassment for the purpose of making
a lawful arrest? Huh? Answer: bullshit! Double bullshit!
It is for the purpose of confiscating Burns's contraband
for the personal gain of the three previously named
agents—of which you are one, Cortese. How old are you?
Huh?"

"What?"

"Pay attention, prick. How old are you?"

"What do you care?"

"How old—twenty-six? Huh? Twenty-seven? Boy, you're
gonna be thirty-five when you get out. Oh yeah. It's fifteen
to life for you, oh yeah."

"Knock it off," Cortese said through closed teeth.

"Ho, boy, sure. Knock it off. Sure. Knock this off, prick!
What's your mother gonna say, huh? What's she gonna say
when that judge brings down the gavel? Bang!"

"Knock it off."

"She'll be standing there with a priest holding her by the
shoulders, huh? You Catholic, prick? What's your priest
gonna tell your mother, huh? Better yet, what's your mother
gonna confess to the priest about how she raised you,
huh? You're sitting here rubbin' your forehead until it's
turning like a tomato and tellin' me to knock it off, and
your mother don't even know what kind of son she got.
Does she? Hey, prick, answer me! Does your mother know
or not?" Balzic was screaming into Cortese's face.

"Get away from me. Get out of my face," Cortese said.

"Ho, ho, listen to him. 'Get away from me. Get out of my face,' " Balzic mimicked him. "Who's gonna get out of your mother's face, clown? Huh? Think of all the people that are not gonna speak to your mother any more, just 'cause she had the bad luck to have you for a son, just 'cause you had the bad luck to get paired up with a couple of rats like Franks and Gensheimer.

"But how's your mother supposed to know about them, huh?"

"Will you shut up about my mother!"

"Shut up about her!" Balzic shouted. "Shit, I haven't even got started about what her shame's gonna be. Christ, this dope stuff, this is one thing. This murder, that's something else. But, hey, Cortese, my young prick, what's she gonna do when she finds out about the little girls, huh? The little girls you and Franks worked over to get your guns off."

Cortese jumped up suddenly and stepped to the far edge of the cell. "You're nuts, pal. You're whacko. You're coming right off the wall with this routine."

"Sure I am," Balzic said, stepping close to Cortese. "Right. You just keep believing that. But when those little black girls get up on the stand and the doctors explain what's been done to them, shit, Cortese, just imagine trying to look your mother in the eye."

Cortese said nothing. He was forcing himself to say nothing, to do nothing, and was having a very difficult time of it.

"Yeah, prick. What's your mother gonna say, what's she gonna tell the priest about how she raised you, when the doctors testify about what happened to the little black girls, nine years old, eleven years old, huh?"

"I know what you're doin'! You think I don't know what you're doin', huh?" Cortese cried out.

"Cortese, hey, Agent William Cortese," Balzic said, sneering, "what difference do you think it makes to me what you just said? I don't give a shit what you think you know about what I'm doin'. Piss on that! What's your mother gonna know? Huh? How's your mother gonna look anybody in the face after seeing those little black girls, the ones who had their nipples bitten off by Franks and by you, Cortese! BY YOU! What's your mother gonna tell her friends—"

"You're crazy! You're nuts!"

"—and your relatives—"

"You're out of your mind!"

"—most of all, what's she gonna tell her God, Cortese? Huh, what's she confess to the priest—"

"Shut up! Shut up!"

"How can she look up at the Virgin Mary, Cortese, and know in her heart what you did to little black girls, you piece of shit, you? Huh?"

Cortese began to tremble. It started in his fingers, but soon it was traveling up his arms like a current of electricity.

Balzic wheeled away from Cortese suddenly, went to the cell door, and pounded on it with the flat of his hand. "Come and let me outta here before I puke. The sight of this scumbag, the stink on him—come on, open up."

"You bastard," Cortese said. "You bastard . . . "

"Hey, prick, how's it feel? Huh?" Balzic said, looking over his shoulder.

The door was swung open, and Balzic stepped out.

"He's all yours, Walk."

Johnson made no effort to step in. He took Balzic by the arm and led him away from the cell, searching his face.

"What's the matter?"

"You weren't playin', were you? You meant all that stuff."

"You have to ask? Goddamn right I meant it."

"Aw, Mario, God . . . "

"Hey, Walk. You get in there and lay your sugar on him, and when you get tired, you pound on the door, and then I'll go back in, and if we do it right, we'll have this sonofabitch before his lawyer gets here."

"Mario, we can't do it like that and you know it."

"Walker, we're wasting time. Now are you gonna help me or not? If you don't want to, just say so. And I'll go back in there and do both numbers myself. I've done it before, I know how to do it."

"Mario, that's not the point."

"What is, then?"

"You, uh, the point is, you're losing your cool, pal. You sounded like a maniac in there. And you even said it, you weren't playin'."

"Walker, are you goin' in there or am I? 'Cause you want the truth, you fuckin'-well-told I mean it. I want these guys. And I want them out of the business they're in, and I want them to lose something for what they did. That pig Franks mutilated an eleven-year-old girl, Walker. And I don't give a shit how I get him—and I mean that—one way or another, with your help or without, but I'm gonna get that scumbag, and if—"

"Yeah, but, Mario, at what price? At what price? You gonna—"

"—and if I got to do it alone, I will. I have daughters, Walker, in case—"

"You know goddamn well I haven't forgotten. I didn't deserve to be reminded of that, and—"

"I have daughters, and it was not very long ago that they were nine and eleven, and I want this pig off the streets for as long as I can keep him off."

Johnson threw up his hands. "Okay, okay, okay, okay." He sighed. "Take it easy. I'll do my job."

"Good. I'm glad, Walk. I never thought for a second you wouldn't."

Balzic and Johnson turned at the sound of approaching quick steps, and around the corner came a short, thin, wiry man in a gray silk suit. His burgundy tie was silk, his oyster-white shirt was silk. Balzic guessed that his underwear was probably silk.

"Which of you gentlemen is Lieutenant Johnson?" said the man in silk, in a voice that seemed as though it should've come from the throat of a man considerably larger.

"He is," Balzic said, drooping with the suspicion of who the man in silk was.

"Lieutenant, my name is Orlando Prudente. I am an attorney. I believe you have my client William Cortese under arrest."

"That's correct," Johnson said, glancing quickly at Balzic as though to say, well, so much for Mutt and Jeff.

"Very good," Prudente said. "I wish to speak to him, please. Now, if you don't mind."

Johnson stepped to the door to Cortese's cell and held it open for Prudente.

Prudente started in, but stopped, canted his head, and backed out. He turned obliquely to Balzic and Johnson and said, "Gentlemen, I have, suddenly, a disquieting sensation. I believe—something tells me—because of your proximity to this cell, and because the door was not locked, I believe that you were either interrogating my client or were contemplating an interrogation of my client. Gentlemen, say not so." Prudente glanced from Johnson to Balzic and back. "No answer? Hm. What does silence mean, gentlemen?" Prudente nodded his head quickly several times, stuck out his lower lip, and, turning back, stepped into Cortese's cell, pulling the door shut with a clang after him.

Balzic probed a molar with his tongue. Johnson looked up at the ceiling.

In less than a minute, Prudente was slamming the flat of his hand on the door and demanding that it be opened. When it was, he confronted Balzic and Johnson with his jaw set and his face flushed with anger.

"What in hell's unholy name do you think you were doing? I demand to know which of you harassed my client, insulted his mother, accused him of assaulting young girls, to mention only a few of your travesties—I demand to know! Which?"

"Aw fuck you," Balzic said, and, motioning for Johnson to follow him, set off at a quick pace toward the front of the building.

"Indeed," Prudente called after them. "We shall see who it is that takes what. I assure you it will be neither me nor my client."

Balzic put his left hand behind his back, middle finger thrust upward, before he turned the corner and went out of Prudente's sight.

"Mario," Johnson said, trying to catch hold of Balzic's arm to slow him. "Where the hell you going?"

"I'm going to see a magistrate I know, the guy owes me a couple. I'm gonna charge that sonofabitch Cortese with everything I can think of, and I'm gonna get that magistrate to set bond just high enough to where he'll think he can afford it to get out. I think about a hundred thousand'll be about right. No. Maybe seventy-five thousand—"

"Mario, wait a minute—"

"—yeah, seventy-five thousand'll do it. He'll come up with seventy-five hundred. He'll have to sell something. This sonofabitch is gonna think how much his buddy Franks is worth. I gotta find out how much property he owns—"

"Mario, hold on a while, will you?"

"—maybe we can get into his mother's money, make her sell something, really put some heat on this prick."

"Mario!" Johnson snapped.

"Mario me no Marios, Walker. I'm gonna put so much on this prick's mind, he'll think anything's better than what I do to him. That refugee from a silkworm farm, Christ . . . "

"Mario, we need a witness who wants to play on our side."

"Right. You couldn't be righter. You go back there and talk nice if you want to, tell him all the options. But I'm gonna put this prick in a bind. I'm gonna get him publicity, a nice, fat bond, the works. You get ready to charge that clown, you bring him to Aldonelli, down from City Hall. You know where his office is."

"Aw, Mario, Mario, this isn't gonna, uh, this isn't—"

"I told you, Walk, Mario me no Marios. I'll see you in Aldonelli's office. Don't be long." Balzic called out over his shoulder.

He left Johnson, his hand over his mouth and rubbing his cheeks, standing in the middle of the duty room.

On the way to Magistrate Anthony Aldonelli's office, Balzic stopped at a pay phone near a gas station. When he got out of the car, he was sweating. He looked around at the people in the gas station, the attendants, the customers in two cars, one a station wagon with two women and four preschool children, and it was a moment before Balzic recognized what was different about the day. When he did, he knew that his family was probably catching hell because of his preoccupation with Franks and Cortese and Gensheimer. The people were all in their shirtsleeves. The pump attendants, the customers, the children, all had bare arms. Spring had happened and Balzic hadn't noticed it and he felt—as he always did when his preoccupations turned him away from the present—like an insensitive jerk.

He took off his coat and loosened his tie and watched the children bounding and romping in the back of the station wagon and felt himself smile at the memory of his own children doing that. And then the station wagon was in front of him and the driver was talking, but Balzic could not hear her words.

"Beg pardon," he said.

"What're you, some kind of pervert? Huh? You like little children? Go somewhere before I report you to the police."

"What?"

"He's not only a pervert, he's deaf," the driver said to her companion, and spun the wheels on gravel pulling away from Balzic and out of the station.

Balzic scratched wax out of his ear and swore, and went into the phone booth and called Russell at the Bureau of Drug Enforcement.

"I won't help you, Mario. I will not, so stop asking," Russell said when he heard what Balzic wanted to know.

"Listen, your guys didn't do shit—"

"Don't tell me what my guys did. I know what they did."

"—didn't! Did not! Not did, Russell. They gave these three pricks a bath. They did not—despite all the information sent their way from me to Carlucci to you—despite all that—"

"Mario, I don't care, I'm not gonna do what you want."

"—despite all the corroborated information that went to you, your guys did nothing—"

"Mario, I'm gonna hang up on you, honest to God I am. I will not get that man's files to find out how much he's worth."

"—I'm not talking about you, Russell. You did everything I asked and more. It was those guys from the other end of the state—"

"No, Mario. No. Good-bye." And Russell hung up.

"I'll be a sonofabitch. You actually did it. You did it," Balzic said to the phone.

Balzic talked to himself all the way to the magistrate's office, and he was still talking when he walked into Aldonelli's musty, cluttered office, which, with the desk and four folding chairs and two file cabinets, seemed hardly larger than a refrigerator. Aldonelli was in his shirtsleeves, fanning himself with part of a newspaper, sipping a beer, and watching a game show from New York on a cable TV station.

"Mario, hey, hiya doin', long time no see, paisan." He stood up, wiped his right hand on his pants, and shook Balzic's hand vigorously.

"Anthony, I'm fine. Got a problem, but I'm fine. How's your wife?"

"Oh, you know. She has her good days. They don't come as often as they used to, but it's to be expected." Aldonelli shrugged, and his eyes closed, and he cocked his head first to the right and then to the left. Finally, he reached up and shut the TV off. He took another sip of beer. "Can I get you one, huh? C'mon, have a beer with me."

"Sure, okay." Balzic pulled one of the folding chairs up beside the desk. He took the cold can that Aldonelli got from a small refrigerator beside his desk. "She's been sick a long time, Anthony. That ain't right. It ain't. I know nobody can do anything about it, but it ain't right."

Aldonelli nodded slowly, and then he shrugged again. This time his eyes filled up. "Hey, so, uh, what's your problem? Huh? Let's take care of things we can take care of. Right? What the hell."

"Okay," Balzic said, and went on to explain in detail what he wanted done and why.

When Balzic had finished, he was sweating from the effort to recall all the details, and from the emotion.

Aldonelli took it all in without comment; occasionally his eyebrows would go up, but not much.

"Is that all, Mario? Hell, the murder thing itself is enough for a hundred thousand. You add on there, uh, one count of conspiracy and, uh, one of to obstruct justice—er, no. Make it, uh, violations of the Drug and Device Act, uh, possession to sell, and conspiracy—hey, no problem. I don't have to stretch anything for this guy. I could make it, with the murder, and with the idea that he might have everything to gain to flee, why hell, I could legitimately make it a hundred and fifty thousand. You want that?"

"No, no, seventy-five's plenty. Just big enough to make him go for the cash."

"Well, that's no problem, no sir, not at all."

They both turned toward the door as a state police cruiser pulled up at the curb outside the office.

Balzic was pouring sweat; it was running in rivulets down his sides and down his chest and over his stomach. "Anthony," he said, as the car doors were opening and closing, "listen to me. I can only say this once."

"Huh? What?"

"Anthony, the information I have against this guy is not a prima facie case. We get to the preliminary hearing, you'd throw it out. But I need to turn this guy into a witness, and I have to put him in a bind to do it. You understand?"

"Yes."

"No problem?"

"What problem? There's no problem. One thing at a time. You don't have something by the preliminary, well, then, we think of something else. That doesn't have anything to do with today."

The door was pulled open, and a trooper Balzic didn't know led William Cortese and Cortese's attorney, Orlando

Prudente, and Lieutenant Walker Johnson into the room.

"Gentlemen," Aldonelli said, finishing his beer and dropping the empty can into his trash basket, "what can I do for you?"

"Uh, if you don't mind," Balzic spoke up quickly, "I'll get mine in first. You ready, Mr. Magistrate, huh?"

Aldonelli rolled a form and copies and carbon paper into his portable electric typewriter. "Be ready in a sec—here, okay."

"Name of the accused is William Cortese," Balzic said. "You give your middle initial, address—hell, Cortese, you know the procedure."

Cortese gave his middle initial, age, address, and occupation.

"Charge?"

"Several," Balzic said. "Number one, accessory to murder of one Jane Doe, age and address unknown, in the late afternoon of January 20, 1979." Balzic waited for Aldonelli to quit typing. "Murder occurred on South Main Street, Rocksburg, in 700 block. Accomplished by gunshot."

"Other charges?"

"Yes. Assault, aggravated assault, involuntary deviate sexual intercourse, rape, and statutory rape—"

"Jesus Christ, this guy's nuts," Cortese said, moaning.

Prudente, the short wiry man in silk, leaned close to Cortese and whispered to him. Cortese sighed, and shrugged angrily.

"—these offenses were committed over a period of several months from January to March . . . they involved two Jane Does, one age eleven, the other age nine. . . . "

"Okay, uh. Anything, uh, anything else?"

"Yes. Violations of the Drug and Device Act, possession and sale . . . and conspiracy to possess and to sell controlled substances . . . over the period from January to March."

"Okay," Aldonelli said, when he'd caught up. "Anything else?"

"No further charges at this time," Balzic said. "I do want to add one thing, and I want to emphasize this as strongly as I can. I believe that the person I've accused in this information is a great risk not to appear at future proceedings against him, and I urge you to set a bond equal to that, with that in mind. That's all I have, Mr. Magistrate."

Aldonelli looked at the two state policemen and asked if they had anything to say or to add to what had been said.

"The only thing I've got to say," said Johnson, "is that I agree with Chief Balzic about the potential of the accused to avoid an appearance at future hearings and proceedings."

"All right," said Aldonelli. "Now you, sir, you're the, uh, Mr. Cortese's attorney, is that right?"

"I am. Orlando Prudente. Pleased to meet you, Mr. Aldonelli, Mr. Magistrate."

"How do you do," said Aldonelli, rising and shaking Prudente's hand.

"Mr. Magistrate, my client is an agent of the Commonwealth of Pennsylvania. He is an agent of the Department of Justice of this Commonwealth, and, specifically, he is an agent of the Bureau of Drug Enforcement. I will say nothing about the charges contained in this information filed against him—ridiculous as they are on their face—but I must stress that my client has undergone—prior to his employment by the Commonwealth in his present capacity—an extensive and rigorous investigation of his character, his family, his academic history, his military history, his social, political, financial history, and he was not found wanting in any area. I repeat, he was not found wanting in any area.

"So, Magistrate Aldonelli, I ask you to consider these facts about my client and to disregard the pleas of the accusers here, to wit, that my client is a great risk to avoid future proceedings, which is simply not true, Magistrate Aldonelli. My client is a law enforcement officer with an unblemished record of service to the state. As his oath of duty to this state he has sworn to uphold not only its constitution but the federal constitution as well. Your Honor, Magistrate Aldonelli, I urge you to set bond at a reasonable figure so that my client may be free to move about to assist in the defense against the charges filed here today against him. Thank you, Mr. Magistrate, sir. I have nothing to add."

Aldonelli hunched over his desk and dropped his gaze to his hands as he clasped and squeezed and kneaded his fingers. "On the, uh, on the merits of the charges given to me here today, I, uh, under the authority vested in me by the Commonwealth of Pennsylvania, I declare the accused, uh, Mr. William T. Cortese, to stand before me for a preliminary hearing on these charges on, uh, let me see here,"—Aldonelli licked his thumb and flipped pages on a calendar,—"uh, on April 10 at two p.m., and, until that hearing I hereby set bail at seventy-five thousand dollars—"

"What?" Cortese shouted.

Prudente tugged at Cortese's sleeve.

"—and until such time as bond in that amount is presented to me to satisfy that bail, I hereby authorize Mr. William T. Cortese's detention in Conemaugh County Detention Center. That's all."

"What kind of shit is this?" Cortese said. "I mean, you talk about bullshit, Jesus Christ, this cuts it here, I mean—"

"That's enough, Mr. Cortese," Aldonelli said. "I said this is over, but I will not put up with anybody's foul mouth. Now you just get yourself under control or I'm gonna throw some other things your way—and you won't like where they land. Counselor, get your client in order before he gets in more trouble."

Prudente's mouth was working hard, and his eyes were flashing in several directions. He seemed genuinely perplexed. At last he said, "That's an, uh, that's not the bond I thought I'd be hearing, Mr. Magistrate. Not at all. But I can live with it, yes, sir. Come along, William, we have some things to discuss. Lieutenant, I wish to discuss my client's bond outside, if that's all right with you."

Johnson nodded and said, "Take as long as you like. There's nothing pressing here."

Prudente nodded, and led Cortese outside and to the state police cruiser. They got into the back seat, and, despite the heat of the day, rolled up the windows and began to talk, in what seemed to Balzic harsh and heated tones. Prudente was having a hard time calming his client, and Balzic watched carefully to make sure he was not seeing what he wanted to see but what was truly happening, and he observed with great satisfaction that Cortese stepped out of the cruiser and brought his fist down on its roof.

"Good," Balzic said aloud. "Good. . . ."

From the time Balzic watched the cell door shut on Cortese in the County Detention Center— and Balzic made sure that his was the last law officer's face Cortese saw that day, aside from turnkeys'—Balzic knew that every hour was going to be a test of nerve. He knew it and he was counting on it, and he wanted Cortese to know it and to count on it. But more than Cortese counting the hours and testing his nerve, Balzic wanted Michael Franks counting hours and testing nerves.

Balzic stopped at the duty officer's desk and told him

what he would tell every duty officer on every shift for the next four days: "That prisoner Cortese, he can see anybody he wants—under your rules of course—but there is one person I don't want him to see or to talk to on the phone, and that is BDE Agent Michael Franks. If Franks calls or tries to get in there to see him, you tell him that Cortese is talking to me. I don't care what time it is, you understand? Day, night, whenever. Franks cannot see him or talk to him because I am talking to him, understand?"

It worked until the late afternoon of the fourth day when Michael Franks, after having tried so many times to call Cortese that the guard on the switchboard lost count, finally lost his patience and called Cortese's lawyer. Prudente lost nothing, least of all time, in getting a court order from the president judge to halt Balzic's " . . . harassment of his client by refusing to allow free access to those persons who might aid in his defense, namely his colleague, Bureau of Drug Enforcement Agent Michael Franks. . . . "

The duty officer read the court order Prudente handed him in Franks's presence, stepped into his office, and phoned Balzic.

"Stall them," Balzic said. "Give me six minutes. And tell somebody to let me in the South entrance. I want them to see me walking away from Cortese's cell. I'll give you a call from the wall phone to let 'em start toward me, okay? But don't let 'em go before I call you."

Balzic jumped into his cruiser, turned on all the lights, and never let up on the siren in the five minutes it took him to get from his parking lot to the service entrance, the South door, of the Detention Center.

A guard was waiting for him, and led him to Cortese's cell.

"Go call the duty officer and tell him to send 'em back," Balzic whispered to the guard.

"Okay," the guard said. Then he nodded to Cortese,

who had been pacing but who, at the sight of Balzic, had dropped quickly to the metal bunk and sat, glaring at Balzic. "You want to go in there? Or you just want to talk?"

"I'm fine out here. Now go do it, will you? What I said?"

The guard nodded and turned away at once, setting off toward a wall phone at the end of the narrow corridor.

Balzic looked into the cell at Cortese, and, in spite of himself, grinned meanly. "Hey, Cortese, hey, man. How you doin', huh?"

"Get cancer, Balzic."

"Ho, ho! Get cancer, huh? Hey, prick, when I get you where you're supposed to be, you're gonna wish you're the one who gets cancer. Yes, sir, you're gonna be prayin' you get some⁺thing fatal. 'Cause you're goin' to the Wall. You're goin' to Pittsburgh. You know how many crazy nigger drug dealers are locked up there? Huh?"

"I hope your whole family gets cancer," Cortese said. "Of the ass."

"You ever been in there, Cortese? Huh? You ever been in there at night—after the lights go out? Huh? You hear sounds in there, Cortese, you hear things in there at night you wouldn't hear in a jungle. And that's what's waitin' for you.... Oops, here comes your attorney and one of your fellow agents. So, uh, listen, don't worry about what we been talking about. Believe me, that information will get to the right people—"

"The who?" Cortese said, bolting upward off his bunk. "What're you doin'? What're you sayin'?"

"Listen, Bill, don't worry about it. Nobody will know anything until the time it'll do the most good. I give you my word. A deal's a deal."

"Deal my ass!" Cortese shrieked. "We got no deals!"

Prudente and Franks had begun to run at Balzic's word "deal." Cortese was against the bars reaching out for Balzic and cursing him when Prudente and Franks came into his view. Cortese became immediately subdued.

"What the hell're you doing?" Prudente said. "I've got a court order right here ending your harassment—"

"What deal?" Franks was asking repeatedly. "What's he talking about, Bill, huh?"

Balzic held up his hands in a mock innocent protest. "I am leaving. I have not harassed your client. I will obey the court order, Mr. Prudente. At once, I will obey the court's order."

"He's running a game, the motherfucker!" Cortese shouted. "I didn't make no deals! He's running a number here!"

"Bill, it's all right, I'm telling you," Balzic called out as he started to walk away. He brushed past Prudente, and then, when he was even with Franks, he leaned close and said, "Hey, Franks, want some good advice, huh?"

Franks recoiled until his back was against the wall.

"Get a lawyer," Balzic said and walked away quickly, humming a nonsensical tune.

"You cocksucker!" Cortese shouted. "I hope your whole family gets cancer! All of'em! Of the ass and the throat. So they can't eat or shit!"

Balzic looked over his shoulder in time to see Franks looking at Prudente and Prudente looking at Franks and both of them looking at Cortese, who had suddenly stopped shouting his wish for all of Balzic's family to die in pain.

Balzic called back, "Trust me, Bill. I'll get that immunity. Trust me. . . . " Balzic turned away quickly and left the corridor. He heard nothing in reply to his last exhortation. Out of sight and on his way to the front entrance, he said to himself, "We'll see who gets cancer, you sonofabitch. We'll see. . . . "

What Balzic saw when he returned to his office was a succession of petty administrative problems that occupied

him for the greater part of two hours: the first was a
dispute between two patrolmen of equal seniority over
vacation time; the last was a foul-up in the arrangement of
dates for salesmen from two uniform retailers; in between
came a harangue from a mechanic who claimed he should
have gotten the department contract to repair borough
vehicles.

Balzic could not have told anybody, with certainty, how
those three problems were resolved. He was too absorbed
with speculating about how Michael Franks was reacting
to the advice he'd been given. He reached for the phone to
call the Detention Center, but its ringing startled him.

"Yes? Balzic."

"Mario, this is Tony. Aldonelli."

"Oh right, Tony, what can I do for you?"

"Nothing. I just thought you'd want to know. Uh, your
guy, that guy who you wanted bail set for seventy-five
thousand dollars? You know, huh?—"

"Yeah, sure, I know. What about him?"

"He just made the bond. Made it with Frendy."

Balzic said nothing for a long moment. Then he swore.

"Yeah, I didn't think you'd be too happy, I thought like,
uh, you'd want that guy to sweat a little longer, but, uh,
looks like it didn't go your way."

"Whose signature's on it?"

"Uh, that's, that would be his mother's."

"Oh—okay. That's okay. That's the best way it could be.
Hey, thank you, Anthony. I appreciate your call—and I
appreciate your help too. I mean it."

"Well, I know you mean it. Anytime. Yes sir, any time."

Balzic hung up and rubbed his face. He was about to
stand up and go out into the duty room when his phone
rang again. It was Stramsky.

"You got a visitor," Stramsky said. "Says he comes with
the blessing of the Reverend Feeler. Looks like a candi-

date for the space academy. You want him back there or you want to come out?"

"No, send him back, send him back."

"One more thing. He was delivered. The Cadillac's in the Thrift Drug parking lot."

"All right. Good enough, send him back."

Balzic waited. Presently, a tall, lanky black—six feet six at least and no more than 165 pounds, ambled into Balzic's office. He had what appeared to be a chin that receded directly into his Adam's apple in almost a straight line. His lips were enormous, his complexion was grayish brown, and his bulging eyes were extremely bloodshot. His hair grew upward and outward in such a way that he looked to be continually electrically shocked.

"You Balzic?" he said in a rasping bass voice.

"I am. Who're you?"

"That ain't the point. Rufee sent me. You got a cigarette? Rum and Coke? Money? Fried chicken? Potato salad? Greens? Whatever you got, I need it. And I ain't sayin' shit till I eats."

"Well, you may never eat then."

"Huh?"

"You heard me."

"Well, looka here, man, Rufee done tole me you wants a number on a dude name of Franks. I got the number. I been buyin' shit from the motherfucker for two years now."

Balzic sighed irritably. "You better have more than that. Christ almighty, my people have talked to seven or eight people who've done that."

"Yeah. Rufee tole me. But I got pictures."

"You got what?"

"Now whose ears goin' bad?"

"Yeah, never mind that. What about pictures?"

"I done tole you, man. I got pictures. Pho-to-graphs.

Ko-daks. Pol-a-roids, man. I never done no business with
the dude without my man with his cam-er-a on the scene,
can you dig it?"

"Yeah? And where've you been until now?"

"She-it, man. What chu talkin' 'bout? Rufee done tole
me you want some righteous shit, man. He didn't tell me
nothin' 'bout you workin' no number on me, man, no way,
ofay, I ain't doin' that."

"That's enough," Balzic said.

"Huh? Motherfucker, who you talkin' to? I—"

"I—shit. You listen—"

"She-it, man, I ain't listenin' to nothin' 'til I see some
fried chicken, po-ta-to salad, greens, rum and Coke, lots of
rum and Coke, can you dig that? Bal-zeek? My upper
mouth and my bottom mouth and my middle mouth, man,
they's all goin' to sleep, baby, 'til some food done makes it
between my upper and my lower mouth, man, and makes
it right through my middle mouth, man. Otherwise,
sheeee-it."

Balzic ground his teeth together several times and looked
at his fingers, and studied his hands and the nails and the
hair on his fingers as though these were all new to him.
Then he picked up the phone and got Stramsky on the
line.

"Send somebody down to Muscotti's for a fifth of rum
and a six pack of Coke. Tell Muscotti to put it on my bill
and I don't want to hear nothing about they can't sell
bottles over the counter, okay?"

"Okay."

"And then send somebody down to the Flats to the
Hungarian place that makes the fried chicken—"

"Hungarian!" the lanky black said, snorting. "Man, I
want some motherfuckin' chicken, I don't want no honkie
chicken, she-it. Honkies can't make no chicken, man,
wha's wrong witchu?"

Balzic glared under his hand and over the tops of his glasses. He had been rubbing his forehead. "Hey, Rufee's messenger boy. Hey, Western Union, you want to eat chicken or you want to eat your own stomach acid? Name it."

"Oh, man . . ."

"I thought so," Balzic said. "Stramsky, get two orders of chicken, potato salad, whatever else they got. And tell somebody to move it. I don't want to spend more time with this needle freak than I have to."

"Needle freak! Is that what chu said? Motherfucker, I ain't no freak for noth-in', man. I am in con-trol, dig? I don't got no tracks on me no-where."

"Not in the last twelve hours maybe," Balzic said. "But your chauffeur's holding something for you, isn't that right?"

"Chauf-feur, man? What chauf-feur? Who do I look like, man? Roy-al-ty? The Duke of Detroit, man? The Prince of Pittsburgh? No shit, I knew I was lookin' bad, too, Jim, but I did not know I was lookin' bad enough to be like the Count of Corpus Christi, man. Chauffeurs, sheee-it. . . ."

"Yeah, yeah," Balzic said. "So what d'you got to sell? And how much does it cost?"

"Hey, man, the Baron of Brownsville don't sell noth-in' until the chicken get here, man. And it better not be somethin' been layin' round in some grease basket since yes-ter-day, man. I mean, I wants to smell feathers when that bag open up, can you dig it? I wants to hear cluckin' goin' on, man. Crowin' and shit."

"Oh for crissake," Balzic said and took his glasses off and rubbed his eyes until he saw kaleidoscopic colors. "What's your name?"

"Leroy Watermelon, man, what the fuck you care what my name is? She-it."

Balzic's shoulders sagged. He tried to think of more

than one way to get even with Rufee for this one. Nothing of any originality came to him.

"Okay, Mr. Watermelon, what's this about?"

"You sure are jive, motherfucker. I don't see noth-in' I can eat. There ain't even a fork nowheres. No napkin, no po-ta-to salad, no greens, no chick-en.... No vic-tu-als, man, no in-for-ma-tion." That said, the lanky black man with the receding chin folded his arms and closed his eyes and gave every indication of going to sleep standing in the center of Balzic's office.

Balzic gave up asking questions after three got not one word in reply. Apparently Leroy-whatever-his-name-was was going to be good to his word: no food, no information. Balzic, therefore, contented himself with studying the man's angular looks and curious posture. Leroy had spread his feet and lowered his chin, so that he looked like an un-gainly horse asleep on its feet, and he did not change position until Stramsky walked in carrying the rum, the Coke, a plastic bag of ice, and a half-dozen plastic-foam cups.

"We ain't home yet," said the black, opening his eyes first warily at Stramsky's presence and then widely at the sight of Stramsky's goods. "But we leavin' from the right place."

Balzic nodded for Stramsky to put the stuff on his desk and then said, "Help yourself."

The black needed no more encouragement. In quick yet somehow languorous movements, he opened the rum—complaining that it was an inferior brand—the ice bag, and a can of Coke, and mixed the Coke and rum in equal portions over three ice cubes. He drank that down with-out stopping to breathe, and then fixed another. That one he sipped, nodding slowly and making a great show of smacking his lips.

"Can we begin?" Balzic said.

"Say what?"

"Can we get started on what you're here for, or do we—"

"Gots to wait for the bird, man. Rum and Coke, that do right for to start, but I gots to get my molars on fried bird. I'm hongry, man. I ain't ate nothin' for two days."

"Hey, I'm doing my best," Balzic said.

"That's all we can ever do, our bes'. Tha's what my momma said. And you can see I been followin' her ad-vice like it came on down the mountain with Moses."

"What do you owe Rufee?"

"Say what?"

"You heard me. What do you owe him, that you're here?"

"I don't owe the Rev. nothin'. He asks me was I loose, could I do him some righteousness, and tha's all they is to it. 'Owe' ain't in my vo-cab-u-la-ry."

"Uh-huh. Purely mutual interest between you and the Reverend."

You got it. Oh-oh—I smell a warm bird comin'. Yas, yas. Here come de bird. You sure ain't no nigger cooked this bird? Damn, that don't smell like no honkie put the flame to it."

Stramsky appeared in the doorway, one large, foil-lined bag in each hand. He set them on Balzic's desk and was bumped aside by the black, whose eyes glistened with appetite.

Long, grayish-black fingers went to work on the bags, and in moments Balzic's desk top looked like a buffet table at a stag picnic. The black's first bites were tentative, but then his chewing became more robust and his lips smacked and his bony chest heaved with satisfaction.

"Honkies make this chicken, no shit?" When Balzic nodded yes, the black went on, "I'll tell you, Jim, these people got the gift. They got the holy touch. Where this place at? I got to come here and get a whole flock of these birds. This the best I ate since I went to my man's in Rankin. Dude got a little place in his house, man. Speakeasy, dig? That man cook some stuff, make you wanna come, Jim, I ain't lyin'. Make you forget all about pussy, I ain't bull-skatin'.''

"Uh-ha. Well, I give you my word. These people are not black. And the guy who cooked this, his wife's sister is married to a Ukrainian guy who makes kolbassi like nobody makes it. You like kolbassi?"

"Long as it ain't full of gristle and shit and's light on the garlic. There's some dude in Homestead make some good kolbassi, but you can't jus' walk in on him. He only make so much, dig?"

"All the good ones only make so much. You can't turn food into a goddamn factory."

"You ain't lyin'. Worst motherfuckin' thing happened to this country was all them goddamn fas' food joints on the roadside. She-it, I spend half my life, man, lookin' for a decent place to eat, man. And look here, I thought you was goin' get me garbage and damn if you ain't turn up a treasure house. Breast o'chicken, man, that is crisp on the outside and ain't no rubber on the inside— that's the holy touch, man. Ain't every motherfucker got it."

"We got some other places around here where they do some things," Balzic said. "There's a place I know, for example, that makes braciole—you know braciole?"

"Bra-shole? Man, are you shittin' me? Bra-shole? Take that round steak and pound it out real thin and then roll it up over that fillin', man, and tie it, and do it in that sauce, man. But tha's like birds, man, you got to have the touch. Lots of dagos think they can make that stuff, but she-it, they's only one every here and there do it right, man. When it's right, you on the edge of paradise. When it's wrong, you in a gutter chewin' on shoe strings in red paint."

Balzic leaned back and folded his hands behind his head. "After I tell you where to get this chicken, I'll tell you where to get the braciole. Uh, how's the potato salad?"

"Aw beautiful, man. If I'm lyin' I'm dyin'. Beautiful." The black looked at the ceiling and then closed his eyes. "See, they ain't killed everything in here with no one thing, tha's the touch. All the good shit got to be there, but not so you can say, oh yeah, they got this in there or that or onions or cel'ry or whatever—then, too, they done cut the may-o-naise with yo-gurt. See. Got just that little touch, that little lem-on-y touch."

"How come you're so thin?"

"I don't know, man. I always been this way. I eats like three hogs, man, and you could put me in a envelope, man, and put me through a mail slot, I ain't jivin'."

Balzic said nothing, just nodded an understanding, and sat, hands clasped behind his head, until the lanky black had gone through both orders of fried chicken and potato salad and washed it down with nearly a fourth of the fifth of rum and two of the Cokes. Having consumed the food, the black produced a gold toothpick and, between sips of rum and Coke, plucked and poked and scraped at the crevices between his teeth.

Then, biting lightly on the gold toothpick, he pulled up his shirt and peeled off a brown, five-by-seven-inch envelope that had been taped to his stomach. He handed it over to Balzic without a word.

Balzic took it, also without a word, opened it, and found dozens of color photographs of the lanky black exchanging money or cellophane or plastic bags, filled with what appeared to be marijuana, with Michael Franks. On the back of each photograph was written, in a crude scrawl, a date. The earliest was two years ago, the latest was a year ago, more or less.

"Lots more where those came from. I ain't never done no business with the man there without my man and his tel-o-pho-to lens, Jim. I mean all those flicks, man, they was from a quarter-mile away. Ole Franks, he be steady lookin', Jim, steady lampin' all over the place. And I tole him all the time, man, I say, 'My man got chu in the one-eye monster catcher, man.' And he be goin' crazy and sayin', 'Bullshit,' and everything, and then I'd take one of them out of my pocket and lay it on his face, see, sayin', 'Looka here, motherfucker, this was two weeks ago.' And he'd get so crazy, she-it."

Balzic looked quickly at the photographs. The equipment had been excellent and so had the person using it. Michael Franks had been caught—beyond any doubt—with his hands on a controlled substance, or with money, or both, in a series of transactions with an admitted trafficker in controlled substances.

"We only have one problem," Balzic said, after having looked at the last of the photographs.

"We ain't got no problem. I jumped bond on a coke number. I'm lookin' at fifteen federal. And I ain't goin' no fifteen in no motherfuckin' federal joint. I ain't goin' to the farm at Lewisburg for fifteen hours, never mind no fifteen years, and if I ain't goin' there, you can damn sure bet your last nickle I ain't goin' to Atlanta or Danbury.

"So you gets the U.S. Attorney and you tells him I wants a new face, a new place, a new name, and a whole lot of new fame. And I wants that in writin', Jim. All of it. Every motherfuckin' thing. And you gets that for me and I'll give you all those motherfuckers—'specially Franks. Also . . . "

"Also what?"

"Also, you gots to give me the name and number of these honkies that make these birds, man. I'm goin' have those fuckin' marshals runnin' down here every day, I ain't lyin'."

Balzic laughed. "Uh, what about the man in the Cadillac in front of the drug store?"

"Tha's my roadie. That's my bank. That's my life savings. When the man from the U.S. Attorney get here, then you go see my roadie, and he give you all the rest of the photo-graphs."

"How many more do you have?" Balzic could not hide his amazement.

"Lots. Got some of a skinny dago name of Cortese, and got one of some little jive-ass used to be steady drivin' for the other two. Gensa, Gensameimer, somethin'—"

"Gensheimer?"

"Yeah, tha's it. Little, weasely motherfucker."

"Uh, where have you been?"

"Hey, man, I been all over. Everywhere. I am a fugitive from jus-tice. When I came back last week to see how my old lady was doin', Rufee tole me I could do me some good. So here I am, jus' tryin' to do me some good, man. Oh, by the way, Rufee said you got a cold soft leg you wanna get straight—"

"A what?"

"A cold soft leg, a stiff momma." The lanky black looked dumbfoundedly at Balzic. "A dead female!"

"That's what I thought you meant. You know about that?"

The lanky black nodded, and fixed himself another rum and Coke.

"Wait a minute," Balzic said. He picked up the phone, got Stramsky and said, "Find the mayor and tell him to get his butt in here. Now. I want him to learn something."

"He just walked in," said Stramsky. "He's heading for your office and should be there about . . . now."

Balzic looked up to see the mayor at his door. He

cradled the phone and stood up. "Come in, Mr. Mayor, come in. You could not have come at a better time."

"Oh? Why's that?"

"Because, sir, because you're about to see how most crimes get solved." Balzic pointed to the lanky black who was sipping his drink and eyeing Mayor Strohn as if he were a homosexual and syphilitic prison guard.

"Mr. Mayor, I'd like you to meet, uh, Mr. Smith."

The mayor advanced on the black and thrust out his hand in his best political style.

The black looked at Strohn's hand as though it were a snake. Then he looked at Balzic. "This dude the no-shit mayor, huh?"

Balzic nodded and watched Strohn withdraw his hand.

"Mr. Mayor, I'll keep this as short as I can. Mr. Smith is a fugitive from a federal warrant on drug charges. Never mind the specifics. Mr. Smith has told me that he is looking at fifteen years. I have not checked that, but after talking to Mr. Smith for some time I'm sure that when I do check I'll find that Mr. Smith is correct.

"Also," Balzic continued, "Mr. Smith—which is not his name—wishes to become a witness under the protection of the federal marshals. He wishes to be given a new name, a new history—including all the paperwork that goes with it—and I think he wants perhaps a new face. Plastic surgery. In return for which, he has presented photographic evidence—and he says there is much more, and again I won't doubt him until I have reason to—these pictures here showing him involved in illegal traffic in controlled substances with an agent of the state Bureau of Drug Enforcement, namely one Michael Franks.

"And," Balzic went on, sitting down, "just before you walked in, Mr. Smith told me that he knew I had a dead female on my hands. Before he could tell me more about that, I tried to have you brought here, and that's when I learned that you were on your way at that moment. Now, I ask you to listen as Mr. Smith tells what he knows about that dead girl. Mr. Smith?"

"You tryin' to send this motherfucker to school on me, is that what you doin'?"

"More or less," Balzic said. "He needs the education, and it won't hurt you to give it to him. That's a promise. And that is the first promise I've made to you."

"I can dig it. I can dig that, yeah. Okay. You, uh, you got a momma shot in the face, three months ago. Maybe longer. Dude in the pictures did it. He was all the time struttin' over that number, 'bout he did this broad up and wouldn't make no never mind for him to do somebody else up. Talkin' 'bout how he watched her brains go all over the bricks. And I use' to tell him that my man with the Ko-dak was standin' next to my man with a thirty-ought-six with a great big tel-o-scope on top and, anyway, I wasn't no dumb soft-leg gonna let his jive-ass walk up on me with no piece in his hand."

Balzic watched the mayor's mouth go slack. Then Balzic said, "Anybody else hear this?"

"Hey, my man, if I'm goin' be posin' wit' the dude, don't you think I'm also goin' be recordin' the motherfucker? I got a whole box full of tapes with that motherfucker's mouth on it. Those is also with my man in the Cadillac. But I gots to tell you 'bout my man in the Cadillac. Pay attention, now, 'cause this is serious and I don't want nobody makin' no jive mistake.

"My man in the Cadillac is a up-front dude and the message is this: he gots noth-in to lose. My man is part of the number here—"

"What number—what's he talking about?" Mayor Strohn said, exasperated.

"Ohhhh, man," the black said. "Where'd you find this jive motherfucker?"

"Just take it easy," Balzic said. "Mr. Mayor, he's trying to explain to you—"

"But I don't know what he's talking about."

"Just listen and he'll tell you."

"You ain't lyin' when you say this jive-ass need a education. Damn!"

Balzic shrugged as though asking for patience, and made a circling gesture with his hand.

"My man, as I was sayin', is part of the number here. Part of the scene. Only he don't talk too good. Tha's why he's out in the ride and I'm in here talkin' to y'all. But he's in the same scene I'm in here, can you dig it?"

The mayor shook his head no.

"She-it, man, damn! I jus' told you, the man jus' told you. I wants to go into the federal witness program—or whatever the fuck they call it—and so do my roadie. My roadie lookin' at two numbers: a state thing in Florida and a federal thing in Florida. The state thing is murder. The federal thing is coke.

"Now he ain't goin' no murder trip in Florida. And if you don't know why, I'm goin' tell, Mis-ter Mayor. They got more niggers on death row in Florida than they got anywhere. And they got motherfuckers down there wants to kill 'em all on the same day, one right after the other, to make 'xamples of everybody.

"Now, my man ain't gettin' no younger—neither am I. We needs to retire. But 'specially him. My man's pushin' fifty-five. He can't do it no more. He outta shape. His knuckles hurt from arthritis. Young dudes wantin' to take up on his ass all the time, cops stoppin' him every time he turn around, people be knowin' how much he worth so they wants to turn him over, he can't be trustin' nobody. That man's dick don't get hard no more, tha's how bad it be on his mind, all this shit, one motherfuckin' thing after another.

"The man need some peace and quiet. He been bringin' pot into the country for so long now, all these honkie kids gettin' high off his labor, you know, the man feel like he deserve a break."

Balzic was watching the mayor's face. There was a vein standing out in the mayor's temple, and its throb was visible.

"Are you seriously trying to tell me," the mayor said, spit bubbles forming at the corners of his mouth, "are you, uh, actually telling me that this man, this man who by your admission has dealt in illegal drugs and is wanted for murder, is that what you're saying, that this man, that he 'de-serves'—is that what you said? "Dee-serves' a break? A break like, it's almost that you're talking about a retire-ment for this man, is that about what you're saying? Huh? A retirement?"

"Break? She-it. I ain't talkin' 'bout no break. I'm tellin' y'all my man's sittin' on gasoline and dynamite. I'm tellin' y'all the wrong dude go near that Cadillac and don't know the right word, I'm tellin' y'all my man goin' light a match and throw it over his shoulder in the back seat, and all this pretty evidence y'all needs is goin' up with my man, tha's what I'm tryin' tell y'all.

"Y'all's the motherfuckers think you deserve something. I'm just tryin' to tell y'all not to do nothin' stupid. I mean, if y'all wants the rest of those pictures and the tapes, then I got to see the man here from the U.S. Attorney who can make the deal, can you dig it? Y'all with me now?"

"Uh, what he's trying to tell you, Mr. Strohn," Balzic said, "is that the evidence we need to solve our murder will explode because, unless we get things worked out, his man in the Cadillac has nothing to lose—and neither one of them is going to jail. Is that about right, Leroy?"

"Amen, brother."

"This is grotesque," the mayor said. "This is the most

revolting, the most crude form of blackmail I've ever heard of. This is—"

"Aw lay dead, motherfucker. Hey, Balzic, get on the phone, man, I'm tired teachin' this jive-ass. You want him to learn something, don't be doin' it on my time, Jesus Christ. C'mon, man, call Pittsburgh, man, before my roadie get nervous out there. We didn't set no time limit on this number, but my roadie's been stretched a little tight lately. Cat's been livin' a little close to the skin, you know? And I know he ain't goin' sit there forever."

"Uh, Leroy," Balzic said, reaching for the phone, "you have any idea how slow the government works? You really thought about how long it could take to get you set up in this witness-protection thing?"

"Man, all I care is how soon I gets started, can you dig it? I don't care how long it takes. I do care how soon we begin. And the soonah, the bettah. Like now! I needs to be off the street and so do my man. We got the righteous shit, man, and we're lookin' to move it. What more you want?"

Balzic picked up the phone. "Stramsky, get me the U.S. Attorney. I want to talk to the ranking officer on duty there. Also, I want somebody out by that Cadillac to clear the area around it, but they are not to go near it or to make any gesture that could be misinterpreted as being a threat of any kind, clear? I'll hang on. . . . Uh, Leroy, I want you to go out and tell your man what's happened so far, and not to get out of joint when he sees one of my people walking around out there."

"I don't go nowhere until I hear who's on the other end of that phone call."

"Ah, come on, man—"

"Come on man my black ass. I got the pri-or-i-ties in the right order. You get them in the right order and we do some business. You don't and we don't. My man is not wrapped too tight. I'm not goin' out and good-mouth him to make y'all feel nice. I wants him to stay jus' as nervous as he is. Can you dig it?"

"I can dig it," Balzic said, shrugging.

"This is preposterous," the mayor said. "Utterly and completely preposterous. . . . "

Getting a deputy U.S. attorney took six phone calls—Balzic could only vouch for those he was involved with—and five hours. When he showed up—pale, chubby, rumpled, perspiring, and badly irritated from having been delayed in traffic because of highway repairs—he produced two John Doe warrants and not much else.

Long Leroy began to protest at once. "You mean y'all couldn't even type my name on here, got-damn! And where it say me and my man goin' in the witness-protection program?"

The deputy U.S. attorney wiped his face with a hanky and asked for a drink of water. Balzic went to fetch it.

"I am not authorized to offer immunity. I am here merely to see that arrests are made and that—"

"Not authorized!" Long Leroy screeched. "You ain't authorized, motherfucker, whatchu doin' here? Damn!"

The deputy took the water Balzic offered, said thank you, and drank it down without pause, tugging at his collar the while. "It's very warm in here."

"Ain't half as warm as it goin' get, you don't come up with somemotherfuckinthing better than you got so far."

"Chief Balzich, is that your name?"

"Balzic. No 'h' on the end."

"I see. Well, I'm Feinstein. And I want you to understand that I sympathize with your predicament here, uh, you've got a witness to a felony, and his, uh, he appears to be in a predicament himself—"

"Predicament she-it, motherfucker!"

"—he won't help himself at all by calling me those names, uh, but I really am in no position to authorize anything more than the arrest of two John Does, uh, after which if you want to assume the responsibility for their incarceration until such time as something can be worked out, why, uh, that would be satisfactory to me—"

"Ain't no doubt about that. She-it, that's plain."

"Leroy, take it easy awhile until we see what's happening—"

"I can see wha's happening, man. I'm gettin' the government hustle, the penitentiary polka—"

"Really, he's not helping himself at all. He's attacking the wrong person. I'm merely an intermediary in this matter. And, uh, quite frankly, Chief Balzich—"

"Balzic. No 'h'."

"Sorry. Chief, quite frankly, if you'll take custody of this man, we might be able to move in the direction he wishes to go."

"I ain't movin' no motherfuckin' direction 'til I get some guarantee. In print, my man. On paper. Words on top, signatures and official seals underneath, can you dig it?"

Feinstein went to fill his paper cup at the water cooler, Strohn threw up his hands and grimaced at the ceiling, and Balzic rubbed his forehead and chin.

"Look, Leroy," Balzic said after what seemed an intolerable silence, "what would it take to satisfy you?"

"Huh? Say what?"

Strohn made a gagging sound and threw up his hands again.

"What would be the least thing that would satisfy you? I mean, would you take my signature?"

"On what?"

"Oh, uh, a statement, uh, that I would do everything in my power to get you where you want to go."

"Your power? Don't look like your power is too much of nothin'.

"At this moment I'm sure it doesn't—"

"My God, the inmates really are running the asylum," Strohn said.

"Mr. Mayor, please stay out of this. I want you to observe it, that's certainly true, but I want you to stay out of it."

"Balzic," Strohn said sharply, putting his hands on his hips, "you've forgotten something. You're not in charge here. I am. And I'm taking—"

"Mr. Mayor, sit down and shut up or else leave."

"What?"

"You heard me. If you didn't I'll say it again—"

"I heard you, but I think you've lost your mind. Dealing with this trash, if indeed this is what you're used to doing, and I have no doubt of that—dealing with his human junk has got your values the wrong end up."

Leroy searched Balzic's face. "Is this motherfucker talkin' 'bout me? He callin' me 'junk' and 'trash' and shit?"

"Forget about him," Balzic said. "I want to know what would satisfy you."

"You'd better start worrying about what would satisfy me!" Strohn shouted.

Feinstein passed between Balzic and Long Leroy and confronted Strohn. "I don't believe we met. I'm Feinstein. Joel. And you're, uh?"

"Strohn. Ken. How d'you do?"

"I'm doing a little better than you are, Ken, and, uh, the reason for this is, uh, have you ever been present at a plea bargaining before?"

"Is that what this is called? This travesty—a plea bargaining?"

"Not exactly, but, uh, it's very similar. See, uh, this doesn't look like the law's most shining moment, but, uh, that's because it isn't. Bright and beautiful it's not. But essential it is. And I, uh, I hope you don't mind my saying so, but, uh, I think you should let Chief Balzich and Leroy do what they have to do."

"I don't like being patronized," Strohn said sourly. "I don't like your tone, and I especially don't like your implication that I'm some sort of neophyte here—"

"Uh, Ken," Feinstein said, tugging at his collar and wiping sweat off his forehead, "Ken, what you don't like is irrelevant. You obviously don't understand what's going on here. Two men, both wanted on federal felony charges, are willing to trade information to save themselves great pain and suffering, not to mention incarceration, uh, they've put themselves in great danger to do that, and so far they're not getting very much in return. All your bluster here does is cause a touchy situation to become touchier. So take my advice. Shut up. And if you won't do that, then leave the room. Things are getting sticky in here, and your interference is the last thing that's needed."

"Amen, motherfucker."

Balzic studied his shoes. When he looked up at Strohn, Strohn's face was ashen, and his right cheek had developed the minutest of tics. And try as he might—and it was plain that he was trying—Strohn could not disengage his gaze from Feinstein's. The pale, rumpled, chubby little lawyer had locked gazes with Strohn and was staring him into silence.

Balzic began at that moment to wonder about Feinstein, especially about the amount and the kind of authority that Feinstein carried with him.

Balzic turned back to Leroy. "Well, you made up your mind yet? What would it take?"

"I made up my mind," said Long Leroy. "You sign a paper—you, Balzic, you sign it first—and then this dude Weinstein sign it—"

"Feinstein."

"—yeah, that's right, Feinstein, he put his name on it. And what it got to say is where we're goin', me and my roadie, and what for in return. And I want a date on it and I want it notarized. Two copies. One for me and one for my man outside. And then, uh, and then—you got that so far, huh?"

"I'm with you so far," Balzic said, nodding.

"Right. And then, we stay here in this lockup. We ain't goin' no place else. We ain't goin' nowhere where they's anybody can get to us, hear? And, whoever brings us the food got to eat some with us. And we got to have rum and Coke for me and vodka for my man. Vodka and orange juice. You still with me?"

Balzic nodded. "Still with you."

Long Leroy nodded. "And I keep the weed I got on me. And some for my roadie." He looked questioningly at Balzic and Feinstein. Neither objected.

"That all?"

"Hey, man, shit no that ain't all. They's the big thing. When y'all goin' tell me whether we in the program or not? I gots to have my twelve-month, twelve thousand-mile guarantee, man. I gots to have my money-back un-con-di-tion-al guarantee, man. And y'all can't be shuckin' and jivin' 'bout that. 'Bout that, my man, I gots to know. I mean, if they's one thing sure as dope make you high, then, baby, I wants a sure thing."

Balzic sighed. "Feinstein, whatta you say here? What can you offer?"

"Uh, Balzich—sorry. Balzic. I've already presented what I can offer. You do what you must. If you feel satisfied about holding them here, if you'll take that responsibility, then I'll promise what I can, which is to start the wheel turning—and that's all I promise."

"Will you sign a statement and let it be notarized?"

"No problem," Feinstein said.

"Okay," Balzic said, sitting at his desk and taking out several sheets of city stationery. He wrote in longhand what had been discussed—three times he wrote it—giving each when he finished first to Long Leroy and then to Feinstein for their approval. When all agreed, Balzic signed first, then Feinstein, and, at last, Long Leroy.

Balzic folded them three times, put them in a long envelope, and took them out to the duty room. He called for a mobile unit to come in and take the papers to a magistrate to have them notarized, and told the patrolman to have the magistrate call for affirmation of the authenticity of the documents and signatures.

Balzic walked back into his office and slumped into his chair. "It'll be a while, Leroy. May as well have another drink."

Balzic had no sooner spoken to Long Leroy than he turned to see Feinstein nodding to him to leave the room. Balzic heaved himself out of the chair and followed Feinstein out.

"Where can we go to talk?" Feinstein whispered.

Balzic pointed to one of the interrogation rooms at the rear of the duty room, and led Feinstein into it and was starting to close the door when the mayor suddenly rushed out of the room they'd left and practically ran into Balzic.

"Balzic," the mayor began, but was suddenly pulled around Balzic.

Feinstein had grabbed the mayor by the arm and, with a deceptively simple movement, pulled him clear into the tiny room.

"What's going on here?" Strohn stammered.

"You are actually the mayor?" Feinstein said.

"You're damned right I am. And who the hell do you think you are grabbing me like—"

"Mr. Mayor. Answer some questions," Feinstein said. "Tell me, have you ever been arrested?"

"Me? Certainly not!"

"Has any member of your family?"

"Absolutely not."

"Ever been on jury duty?"

"No."

"Grand jury?"

"No."

"Ever been a witness, either before a magistrate or a grand jury or a coroner or in a trial, civil or criminal?"

"No, no."

"Ever been present at a magistrate's hearing?"

"No."

"How about an arraignment?"

"No."

"A preliminary hearing?"

"No."

"How about a trial, jury or non-jury, civil or criminal?"

"Have I ever seen a trial?"

"Yes. Have you ever witnessed a trial—of any kind?"

"Well certainly."

"Uh-ha. What do you remember about it?"

"What do I remember? Well, uh, mostly I remember it was pretty boring."

"Boring. I see. Well how about prison? Jail? Ever been in one—to visit I mean?"

"No."

"Ever been curious since you've been elected to see where people go who break your laws?"

"What do you mean 'my laws'?"

"My laws, your laws, our laws. There's no trick to that. I mean, you and I and the chief here, we are, so to speak, the law. We either make the law or we enforce it or we prosecute it. That's all I mean. Haven't you ever been curious to see what happens to people who don't obey our laws, and who are dumb enough or unlucky enough to be caught? In short, haven't you ever set foot inside a jail? Or a prison?"

"No. No, I haven't."

"Uh, excuse me here a second," Balzic butted in. "I don't know what's going on here. Maybe you don't want to remember, but I was with you when you were in one, uh, the other day, remember? The young fella cut his wrists?"

"Well I—that was so, that was so—I don't know what to say. I forgot. Yes. Yes, I have been inside a prison."

"Okay," Feinstein said. "Just accentuates my point." He sighed and shook his head. "Mr. Mayor, a little while ago you got upset because you thought I was patronizing you, because, uh, you resented the implication, I think you said, that I thought you were a neophyte. But, Mr. Mayor, the truth is, here you are the top official, the authority, in a fairly large third-class city, and you don't know one goddamn thing about how our judicial system functions. By your own words, the only trial you remember going to was 'boring.' 'Pretty boring,' I think you said. It's amazing how many people who think they know how laws are made and how order is maintained, how justice, as it were, is achieved, how many people like yourself don't know the first goddamn thing about it.

"That black man in there, that habitual felon," Feinstein went on, "that dope dealer and murderer and God knows what else, Mr. Mayor, he knows more—knows more, hell—he's forgotten more about our system of justice and law and order than you know. And I assure you that statement is not made for effect."

"I don't—I don't understand," Strohn said. "Why are you talking to me this way? I'm watching a travesty of this thing you're calling justice and you're uh, you're talking to me as though I'm—I'm in the way! As though I'm a roadblock or whatever."

"You are indeed," Feinstein said flatly. "You are confusing some sort of morality—God only knows which brand yours is—with the successful prosecution of serious felonies.

"And that habitual felon in there is a walking resource guide to the commission of serious felonies in at least two states, Florida and Pennsylvania, and certainly others, and has walked in off the street, unrecruited, is that right, Chief? Did you or anybody else in your department recruit this man or solicit his aid in any way?"

"No, sir. We did not."

Feinstein poked Strohn in the chest twice. "Do you have any idea how rare that is? This is not some psychotic with a need to confess. This is an habitual felon who walks in unsolicited, and if that isn't enough, mind you, he walks in with photographic and sound recordings of his dealings with a corrupt state official who is also a murderer—and here you stand telling me that you are not a neophyte and that what is happening is a travesty. For God's sake, man, what the hell do you think the law is all about? It's trade, it's bargain, it's compromise, it's negotiate, it's deal, deal, deal!

"You see a travesty. You know what I see? I'll tell you. What I see is, hell, I feel like the guy who opened up Tut's tomb. That black hustler over there is a treasure house. We open up the tomb of his mind and there's gold. He is a major trafficker in drugs. His roadie, as he calls him, is a murderer with almost certain participation in at least two murders. We've known that for months. For years.

"And now they've walked in with evidence beyond the slightest hint of an illegal search—photos and tapes for God's sake—and all you're worried about is whether we're going to get this man some rum and Coke and some vodka for his friend, and whether we're going to let him keep the weed he's got on him. For the information he'll give us, I will personally buy and deliver to him all the weed he can smoke and I will not charge one dollar in expenses, that's how much this guy means to me personally, never mind the whole Justice Department.

"Am I getting through? Is any of this getting through to you?" Feinstein peered into Strohn's blinking, slightly glazed eyes.

Strohn sidled away from Feinstein and Balzic. "There is no thought of justice here. There is no thought of order here. Or law. Neither one of you is talking about creating a better place to live. I doubt seriously whether either one of you even thinks in those terms," Strohn said, backing away from them.

"All you're talking about is specifics—is the specifics of one case, that's all."

"A minute, please," Feinstein said. "This 'no thought of justice here' or of order or law, or neither one of us thinking about creating a better place to live—is that what you said? Uh, you do not think that the removal from this place of a corrupt public official creates a better, a more lawful, more orderly place? And is not the removal of a murderer from this place, is that not a practical design for greater order, for the public safety—no, I can see from your face. This is just the, uh, the, uh, what what what is this? Huh? What do you call this, this that we do that offends you so much?"

"Let it go, Feinstein," Balzic said, wanting badly to get on with even greater specifics than those he was being accused of.

"No no no," Feinstein said, holding up his hand to Balzic. "I'm amazed. Fascinated. I've been in this business now for a lot of years. I've gone through Democrat administrations, Republican, back to Democrat. My record as an investigator, as a bargainer, as a prosecutor—hey, I put that record against anybody. Democrats, Republicans, they both like it. But this guy, I haven't heard anything like this guy's talking. I'm not kidding. His complaint about what we're doing here is unique. Or maybe I'm just a dummy. Maybe I'm the neophyte. So what's wrong, Mr. Mayor? What is it we do, what gives here that so upsets you?"

Strohn shivered with some inner struggle. He hesitated for a long moment. "It's—it's so dirty. It's so sordid. Messy. That man in there. He's revolting. . . . "

Feinstein breathed heavily through his nose, thrust out his pink lower lip, closed his eyes, and nodded wearily several times. "So. So. Dirty. Sordid. Messy. Revolting. And naturally, we, the chief here and me, we are also dirty and sordid and whatever because we're down there dealing in it. Huh?

"Ho boy," Feinstein said. "You know, that's the same la-de-da I used to hear from my father-in-law. 'Why are you down there in the dirt, in the gutter with those scum?' Took me a long time to figure out an answer for him, but I did. And it shut him up. Now he doesn't ask why I don't work for Duquesne Light, or Alcoa, or U.S. Steel.

" 'Cause here's what I told him. I don't live in the gutter. I don't deal in dirt. What I do is not revolting. What I do is reach down and pull somebody up to my level. I don't stay down there. I drag people up. And for the first time in their lives, for many of them, and no matter what their motives, they are doing a social, sociable, decent, law and order act. They are cooperating with the duly appointed members of the law enforcement agencies of this country, and, Mr. Mayor, if you can't understand that, then you need to go back to study some civics. You got yourself elected, but you don't understand what the law's all about. In the prosecution of criminal justice, you don't deal with saints. You deal with sinners. And sinners sin. And if you don't know that going in, you sure find it out in a hurry. But I can see from your expression that you do not understand and, what's more, you're afraid to even want to understand.

"You're a fearful man, Mr. Mayor. You've got some demons gnawing at you. You're afraid you're going to get dirty merely by understanding what it is that I do." Feinstein shook his head. "If you don't mind my saying so, *that's* revolting."

Strohn clapped his hands over his ears in disgust and frustration, wheeled about, and very nearly ran out of the duty room.

Feinstein shook his head and looked sympathetically at Balzic. "He just began his term?"

Balzic nodded.

"For what—four years?"

"Forget about him," Balzic said. "What about them? Did you really come here as unprepared as you said—with just those two John Doe warrants?"

"My friend," Feinstein said, tapping Balzic lightly on the arm. "All the paperwork that we needed, you took care of. Those little chits that are out being notarized. That's enough for Leroy. That'll hold him until I come back with other things. Besides, you didn't really think I was going to come clear out here from Pittsburgh, miss my supper, make my wife mad, upset my stomach, on the chance that your Leroy was my Leroy, huh? The Leroy I've been looking for for years? You know how many Leroys I deal with, hm? Any idea?

"My friend, Balzich, I—"

"Balzic."

"Balzich, Balzic—what's your first name?"

"Mario."

"Mario it is. Mario, my Long Leroy, ho boy, my friend, I have taken a lot of looks at Leroys and none of them has been my Leroy, no sir. But when I came in here tonight and saw that chin disappearing into that skinny neck, I felt my knees go weak, like rubber. And it wouldn't make any difference what sort of paperwork he required, believe me, I was prepared at the sight of him to bring Washington, D.C., here, if necessary.

"But, let's go get his friend. I want him too, very much. All you have to do is hold them here until I get everything in order. Two days, three at the most. Then we take them off your hands."

"And, uh, do you guarantee that they testify when I need them? You're not gonna give me some waltz about how they're too important to help my little case, are you?"

"I absolutely guarantee their appearance. You have my word. Honest to God," Feinstein said, raising his right hand to the level of his ear.

"Okay," Balzic said. "Then I'm gonna take a few of those pictures and call my friend with the state police and I'm gonna go bust those sons of bitches. You been waiting for Long Leroy, huh? Well, you can just guess how long I been waiting for this moment. These wise-mouth sons of bitches, I've been waiting a while. . . . " Balzic reached for a phone to call Lieutenant Walker Johnson at home. When Johnson answered Balzic said, "Hey, Walker. Get dressed. And get some people. Have I got news for you."

Cortese and Gensheimer were arrested by state police troopers as they were driving out of the BDE parking lot at the end of their watch, about twenty minutes after Balzic had phoned Johnson. Cortese, in spite of the charges made by Balzic against him, had not been suspended from duty; he had merely been reassigned to shuffling files. Gensheimer had been requesting reassignment every day since Cortese's arrest, according to BDE Agent Russellini, who called Balzic after he saw the arrests being made.

Balzic was in his cruiser when he got the call from Russellini. Lieutenant Walker Johnson was sitting on his right, and Mayor Ken Strohn was sitting in the back seat, peering up through the heavy mesh that separated front seat from back. Under other circumstances Balzic might have been wondering where Strohn had come from, or how or when he'd gotten into the back seat, or how he'd even known that Balzic was getting ready to pick up Johnson; the last time Balzic had seen Strohn, he'd had his hands over his ears and was practically sprinting away from Feinstein. But these were not other circumstances and Balzic did not care how Strohn got where he was. All he wanted to know was how Cortese and Gensheimer had reacted to their arrest, and he asked Russellini.

"Gensheimer just looked confused," Russellini said, "Confused. But Cortese took it real bad. I thought for a second he was not gonna go easy."

"Were they separated?"

"When they left? Yeah. Gensheimer in one car and Cortese in another."

"Good. Thank you, Russell. Appreciate your call." Balzic replaced the mike on its hook.

"I hope this sonofabitch tries to not go easy."

"Who?" Strohn said.

"Now, Mario, take it easy," Johnson said.

"Who?"

"Franks—I'll take it very easy. I just hope he doesn't try to, that's all. That's a reasonable wish. It's the sort of wish a reasonable man could be expected to make—"

"C'mon, Mario, slow down—"

"What are you two talking about?" Strohn squeaked.

"Nothing," Johnson said.

"That's not true. You two are talking about something, and I want to know what it is."

"Look," Johnson said. "You might be his boss, but you're not mine. I don't even know what the hell you're doing here. This is not your territory. It's mine. And the arrest is mine. You got that, Mario?"

"I hear you."

"Good. And I hope—I sincerely hope—that nothing causes you to forget that."

"If this is your arrest," Strohn said, "what are we doing in a Rocksburg Police Department car? And what's the chief doing driving it? I thought you were along for the ride."

Balzic ground his teeth to keep from laughing as he heard Johnson moaning and sighing.

"Mr. Mayor," Johnson said after some moments, "if there's anyone along for the ride it's you. Just for the record, I don't know why we're in this car. Or why he's driving. But it doesn't make any difference whose car we're in or who's driving. I'm the one with the warrant. And your chief, here, is here as a courtesy and because he's an old friend. But if he does something reckless because he doesn't like this guy, I'm going to get very upset. And if you do something, I'll—"

"What would I do?" Strohn protested.

"God only knows. I mean, here you are, and here I am, and I don't even know how you got into this goddamn car."

"Well, obviously I got in this 'goddamn car' of my own volition and because an arrest is about to be made and a, a, a case is about to be solved that involves a murder in my city, and as mayor of that city I am by law responsible for the conduct of public safety—"

"What the hell are you talking about?" Johnson said, snorting. "Solved what? What solved? We're gonna make an arrest—a peaceful, smooth arrest, right, Mario?"

"Whatever you say, Walker, whatever you say."

"Right. That's what I say. A nice smooth little bust, and then we're going to the nearest magistrate and start the wheels turning. Nobody 'solved' anything. Where'd you even get such an idea? What do you think we're doing here—working some kind of arithmetic problem? This is just one part in a long series of events, uh, that's supposed to be something called justice, but it might not end for three years—more, by the time all the appeals are done with—and that's assuming the DA gets a conviction, which is a hell of an assumption.

"Hey, Mario, we're coming up on it pretty soon, I think," Johnson said, glancing at a slip of paper he'd pulled from his shirt pocket.

They'd been driving in rush-hour traffic for nearly twenty minutes, and they hadn't gone five miles.

"I remember when this was a two-lane blacktop and there wasn't a gas station on it for ten miles. Now, shit, look at it. One goddamn thing after another. I'll bet there are six gas stations in the little way we've gone," Balzic said. "Never mind all the rest of this junk. Boy, somebody named it right when they called it junk food. What can people be thinking of themselves eating that stuff and knowing that's what it's called—junk?"

"Wait a minute, Mario," Johnson said. "Shit, you missed it. It was that road back there. Here, pull over here and go behind that laundromat and see if we can't get on it."

Balzic wheeled off the road without a turn signal and caused a protest of horns and squealing tires behind him.

At first there appeared to be a road behind the laundromat, which was the last in a series of seven or eight businesses under one roof, but the road behind was blocked at the far end by garbage containers. Balzic put the car in reverse and backed up, and started out around the corner of the building.

"Shit," said Johnson. "We got to find a way to get back along the highway there and—"

"No we don't," Balzic said, very excited. "No we don't. Look there!"

"Huh? Where?"

"Coming right at us. Carrying that basket of clothes. It's our boy."

"I'll be goddamned if it isn't," said Johnson.

"Who? Where?" said Strohn.

Balzic tramped on the parking brake and started to get out.

"Mario! You stay right here. I'll do this," Johnson said.

"Okay, okay. I'm just opening the door to get a little air, that's all."

"What's going on?" Strohn said, pressing up against the mesh and screeching in Balzic's ear.

"We've found our man, Mr. Mayor," Balzic said, watching Johnson go around the front of the car and approach Michael Franks, who seemed intent only on not dropping his laundry. He looked up, more curious than startled, when Johnson held the warrant out across his path, chest high.

"What's that?" Franks said.

"Read it," Johnson said.

Franks put his plastic basket of dirty clothes down and took the warrant. He glanced at it quickly and smiled without showing his teeth. "You got to be out of your mind. General charge of murder, shit." Then Franks noticed who was driving the car. "I should've known. I should've known it would be that asshole."

"Watch your mouth, Franks," Balzic said, getting out of the car.

"Mario, get back in the car, please," Johnson said. "As for you, Franks, you know what your rights are as well as I do, so I'm not gonna bother with that except to tell you that you should consider that you have been told your rights. Now go put your laundry in your car and lock it up."

"You have the right to remain silent, prick," Balzic said, stepping up onto the sidewalk in front of the laundromat.

"Mario," Johnson said wearily. "Don't start fooling around. I'm telling you."

"I'm not fooling around. I want it observed by two witnesses that this prick was advised of his rights, and that's all I'm doing."

"Okay, Mario, okay. Have it your way."

Franks was breathing heavily through his nose and looking every which way, and his shoulders were heaving with furious sighs.

"You have the right to have legal counsel present and if you don't have counsel, you have the right to have one appointed for you by an officer of the court."

"Aw go fuck yourself. Tellin' me what my rights are, you asshole, you've been harassing me for months."

"I have not even begun to harass you, you, you goddamn pervert."

"Mario! Goddamnit, now that's enough!" Johnson said.

"Ho! Ha! Did you hear that? Huh? The anti-Semitism, huh? That's what this is really all about. The chief here is a Jew-hater. That's what this whole thing's been about. For months! And now it comes out. Finally!" Franks was practically jumping in place.

Johnson frowned at Balzic and screwed up his face and looked back at Franks. "What in the hell are you talking about? Jew-hater? Huh?"

"You heard it! You heard him!" Franks said, still bouncing up on the balls of his feet. "You heard what he said. Oh you fucked up this time, Balzic. This time you really blew it. Call me a 'Jew pervert' in front of two witnesses, you pulled the cover off. I'll be goddamned if that's what this whole thing's been about. Right from the start, I knew it!"

"What the hell's he talking about?" Johnson asked Balzic again.

"Oh he knows what he's doin'," Balzic said. "Hey, Franks.

Hey you! Hey you, you goddamn pervert, you! You hear me?"

"There he goes again!" Franks shouted, jumping next to Johnson and grabbing his arm. "D'you hear him, huh? You heard him. Hey, you in the car, d'you hear him?"

Mayor Strohn got out of the car, his face slack with confusion.

"Mario," Strohn said, advancing toward him and trying to keep his voice down, "is this true?"

"What? Is what true?"

"These charges he's making. This business of anti-Semitism. This—"

"What! Oh for crissake! Will you cut it out? Huh? This clown's trying to throw smoke in your face, don't you understand that? He heard me say, 'You, you pervert,' and he's gonna try to make people think what I said was 'Jew pervert,' and you both got to know that's bullshit. But what it is—"

"What it is, is blatant harassment!" Franks shouted. "And because of what I am. That's what it is."

"Walker," Balzic said, "you better get that sonofabitch away from me or I'm gonna light him up, I swear—"

"Mario, is there—was harassment, did, uh, harassment have any part in your investi—"

"Mr. Mayor, I cannot believe you. I mean, I have not believed you from the start. It was just one goddamn thing after another with you, but I'm telling you, if you think this bastard is doing anything other than setting up his defense on a murder charge, you're even dumber than I thought."

"Mario, I resent this," Strohn said. "I resent this. I want to know—"

"I just got through telling you. This is smoke! Pure and simple smoke! How many times you think this guy has busted black guys who start yellin' the second the cuffs go on, the only reason they're gettin' busted is 'cause they're black? Huh? How many times?"

"Not the same thing," Franks sang out. "I'm an officer of the state! Of the courts! And I've been harassed!"

"Shut the fuck up," Balzic snarled.

"Go ahead, say it," Franks cried. "Say it. Call me a Jew pervert again. That's what you want to do. Go ahead."

"Walker, I swear," said Balzic, "you don't get him away from me I'm gonna kick his balls clear up to his stomach."

"You heard him, Mr. Mayor," Franks said. "You heard him. Threats, anti-Semitic harassment and threats of violence against me. You're my witness! You are my witness! These two will cover each other in court, but you are my witness!"

Johnson jerked Franks by the arm, away from Balzic and Strohn and toward Franks's car. "Come on, Franks, before I hit you myself. Mario, I'm taking him in his car."

"You tell him his rights!" Balzic said. "All of 'em. The whole number."

"My rights have been violated already," Franks said over his shoulder.

Balzic could not contain himself. He raced to Franks's side and spun him around. He took one of the photographs he'd gotten from Long Leroy and thrust it under Franks's nose.

"Hey, Franks. You can throw all the smoke you wanna throw. But you're not gonna be able to bullshit your way out of these. I got dozens. Dozens and dozens. And that ain't all. So you can run the persecuted nigger routine on me all you want, but it won't work. The DAs and the judges are wise to that one. And when the DA starts showing these pictures to the jury—"

"Hey, Balzic," Franks said, smiling meanly. "The persecuted nigger's one thing. The persecuted Jew, that's something else. How many nigger lawyers are there? Huh?

Well, for every nigger lawyer you know, I know a thousand Jewish lawyers. You can bring all the pictures you want. But I guarantee you my lawyer—whoever he is—he's gonna call your mayor as a witness. Bet your ass on that one. There'll be so many civil suits filed on this one, nobody'll even remember who got killed or when."

"Give me your car keys," Johnson said.

"You want 'em, find 'em."

"Why you makin' this so hard, Jesus Christ," Johnson said, turning Franks around and reaching into his pants pockets to find the keys to his car.

"This—shit, you think it's hard now? This is nothin'. Nothin'," Franks said, sneering. "This is gonna be the hardest work you ever did. You're gonna testify in so many suits, you're gonna think you're a professional witness."

Johnson found the keys and started to lead Franks to his car.

"Hey, my clothes, huh? My laundry basket there?"

"I'll get it," Balzic said. He did, and carried it along behind Franks and Johnson as Johnson led Franks by the arm to his car. Balzic set it on the pavement. "You gonna put cuffs on this, uh, this pervert, or am I gonna do it?"

"What cuffs? Cuffs," Franks snorted. "Jesus, what d'you think I'm gonna do? Huh? Run? Christ. What for? You got a picture of me and some nigger. So what? You can have a hundred—"

"I got more than that."

"A thousand then, who cares? When I get through talking to B'nai B'rith and to the Civil Liberties Union, what kinda case you gonna have? Huh? What makes you think I don't know lawyers who'll make sure those pictures don't get admitted as evidence? The hearing on just whether to admit the pictures'll last a week, for crissake. Guys I know'll have those dumb-ass DAs talkin' to themselves."

Balzic turned around to see if Strohn was listening, and almost bumped into him.

"You payin' attention, Strohn? You takin' all this in? Huh? Franks here is givin' you the short course in how to use the very thing you shit on when you're dealing with other people, but when it comes to you, oh brother, then it's use every trick in the book.

"How many times you think he's shaken down prisoners? Huh? How many illegal searches you think he's made? Huh? How many bribes you think he's solicited? Huh—"

"Aw fuck you, Balzic. What is this—Romper Room School?"

"But when he gets the collar, then it's everything his way. He reminds me of that fuckin' attorney general who got preventive detention in D.C., yeah. Oh yeah, and then he broke the fuckin' law, the look on his face when he found out he was actually gonna do time, hey, that one didn't have a price.

"And here we got another one. You better take him, Walker, before I lose my temper and hit the sonofabitch."

Balzic walked quickly back to his car and got in. "You coming, Mr. Mayor?"

Strohn turned around, his face still slack with bewilderment. "Yes. Oh yes." He trotted toward the car and got in.

Balzic turned the ignition key and held it past the start of the engine, causing a whine to come from under the hood. He put the car in gear and wheeled away from Johnson and Franks. He turned the lights and siren on to get into and across traffic, and took his frustration out in speed.

"Aren't—aren't you going a little too fast?"

Balzic looked at the speedometer needle and quickly lifted his foot until the needle returned to near fifty mph.

The mayor sighed noisily and relaxed downward on the seat. "I—I really am completely confused."

Balzic was going to say something sarcastic, but thought better of it.

"I mean, I've seen things and heard things that are so contrary to what I know—or at least what I think I know—or at least what I thought at one time that I knew—I'm not making sense," Strohn said. "Do you have to keep the siren on?"

Balzic switched the siren off, but kept the flashers going. He also slowed down to fifty again. He had speeded up without thinking about it.

"Mr. Mayor, all you have to know is one thing: I did not call Franks a 'Jew' anything. A pervert, yes. A bastard, yes. A sonofabitch, yes. Probably some other things, I forget. But I did not call him a 'Jew' anything. Also, the persecution hustle is a very old hustle, and the blacks, a lot of blacks, worked it pretty good until the judges and the DAs and even the ACLU got wise to it.

"But that's what he's gonna do, and it makes me sick, but he'll work it for a long time. A long time." Balzic grew angrily quiet. His frustration caused him to breathe more quickly and more noisily, and he knew that if he didn't stop biting hard, he was going to have a bad headache.

"But you have all this evidence. All those photographs and those recordings. You made that deal with that, that Leroy character. Doesn't that all mean—what does that all mean? You sounded so sure of yourself when you were getting that."

"I was sure of myself. But I forgot how much smoke he could blow. Because the thing is, if they all hang tough, all three of them, then it's gonna be the word of two admitted felons out to make a deal for themselves. And any lawyer worth fifty bucks an hour will turn a jury's head right around on that. Shit, I can hear him now. . . .

" 'Leroy, are you under indictment at the present time, and, if so, would you tell the court what for?' And the assistant DA jumps up and objects. And the judge says, 'I think I'll allow the witness to answer that. I think the jury should be allowed to judge whether this witness's testimony is tainted in any way, la da da, la da da.' "

"But what about the pictures? And the tapes?" Strohn asked.

"You heard Franks. He said it himself. The hearing to suppress the evidence will last a week. And he's right. Any lawyer worth his money will make a case out of each fuckin' picture. He'll bore the shit out of the judge, make him get impatient, and then testy, and then short-tempered, and pretty soon the judge'll start saying, 'Yeah, throw that out, what's the point of that one.' Shit. I've seen it happen before. More than once."

"But—but that's not right," Strohn said.

"Oh yes it is. The hell if it isn't. That's what court's all about. How d'you get this evidence? And why? And who from? And when? The fuck it isn't right. I wouldn't have it any other way. 'Cause it could always be me sitting in front of the jury. And I'd want some lawyer askin' the same fuckin' questions. Yessir. I believe in that with all my bones. I believe it when they say 'innocent until proven guilty.' Goddamn right. That's the only way. It's just that sometimes you get a fuckin' pervert like Franks and he knows all the twists and bends and it makes you work. So you want to make it simple and hope he does something stupid so you can have the holy satisfaction of beatin' his brains out, but that's just ego workin', that's all. Nah, with guys like Franks, you earn your money. You earn your money twistin' the head of his partner. The good thing about this is he got two partners. And I guarantee you one of those two bastards'll get turned around. I guarantee it. I'm gonna stay on their ass until one of 'em does."

   Balzic did as he said he would. He stayed on their asses—Cortese's and Gensheimer's—for two weeks. And because Cortese was in Southern Regional and

Gensheimer was in the county lockup ten miles away, Balzic, for all practical purposes, became a single man. When he wasn't working on routine matters for the city, he was working on Cortese or Gensheimer, or driving from one to the other. Lieutenant Walker Johnson assigned two men to work with Balzic—administratively, legally, Balzic was working with them—but one of them got the flu and the other thought Balzic was a fanatic and refused to cooperate more than superficially. Balzic never even bothered to bring it up in his conversations with Johnson.

The truth was that Balzic *was* working fanatically. He had never wanted in his professional life to gain a conviction against anyone as much as he wanted this one against Franks. So he drove not only himself but Detective Rugs Carlucci as well. Balzic made Carlucci triple-check the evidence of contraband weight submitted by Franks at all the magistrates' hearings, and made him tape-record again all statements made by convicts prosecuted by Franks. The testimony about the weight of contraband drugs was correlated with the weights actually submitted by Franks— all of this was made necessary because the same information, gathered by Carlucci once before and turned over to the BDE through Agent Russellini, had disappeared after BDE agents had cleared Franks.

Now Balzic had it again, and again Carlucci's mother was cursing him for the hours he made her son work. Some things changed, some things didn't.

Among the things that had changed was the bond status of Cortese, Gensheimer, and Franks. Bond for Cortese and Gensheimer had been set at one hundred thousand dollars cash. Neither could come close to raising it. Bond for Franks had been set at two hundred thousand dollars. His lawyer produced twenty thousand dollars in twenties, fifties, and hundreds within forty minutes of Franks's arrival at the magistrate's office.

While Cortese and Gensheimer lived their lives in isolation cells away from the general prison population in Southern Regional and in the County Jail, Michael Franks led an exemplary, uneventful, and routine life as a suspended officer of the Commonwealth of Pennsylvania. He was a regular at three restaurants in the city of Pittsburgh: Poli's, Klein's, and the Grand Concourse. He never drank more than three glasses of wine with his meals, but he was apparently addicted to escargot, oysters Rockefeller and clams casino, scallops broiled in butter and garlic, and swordfish steaks with Bearnaise sauce. He paid cash for all his meals; his lunches averaged ten dollars a day and his dinners fifteen.

Balzic made it a point to arrive at lunchtime in Cortese's cell and at suppertime in Gensheimer's cell every day, to inform them of what Franks had eaten the day before and how much it had cost.

Cortese was unflappable, imperturbable, unshakeable—a rock. It made no difference what Balzic said or how he said it, Cortese sat on his metal bunk, said nothing, and just stared at Balzic.

Balzic showed photographs and played tapes; he brought copies of testimony given in magistrate hearings and tapes of convicts contradicting that testimony; he described in detail where Michael Franks ate, and who his dinner companions were. Those last, Balzic described in great detail. On two occasions, he even brought pictures taken through a three hundred-millimeter lens by one of the state cops Johnson assigned to maintain surveillance on Franks. Balzic might as well have played music for a deaf-mute. Cortese sat and stared and said nothing until Balzic was getting ready to leave at the end of each session.

Then Cortese would say, "Get cancer. Get it soon."

To which Balzic would say, "What I'm gonna get is you."

And then Cortese would say, "If you had a case, you wouldn't be here. We both know it."

"I've got a case," Balzic would then say. "I've got a damn good case. I just want one that doesn't have a hole or a crack or anything that that degenerate sonofabitch can slip through. He mutilates children, Cortese. Little girls. He's perverted, twisted, a scumbag. And I'm gonna get him, but I just want to make sure. You could help me make sure. And you could do yourself the best favor you could ever do for yourself."

"If you had a case," Cortese would then say, staring meanly at Balzic, "you wouldn't be here." Then he would fall silent again, and go back into himself, leaving only a pinched expression of anger and contempt on his face. His body seemed to Balzic to visibly grow smaller, while his face grew more defiant.

It was after the fourth of those conversations that Balzic decided to forget about Cortese. Cortese had made a vow—that was obvious—and nothing Balzic knew or hoped to know was going to get on Cortese's nerves enough to make a collaborator out of him.

So Balzic turned all his efforts to Gensheimer, the stocky, almost chubby third wheel after Franks and Cortese. For four days Gensheimer, too, tried to contain himself, to live on his own resources, to say nothing, to stare sullenly and meanly. But on the fifth day, when Balzic recounted that Franks had spent sixty dollars at Poli's for dinner for himself and a woman wearing silver shoes and a black dress slit to the middle of her thigh and carrying a clutch bag that matched her shoes, and that Franks had spent at least twenty dollars more on admission and drinks at a disco in Monroeville, Balzic saw very soon that Gensheimer was having a hellish time containing himself.

"You all right, Gensheimer? You look a little sick."

"Why's the bond so goddamn high? Huh?"

"You know as well as I do why it is. This is a murder thing. You're accessory to—"

"I'm shit accessory. I'm accessory to nothin'. I'm just goin' to waste in here. My mother and sister are goin' crazy without me. They're goin' broke! This ain't fair."

"Well, let's talk about it."

"Talk about what?" Gensheimer jumped up from his bunk and started to pace. "We got nothin' to talk about."

"We got your mother and sister to talk about. Your family. Maybe I can help."

"Help! Shit. It's you got me in here."

"Well, uh, how can I help your mother?"

"Get me the hell out, how else?"

"Does your mother need your financial support?"

"Whatta you think, huh?"

"I'm just asking, Gensheimer. Uh, doesn't she have, uh, any other income?"

"No, she—yeah. Yes. She works. So's my sister. They work in a hamburger joint. Both of them together don't get fifty hours."

"What about, uh, what about your father?"

"My father's a lush. If he was a magnet and jobs was steel, he couldn't hold one for a minute."

"Did, uh, did your mother visit you today?"

Gensheimer nodded and put his head down and rubbed his eyes.

"Sister too?"

"Yeah."

For a long moment Balzic felt a little queasy. His vision wavered, as though he were looking at heat rising off a road in August. His stomach rumbled and he belched and tasted sour juice in the back of his throat. It brought tears to his eyes. He tried to clear his throat and nearly gagged. He turned his back to Gensheimer and settled himself by forcing his thoughts to a nameless girl lying on her side, her blood running off a curb, and to two black girls, one of whom would speak with difficulty if at all, and to Randolph Kolesar, his blood covering half the floor in a cell and with the words, "Balzic, your all alike" written in it. Well, shit, he thought. Everybody's got a mother. Judas had a mother, and nobody said where he was buried, and she couldn't have felt any better than Jesus's mother when she got the news. Nobody knows her name. All anybody knows is her son kissed cheap.

"Well," Balzic said, "what about your mother?"

"What d'you mean what about my mother? She wants me out. She thinks I'm getting screwed. I am gettin' screwed! I ain't supposed to be here. I didn't do any goddamn thing."

"Is that what you told her?"

"Hell yeah. 'Cause it's the truth!"

"Shit, that's probably what Judas told his mother. 'I didn't do anything wrong. I just kissed him a couple times. I didn't kill the sonofabitch or anything. I didn't even hit him. I just kissed him. I didn't know what they were gonna do. I just thought they were gonna pick him up and hold him for a couple days. Question him, maybe break a couple bones, but I didn't think they were gonna kill him, shit, how was I supposed to know—' "

Gensheimer was looking, slack-jawed and bug-eyed, at Balzic, and then he put his hands over his ears and started to speak in a monotone. "I heard you were a bastard. I heard you'd tell any lie, but I don't believe this . . . I don't believe this . . . I don't believe this. . . . "

"—I'm just pointing out how old the story is, Gensheimer. Guys have been lyin' to their mothers as long as there have been guys and as long as there've been mothers. I never saw one yet go up to his mother and say, 'Hey, yeah, right. I did it. So what?' 'Cause guys know, Gensheimer. They know! You get your mother down on you, man, that's the goddamn worst. If the whole world knows you're a scumbag, but your mother still pats you on the head, gives you a little hug, there's still something left. Something! But when momma goes thumbs down, when momma says, 'Hey, lock him up, I can't do anything with him,' then school's out, Gensheimer. I've seen it too many times at the juvenile hearings. The kids just sag. All the starch goes out of the bones. They come in there spittin' on everybody, snarlin' and snappin' like dogs, tellin' the whole world to go piss up a rope, but when momma says, 'Do it, lock him up,' there's a split-second there, I don't care how tough those little bastards are, there's that split-second when the breath gets a little short and the face goes slack and they know, Gensheimer. They know! From then on, they're in it alone. There's never gonna be anybody ever again who's gonna do them some good without a reason. You want to help your mother? Shit, you're lucky. You're damn lucky. You still got a mother who believes you should be doing things for one another. And a sister, too. Jesus Christ, I can think of half a hundred guys who don't—"

"Aw come on, Balzic. Please stop. Goddamn. What're you tryin' to—"

"I've been telling you for days what I'm tryin' to get you to do. And it all comes down to helping your mother out. And your sister. Hell, Gensheimer, I've got a mother. I support her. I look out for her. I've got a wife. I've got daughters. I know what you're going through. You're turning yourself inside out trying to figure out who you ought to be loyal to. Shit, that's no mystery to me. I know it exactly—"

"The shit if you do."

"Oh but I do, Gensheimer. I do. I've been away from my family for weeks. My mother's an old woman. She's not well. I leave before she wakes up, I don't get home until she's in bed. Same with my daughters. Hell, I see my wife maybe a half-hour a day. I know the problems here—"

"They're not the same," Gensheimer said.

"You think they aren't, but they are. They are," Balzic said. "You just haven't seen it that way yet."

"'Cause I can't see it that way. 'Cause it ain't that way."

"Yes, it is," Balzic said, nodding emphatically. "We both got the same problem. You and me. We got families. We got people we love, people who love us, people we want to help, and people who want to help us, and there's a guy walkin' around with no responsibilities, no problems like we got, because he made the bond. In cash, Gensheimer. Big bucks. Twenty-thousand big bucks. And now he's out there spending forty, forty-five dollars a day for food on himself. Who can afford that? Gensheimer, think of that. Forty, forty-five a day just on himself, and what're your mother and sister eatin', huh? What're they doin' for food with you in here, huh? Man, you're needed out there! You're not doin' anybody any good in here. . . . "

The next day Balzic was back to see Gensheimer at noon, and he brought a picture of Franks eating a clam at the Grand Concourse. After Gensheimer had handed that back without a word, Balzic produced another picture, this one of Franks using scissors to cut the tail of a lobster for his dinner companion, whose hands and smooth, bare arms were just in the left of the photo. The next picture was a profile of Franks's companion, a girl barely out of her teens with lush black hair and a deep tan.

Gensheimer returned all the pictures without so much as a shrug or a sigh.

"So," Balzic said. "How's the food here? D'you enjoy your meal last night? How was your guest? Pretty? Huh? D'you get laid?"

"Come on, Balzic, knock it off."

"Why? Am I being too direct? Huh? You want me to be a little more subtle, maybe. Excuse me if I can't, Gensheimer. This is a simple matter. While you're sitting on your ass in here, getting blisters on your soul, your pal Franks is out there walking around, feedin' his face to the tune of forty-nine dollars plus tip, and then going to the little girl's apartment for a very long nightcap. This is not subtle stuff, Gensheimer. This is basic stuff. Elemental stuff. Everyday down-to-the-belly stuff. How much does he eat, where does he eat it, who with, and where do you eat and where does your mother eat and your sister? That's how basic this is. This is food, clothing, and shelter stuff. You got that wonderful little blue jumpsuit on and those nice slippers and you—"

"Jesus fucking Christ, Balzic, are you gonna spell out every little goddamn fucking detail of the difference in my life between me and—the, uh, the difference between how Franks is living and—"

"That's exactly what I'm gonna do."

"Shit shit shit I don't believe it. . . . "

"Gensheimer, you have to believe it. This is real. This is fact. This is truth. You are here getting bedsores on your brains, gettin' blisters on your soul, and your mother and your sister are countin' the days, and, Gensheimer, it could be five months before you come up for trial. And this delay and then that—"

"How long?" Gensheimer was on his feet. "How long did you say?"

"Five months."

"But what about the 180-day rule? I got to come up before . . . " Gensheimer's face sagged. His eyelids squeezed shut. "Oh my God, oh my God. . . . "

"Amen, Gensheimer," Balzic said. "A hundred and eighty days is six months. Never thought of it that way until just now, did you? Six months, 180 days. Comes out even every time. And there are always delays, Gensheimer. The judge gets sick, the assistant DA's got some other fuckin' thing to do, your attorney's kids get the mumps or something. One thing after another. Six months is now eight months. And eight months is now ten months, and here you sit in your little blue jumpsuit and slippers, and your mother and sister—"

"Stop it stop it stop it STOP IT!"

"Ah, Gensheimer, I'm not the one to stop it. You are. All you got to do is—" Balzic suddenly looked at his watch and said, "Oh shit," and snapped his fingers. "I forgot. I got to go. Hey, Guard, ho, Guard!"

"Where—where you got to go?" Gensheimer said. "How come you're—where you goin'?"

"Got to go. Cortese said he'd have his mind made up today for sure."

The guard came then and opened the door, and held it open.

"About what? What did—what d'you tell me that for?"

" 'Cause it almost slipped my mind. Cortese has been thinking about it really hard, and he told me today he'd let me know. So I got to go."

"Let you know what?"

"Hell, Gensheimer, what d'you think? He's gonna let me know today whether he's gonna roll over. And if he does, that's it. I just need one of you. You got to understand, I can't use you both."

"What?" Gensheimer screeched. "You're not gonna give me—hey, you mean Cortese is gettin' ready—aw bullshit. This is another number here, Balzic. This is another—go on. Go get Cortese. Go ahead! Go on! You're not gonna jerk me around any more. Jesus Christ. . . . "

"Sorry you feel that way," Balzic said. "Well, if you don't see me again, you'll know what that means."

"Ho brother. 'If I don't see you again' means that you'll

stay away for a couple days and that way you'll think I'll be floatin' around inside my head here, and when you show up I'll be so goddamn happy to see you that I'll go the whole route. Shit, Balzic, you're about as subtle as a kick in the nuts."

"Well, maybe I'll be seeing you and maybe not," Balzic said. "Right now, I'm late. Goodbye, Gensheimer. Good luck."

"Go fuck yourself," Gensheimer said as Balzic stepped out of the cell. As hard as Gensheimer had tried, there was no conviction in his voice. Even though he knew the scenario, even though he knew that it was exactly what Balzic was going to do, and even though he wanted to believe with all his being that he was right and that he was being hustled, Gensheimer did not curse convincingly.

Two days later, when a guard brought Balzic's message that Gensheimer, for the good of his mental health, ought to be taken out of isolation and allowed to mingle with the general prison population, Gensheimer began to sweat and to belch with fear. He grabbed hold of his metal bunk and began to shriek that it was his right to be left where he was, that if he was forced out among the other prisoners he'd be killed or worse, and that he had a right to see his lawyer right away.

The guard who brought him Balzic's message tried to coax Gensheimer out of the cell to call his lawyer, saying that he wasn't going to call anybody's lawyer, that it wasn't his responsibility, and that if Gensheimer wanted to talk to his lawyer, he'd have to come out of the cell and call him himself.

Gensheimer sank onto his bunk and began to shake his head no, all the while belching more often and louder.

Balzic was waiting just out of Gensheimer's sight, and heard the reaction. He walked softly to the door of Gensheimer's cell and stood there, watching Gensheimer push himself farther back on his bunk and into the corner, his eyes wild with fear.

"Hello, Gensheimer, how you doin'? Hey, I thought I'd drop by and tell you that I talked to your mother today," Balzic lied. "She called me and asked me what was goin' on, and so forth, and I gave her the good news that you were gonna get out of isolation. That you, you know, you were gonna be allowed out to mingle with the other people here, maybe make some—"

"You motherfucker!" Gensheimer shouted, standing suddenly. "You motherfucker! D'you tell her what this means, you motherfucker, what's gonna happen to me if I get let out of here? I can hear 'em talkin', Balzic. Every time I go to the shower I can hear 'em talkin' about what they're gonna do to me. You motherfucker, d'you tell my mother what's gonna happen if you do what you want and make me go out there with all those fuckin' niggers? Huh? They can't wait to get me, you sonofabitch, they wanna shove bottles up my ass and that's the easiest thing they wanna do! Are you listenin' to me?"

"I'm listening, Gensheimer," Balzic said quietly.

"Well goodammit I won't do it, I won't go outta here, you have to put me in a jacket, that's the only way I go, I don't care I don't care I don't care. . . . "

"That's nice, Gensheimer. That makes you like everybody else here. They don't care either. The turnkeys don't care whether you ever come out of this cell. They can work around you. And the cons? They don't care. If you don't come out, it's no big deal. But if you do come out, it'll give 'em something to do. Either way, nobody's gonna come in there after you."

"Oh God oh God oh my fuckin' God. . . . "

"Gensheimer, there's only two people that care about you who can do anything for you. Are you listening to me?"

"Oh God oh God . . . "

"Quit bitchin' and listen! Of all the people who are in a position to do something for you, there are only two who care enough to do anything at all. And both their motives are pure selfish, one hundred percent pure selfishness. You hear me?"

"Yes," Gensheimer croaked.

"Those two people are you and me. You need to save your life, to keep from having bottles shoved up your butt and from doing sodomy on every con in here—you listening?"

"Yes!" Gensheimer hissed, and began to sob.

"You need to save yourself, Gensheimer, and I need your testimony against Franks. You got your motive, and I got mine. And you know what your options are—don't you?"

"Y-yes."

"I can't hear you, goddammit!"

"Yes! Yes! Can you hear me now?"

"That's better. Now I want you to think about it. Take all the time you want. Think it over carefully. But I'm leaving here in one minute and you better tell me something—or you better hope the turnkey forgets to collect your razor blade."

"Oh God, oh Christ," Gensheimer sobbed. "I don't know when you're lyin', I don't know when you're lyin' . . . you lie so much. . . . "

"Hey, don't waste my time and your life talkin' about my ethics. You got a decision to make. You better make it."

"Balzic—Jesus Christ, Balzic, the state can't protect me. You know that! There ain't any witness protection here. That's federal stuff, that witness protection crap. You can't give me any protection! You're lyin'!"

"Gensheimer, why are you such a hard-head? Huh? Why are you so narrow? Huh? Why do you always assume you know the goddamn answer? Why don't you ever ask?

It would be so much fuckin' simpler. I've already got two people in the witness protection program on this case. You know Long Leroy and his roadie, huh?"

"Oh shit," Gensheimer said. "Oh shit. . . . "

"The U.S. attorney turned them both over to the marshals a couple weeks ago. It's simple, Gensheimer. All I have to do is charge you—through the U.S. attorney— with a violation of somebody's civil rights, don't you understand? Then you're their problem. How much simpler could it be?"

Gensheimer's gaze began to dart around the cell. His eyes became less and less frantic as he began to assimilate the information he'd just heard.

"Don't shit me now, Balzic. Don't blow smoke. This is my life here."

"I'm not blowin' smoke. I'll take Franks any way I can get him—in state court on a murder rap, or in federal court on drugs, or on a violation of somebody's civil rights, I don't care how. But the only way you're gettin' out of here is on my word. Nobody else gives a shit. So you're with me or you're here."

"I know, I know, oh Jesus fucking Christ I know."

"So decide! C'mon! Now!"

Gensheimer sobbed and tried to cover his face with his arm. "I'm with—I'm with you. I'll tell you. Anything. Please God don't let the niggers get me. Please God don't. . . . "

Balzic began his day, the Friday after Gensheimer agreed to testify against Michael Franks under immunity from prosecution, with a feeling of elation such as he had not known in months. Much of it was caused by the day: the sun was warm even at nine o'clock in the morning, and it was the first time this spring that he

remembered feeling that. There had also been a heavy
rain the night before, and so streets and gutters and sidewalks all looked cleaner than usual, and smelled fresh—or
as fresh as they ever smelled in Rocksburg.

Balzic had not left home until he'd seen and talked to
his mother. They'd talked about this and that, the weather
mostly, and how her ankles felt. He had not seen her for
two weeks, and their conversation was a little stiff. She
seemed older to him, and weaker, and shorter. It took a
while talking to her before his elation returned to him; he
was almost at the station before he felt it as fully as he had
when he'd first gotten out of the shower and remembered
what he'd accomplished with Gensheimer.

There were two things that remained to be done about
the girl who still had no name. Balzic had never talked to
the warden at the Allegheny County Jail about Randolph
Kolesar. Balzic wasn't even sure why he thought he had to
call him now, but if Kolesar had not panicked and if Balzic
had lived up to the bargain he had struck with him, then
Balzic was supposed to have taken the warden's call to
confirm what Kolesar had given as his reasons for wanting
to get out of that jail and into Southern Regional.

Balzic made his way back to his office through the duty
room, chatting along the way with the desk man and with
one of the clerks from the sanitation department who had
just dropped in and had brought doughnuts.

Balzic called the Allegheny County Jail, but the highest
ranking officer he could talk to was the senior guard on
that watch. Balzic identified himself and told why he was
calling.

"It's all after the fact, understand, I mean, the kid is
dead and, uh—"

"Just what do you want to know?" the senior guard said.

"Well, for one thing, I want to know, uh, did you yourself,
did you know him?"

"Kolesar? Oh yes. I knew Kolesar very well. Shouldn't have been here."

"Uh, that's what they all say," Balzic said.

"No, that's not what I mean. He was dangerous to himself. He should have been in a mental institution. Well, not these corrals we call mental institutions. But, given an ideal world, he would not have been in jail. Of course, ours is not an ideal world."

"Uh, how was he dangerous to himself?"

"Oh, Kolesar was very violent. He was always cutting himself, injuring himself. One time, it was the first time he was here, oh, seven, eight years ago, I saw him put his head down and get at the other end of his cell and run at the bars. And I don't mean he trotted up to those bars, I mean he ran. And he got up and did it again. By the time we got in there and got him out, that boy needed seventy stitches in his scalp."

Balzic suddenly felt a rush of uneven and unequal and grossly conflicting emotions. "Uh, this last time he was there, did you see him?"

"Yes."

"And did you know what happened?"

"You mean when he cut himself? In his genitals? Is that what you're talking about?"

"Uh, he did that?"

"Oh yes."

"Two niggers didn't do that?"

There was no reply. There was no reply for so long a time that Balzic repeated his question.

Finally, the voice on the other end said, "Perhaps I should have identified myself more fully. I am Senior Guard John Wilson. I am black. I do not like that word."

"I'm only telling you what he told—what Kolesar told me."

"And I don't care what he told you, I don't like that

word. Never mind. Kolesar was dangerously diseased. I
don't know why he was like he was. But he cut himself
with a spoon he'd filed down. Two other prisoners—both
white—saw him do it. And many people here, staff and
prisoners alike, have testified, and will testify again if
that's necessary, that he refused treatment. He said finally
he'd agree to be treated after we transferred him to Southern Regional. All here agreed, without much argument,
that Kolesar was an administrative nightmare and a legal
nightmare waiting to happen, and so he was transferred.

"In conclusion, my name is John Wilson, I am senior
guard here, and I will be happy to testify to these facts—
if I am subpoenaed.

"Now, if you'll excuse me, I have work to do. Good-bye."

As elated as Balzic had been within the hour, so now
was he rushing downward toward what had all the symp-
toms of an unresolvable funk. He sat hunched over his
desk and, mouth agape, he toyed with the flesh on his
neck with his left hand, rubbing this way and that, pushing
it, tugging, feeling the bristle of his shaved hair as his
fingers went one way, and then feeling the smooth flesh as
they went with the grain.

Then he fingered his nose and then his eyebrows and
then he sat back and tried to think Senior Guard John
Wilson's information through. His thinking came to nothing;
rather, what his thoughts brought him to was the inescap-
able fact that Kolesar was dead and that no amount of
thought would change that fact. But Balzic was dipping
dangerously low and, try as he might, he could not stop his
emotional slide with the memories of his success with
Gensheimer.

He jumped up suddenly, buoyed by the thoughts of the
Reverend Rutherford Feeler and of taking news of the
Gensheimer success to him. The Reverend had provided
Balzic with all the preliminary work; Balzic felt now that it

was essential to show Feeler the last stages of the work, before the trials began.

Balzic was just reaching for the door when someone knocked on it. He opened it and found Mayor Kenny Strohn, smiling one of his better political smiles.

"Good morning, Mario."

"Good morning."

"I—uh, I've come to offer my congratulations. I've heard the news. It looks like—well, it's, uh, everybody's talking about it."

"Everybody?"

"The people here, I mean."

"Oh. What people?"

"Well—the people all over the hall. City Hall." The mayor laughed uncomfortably. "Listen. Congratulations. I know I tried to, well, uh, I tried to hurry this, this whole thing along and I probably should never have opened my mouth, but I still want you to know I—"

"You ever been to Rufee's, Mr. Mayor?" Balzic interrupted him.

"Beg pardon?"

"Rufee's. You know. Ever been there?"

"Uh—no. No."

"Ever wanted to go? Never mind. Don't answer. Just come on. I got to tell him something." Balzic didn't wait for the mayor to respond. He just led the mayor out to his cruiser and set off.

They were a mile out of Rocksburg before Balzic spoke, and then it was not to the mayor but to Desk Sergeant Royer, over the radio, to get Royer to send Detective "Rugs" Carlucci out to Rufee's. "Tell him to wait for me in the parking lot."

"Mario, wha-what's going on?" the mayor asked.

"I just have something I want to tell Rufee, and I think Carlucci ought to be there. And you too."

Balzic fell silent again until he pulled into one of Rufee's parking lots, past an old man sitting in a sentry box waiting for the phone to ring. Carlucci arrived about five minutes later.

" . . . looks like it's ready to collapse," the mayor was saying as Balzic got out.

"What does?"

"The building. It's just a big old house. I'd always imagined it was a lot more—I don't know—imposing."

"It's the time of day," Balzic said, walking to meet Carlucci, who held out his hand in congratulations.

"Heard you broke him," Carlucci said.

Balzic shrugged as he shook Carlucci's hand. "Hey, how hard is it to break a narc when he can't make the bond? Shit, it was, uh, never mind." He looked at the Cadillacs and Lincolns parked near the house, three Cadillacs, two Lincolns, bronze and white and powder blue.

"What d'you think they're doing? Little cards maybe, huh?"

Carlucci shook his head. "Driving these cars? Huh? Nah. They're countin' the money."

Balzic shrugged his agreement and set off toward the front door, with Carlucci and Strohn close behind. When they got to it, Balzic pounded on the door with the flat of his hand.

There were footsteps, then silence, then the locks—four of them—being opened. The man who opened the door said brusquely, "What's on your mind?"

"Tell the Reverend I want to see him. I have some news."

The doorman looked at Strohn. "Who's he?"

"The mayor of Rocksburg."

"He got news for the Rev too?"

"No. He's just with me."

The doorman's head and torso bobbed with silent, toothy

laughter. He had a solid gold incisor, and he was wearing an automatic pistol in a shoulder holster. His laughter started to make a breathy noise, then he shut the door.

"This is—this is incredible," the mayor said. "Doesn't he know who you are? He looked as though he knew you."

"He does."

"Then why are we standing—why did he shut the door? You're the—uh, you're the—he's carrying a concealed weapon—"

"He knows who I am," Balzic said. "He knows who Rugs is, and now he knows who you are. But it doesn't make any difference. Down here we're just three white guys waitin' to see Rufee. If Rufee says we're okay, the door opens. If Rufee says we're not, we just stand here until we get tired being made a fool of, and we leave. Also, Mr. Mayor, the weapon wasn't concealed, I mean, we all saw it."

After a minute, the sound of heavy footsteps approached, the locks were opened and then the door, and the doorman with the gold incisor stood out of the way. "The Rev says this better not be bullshit and he had a long night and he ain't in no mood to listen to no bullshit and he was 'sposed to be 'sleep a hour ago. Can you dig it?"

"I did not drive down here to bullshit. Where is he?"

"Upstairs. But I'm goin' tell y'all one more time. This ain't the time to jive the Rev. He done had a long night."

"And I told you I had news."

"Um-huh. Better be some good fuckin' news, man." The doorman stepped aside and let them pass.

They went upstairs and found Rufee sitting in his great white peacock chair, and drinking what appeared to be milk. He took a swallow and scowled fiercely at the glass and set it down on a small round table to his right.

"Whatch'all want, Balzic?"

"Reverend," Balzic said, "good morning. I'd like to introduce the—"

"The mayor," Rufee said. "I don't need no introduction, Balzic. I know who the mayor is, and some other time, Mr. Mayor, you and I will have to discuss how many votes I had sent to you—well, not to you so much as they didn't get sent to that little dago you replaced. But not now. Now all I want's the news."

"Okay, okay. Take it easy—"

"Balzic, man, just so you know," Rufee said, leaning forward and emphasizing each word, "I had me a long-ass night. I'm tired, my stomach hurts, my head hurts, get to the motherfuckin' point."

"Okay. I think we got Franks."

"You think! Jesus Chris', man. You think! Don't chu know? Got-damn. I sent you all that information, I sent you all those numbers and that wasn't enough, so then I sent you Long Leroy with all his pictures and tape recordin's and you tell me you think you got the motherfucker? Balzic, you a bitch! You a top class, a number-fuckin'-one bitch, man, you know that?"

"Is that a compliment?" Balzic said, smiling.

Rufee put his head down and shook it and sighed noisily. "This the good news you brought me?"

"Rufee, you got to understand. Franks knows how the law works—not how it's supposed to work, or how people think it works, but how it actually works. He knows that all the stuff we had—including the stuff Long Leroy had— all that stuff in the hands of a good lawyer and in front of a dumb judge, all that stuff is useless if we can't answer the question of probable cause. We have to show in court why we began to look at this man—of all men—why him, that's what we have to show. And all the stuff you gave me was full of self-interest, and that doesn't look good to a jury of retired white people. Plus, the one witness I had that could link Franks to that girl is dead. He killed himself. So the chain got broken. And that's why all the tainted stuff has to be corroborated by one of his own. Otherwise, all we got is a pile of facts that don't necessarily point to Franks. I wanted something else. Somebody else. One of his own. And I got him. That's what I came to tell you. I got one of his fellow officers."

Rufee picked up his glass of milk and swallowed some, scowling the while, and set it down again.

"So you think you got him?"

"Yes, I do."

"If you had to make a bet, what odds would you give?"

"I don't have to make a bet. I know this much. If we lose him in the state court, the federal guys will go after him for a violation of that girl's civil rights."

"Oh no, I don't want that civil rights shit. I told you, I want that motherfucker in Pittsburgh, without a friend, without a voice."

"Well, Reverend, I've done as much as I can to avenge those three girls, I've given it my best—"

"What three girls?"

"The girl who was shot, and the other two you told me about, the ones Franks mutilated—wait a minute. What d'you mean, 'What three girls'?"

Rufee began to smile, and then to laugh. He shook with laughter and slapped his knee and ran in place while still seated so that his shoes made a steady thumping for a long moment.

"Uh, what's so funny?"

"You are, Balzic. You're so goddamn serious you're funny. But if you weren't serious I wouldn't be laughin' now," Rufee said, wiping his eyes. "You the most serious cat ever was. I made book on that."

"What?" Balzic canted his head. "What're you trying to tell me? And what'd you mean, 'What three girls'?"

"Just tryin' to tell you, you a serious dude, that's all, and I'm damn glad you are, otherwise, sheee-it."

"You're having a pretty good laugh on me, Rufee. I want to know what's so funny, goddamnit."

"Oh, Balzic, man, sheee-it, can't you dig it? I mean, don't you know, man? Can't you get it together? Huh?" Rufee stopped laughing and squinted at Balzic. "Hey, Balzic, man, I owe you one. I owe you a big one. I want you to know that."

"Uh-huh. So owe me later. What's so funny?"

"Balzic, your Jew-boy Franks ain't the only one know how the law work. I mean, they's lots of us poor folks know dat." Rufee was talking like an uneducated street black now, but there was no attempt to be comical.

"Balzic, that Jew-boy was robbin' and stealin' from poor folks and sendin' poor folks to the joint, the same ones he was robbin' and stealin' from. And he wasn't 'sposed to be a robber or a stealer, he was 'sposed to be a cop and 'sposed to protect people from being robbed and stole from.

"Now that's what he be doin', and all my friends know that's what he be doin', and now the problem come up right quick—since we know the dude know de law—the problem is, how do we get rid of this thief? That was the problem, Balzic.

"I mean, do we call the cops and say, 'Hey, y'all, one of y'all's robbin' and stealin' us blind and sendin' poor folks to the joint'? 'Cause you know we can't say that, Balzic."

"Maybe he does, but I most certainly do not," interrupted the mayor.

Rufee smiled. "I thought you would not. Yeah. So I will explain to you. The man was robbin' dope and stealin' cash and lockin' up poor folks just because they was dealin' in dope and cash." Rufee held up his hand to stop the mayor from speaking. "Uh-uh. I know what you're

thinking. These poor folks, these dope dealers and cash
dealers, *they* were breakin' the law. And they were. Your
law. Not theirs. Yours. But I ain't gonna get into how
stupid your dope laws are. One example of that is enough.
Everybody knows heroin is the best pain killer there is,
but y'all won't give it to people dyin' of cancer and got
terrible pain because y'all is worried about them folks
turnin' into addicts! I mean, of all the jive white folks puts
out about dope, that got to be the dumbest.

"But never mind. Your man—your *law* man—was robbin'
a cash crop and lockin' up the farmers. And how were we
'sposed to deal with it? Been a black dude or a white dude
who wasn't a cop, there wouldn't be no problem. He'd've
just had an accident, a garbage truck back over him or
somethin'. No sweat. But not with this Franks. Oh no, he's
a cop. So he can't have an accident. 'Cause if he had,
every motherfuckin' cop in white America'd be looking
for the cause of that accident. Ain't that true, Balzic?"

Balzic shrugged.

"Don't just be shruggin'. Nod your head. 'Cause you
know got-damn well what I'm sayin'. 'Cause that's where
you came in. And I already told you, you a serious man.

"Balzic, it came down to this. If I told you my product
was gettin' ripped off and my employees were being sent
to the joint by a cop, would you have helped me? You and
I both know the answer to that. Isn't that right?"

Balzic shrugged again, this time less comfortably.

"Don't shrug, Balzic. You know it and I know it and
Rugs here know it and if Mr. Mayor don't know it, he'll
just have to catch up. But the rest of the world know what
I'm tellin' you. Ain't no white cop goin' bust no other white
cop for fuckin' with me and mine and stealin' and robbin'
from me and mine and for sendin' mine to the joint, now
say it out loud—am I lyin' or not?"

"You're not lying," Balzic said, coughing on phlegm. He

knew what was coming and he could not believe he was still standing where he was standing, waiting to hear what he knew he would hear.

"So if we both know that, Balzic," Rufee went on, "then what choice do I have? I got no choice. I have to find me a serious man who will respond in a serious way to a problem he—and only he—will believe in all his white soul is a serious problem. And that, Brother Balzic, that serious man was you. A serious man, with daughters, and with the feelings any serious man who has daughters would have, if he heard a certain story."

Balzic felt himself growing very warm under his sternum. The heat radiated outward. His mouth got dry and he tried to swallow. His hands began to clench and unclench and then he began to flick his thumbs with his index fingers, and the sound from that flicking became very loud. The noise seemed to be amplified and he found himself—utterly distracted for a moment—trying to decide whether the sound he heard was that of his thumbs or of the pressure points in his neck.

"So," Rufee said after some moments had passed, and speaking now in his West Indies accent, "I told you the story . . . young girls . . . a suggestion of sex . . . a stronger suggestion of violence, of perversion. . . . " Rufee shrugged. "It was necessary, Balzic. A disease was loose in the streets, mon. A monster. . . . Somebody said once, I think it was that crazy German, that Nietschze, I think he said, 'Be careful when pursuing monsters lest you become one yourself.' But, Balzic, you and I both know there is no other way. To pursue the monster, to catch him, to crush him, you have to *be* a monster. Or else. Or else you have to *know* somebody who can be a monster—and get away with it. Hmmmm?"

Balzic was seething. But he didn't know whether it was for being gulled, or whether it was for having his being gulled stripped bare in front of Mayor Ken Strohn and Rugs Carlucci. Balzic tried to bluff it out by staring at Rufee; it was a poor effort and Balzic soon found himself looking awkwardly at the floor.

Besides, Rufee wasn't having any. "Oh come on, mon. Balzeek! Hy'ah. Peevish 'bout some little black lies, mon? Well, now. Look at the scoreboard, Long Leroy and his roadie. Several very large federal cases taken care of there, hm? Then there's Gensheimer and Cortese and Franks. Three very big stinkballs. Won't be smellin' up our noses no more, mon. And Black Mary, mother of Black God, Balzeek, think of all the poor black folks who'll come out the joint, mon. Cases overturned left and right. Justice, that blind, black, big-nippled beauty, just goin' about, settin' things right, mon.

"And there you stand, Balzic, lookin' like a motherfuckin' jive honky, tryin' to get yourself in order. Balzic, how was I goin' do it without chu? Huh? I went your way, mon. I went the way of law and motherfucking order. I just came in the back door, that's all. She-it. Us niggers been usin' that door a long time. Now why you lookin' at the floor? Balzic, the good guys won! All you got to do is 'splain it to Mr. Mayor here, that's all. Mr. Mayor need to know how this shit work."

Balzic looked up from the floor at Rufee. Then he looked at Carlucci, who was trying not very successfully not to laugh. Then Balzic looked at Mayor Strohn.

Strohn's face was stiff, blank, and pale, and his shoulders were raised as though caught at the top of a shrug of profound confusion and elemental dismay. Then he began to shake his head from side to side, and he turned rigidly and stumbled toward the steps, muttering darkly.

"Carlucci," Rufee said, "go walk with the mayor and make sure he don't trip down the stairs."

Laughing to himself, Carlucci trotted to catch up with

the mayor, and, once beside him, took him by the arm and steadied him.

"You sonofabitch," Balzic said.

"Now don't you call me no names. I done worked your whole motherfuckin' case for you, practically. Two of my good friends are goin' to be lost to me forever—"

Balzic felt his chin dropping until he was looking over the rims of his glasses at Rufee. "Two of your friends are gonna be lost forever—"

"Tha's right."

"My fuckin' heart bleeds for you and your two friends." Balzic began to pace in small half-circles and to shake his head and to moan to himself.

"Balzic, what's wrong witchu? You moanin'? You actually moanin'?"

Balzic continued to pace. "You know how much explainin' I'm gonna have to do?"

"To who? The mayor? She-it, Balzic. Tell him 'bout Snow Black and the Seven Honkies. Honkie-Dumpty—"

"Very funny," Balzic said, stepping close to Rufee and lowering his voice. "But what you don't understand is I got three and a half more years with him, and he thinks it's part of my job to make people care about one another . . . good people. Nice people. Upstanding people."

"Well?" Rufee said. "Ain't that what you done?" He was chortling and grinning, and his stomach was bouncing with quiet laughter. "Who's more righteous and upstandin' in this community than me?"

Balzic began to pace again and to breath heavily through his nose. "Yeah, you're righteous all right. You sonofabitch, you don't pay taxes to nobody. Name me one taxing body that touches your money. Go ahead. Name me one!"

"Now wait a minute, Balzic."

"Don't now-wait-a-minute me nothin'. You sit down here in the middle of this little empire and you con me into gettin' trouble off your black neck and who do you pay for my services, huh?"

Rufee rolled his eyes and swayed backward in his chair. He squinted meanly at Balzic. "Are you gettin' ready to shake me down?" He leaned forward and put his right elbow on his right knee and began to clench and unclench his fists.

Balzic didn't stop pacing. "Now you got it. That's exactly what I'm gonna do—"

"For me making you look a fool in front of this mayor? I'll-be-go-to-hell-and-come-back-white if you ain't a bitch."

"Wrong. Wrong! Wrong! Wrong!"

"Then tell me what's right!" Rufee bellowed.

"Don't you shout at me. Every part of this hustle was on your edge, and don't even look like it wasn't. I mean, don't you even look like it wasn't. And—and, goddammit, you don't pay taxes to anybody! You run your church number at Uncle Sugar, and whatever you make in here you run through your collection baskets in your church, shit, everybody knows that. So who do you pay taxes to? Huh? Well, goddammit, you're gonna start."

"To who? You? Huh?" Rufee said, smiling. "To Mr. Clean? All you need to do is shave your head, Balzic, and you'll look like a got-damn ad for a liquid cleaner. 'Cept it's all bullshit. Even you . . . even you!"

"Rufee, it ain't me. I don't know who it's gonna be for, but it's not me."

"Even you. I'll be a sonofabitch, even you!"

Balzic quit pacing and walked close to Rufee. "Don't say that again."

"Give me a reason why not," Rufee said, standing.

"'Cause you're gonna do this on the square. You're gonna open a checking account and you're—you're gonna write the checks and they ain't gonna be to me. And that's why you're not gonna say that anymore. So sit down!"

Rufee thought and grimaced and scowled and thought some more. He sat back down. "I don't put my name on nothin', Balzic. You know that."

"Then get somebody to do it for you, I don't give a shit who signs what. Get that woman with the striped hair, what difference does it make? All I'm tellin' you is you're gonna get off some bucks. You're not gonna ride free anymore."

Rufee tilted his head and squinted and chewed his lips. "If you're jivin' me, Balzic, I swear, I don't know what I'll do, but I'll do something bad, I swear on my momma, I'll do somethin' bad."

Balzic turned and walked slowly away, stopping in the doorway to turn and wave his finger at Rufee. "I can't say right now how much you ought to pay or where it'll do the most good, but you'll know soon. In a week, maybe. I don't know whether you'll be giving parties for people in the county home, or whether you'll be buying food for those kids in that school where they're all retarded, or what you'll be doing. But you'll know. And one thing."

"Yeah. What?"

"Don't even think about not doing it."

"Hm," Rufee snorted. "She-it, Balzic. For a little while there, you had me worried. Now that I see where you're goin', I think I can maybe make me a real public relations score out of this."

"Yeah, well keep thinking that way."

"Hey, Balzic, I ain't got no problem with this—I mean as long as it ain't too heavy—but what chu goin' do with your mayor there, huh? What chu goin' tell him?" Rufee found that thought comical indeed and he laughed mightily.

Balzic looked at Strohn, still being supported by Carlucci. Balzic stepped close to the mayor and looked into his glazed eyes.

"Mr. Mayor, do you know what's going on here?"

No response.

"Mr. Mayor, do you understand any of this? Do you understand that there're only a couple options open to us here? I mean, we can't prosecute the preacher here. All we can do is arrest him and charge him with something every couple of weeks and make him pay the bond—you understand?"

No response.

"But if we do that, we do it knowin' that goin' in it will never get past the preliminary hearing. 'Cause we won't have a case. Even if by some dumb luck it got to trial, we'd never get a conviction. Mr. Mayor? Are you in there?"

Strohn focused on Balzic and, just as quickly, his eyes seemed to cloud over. Balzic had to overcome the urge to shout.

"Mr. Mayor, whether you understand this or not, this is the only way. This man," Balzic pointed repeatedly with his thumb at Rufee, "this man has to pay some taxes. What I'm doing to him is a lot simpler than going the legal route of busting him, getting him in front of a magistrate, making him come up with ten thousand dollars in cash to cover a one hundred thousand dollar bond, and having the thing get thrown out at the preliminary hearing, just to make him spend the ten thousand dollars. All we do there is make the bondsman rich, you understand? Mr. Mayor, are you with me?"

Balzic looked at Carlucci. "You don't think this guy's not okay, do you?"

"I think he just had a real shock to his nervous system," Carlucci said. "If you know what—"

"I know, I know. Christ, he don't look good."

"Probably," Carlucci whispered, "probably 'cause he never thought it was supposed to work like this, huh? Whatta you think?"

"God Almighty, I think we better get him out of here."

"By all means," Rufee said. "I, too, am beginning to feel ill."

"Hey," Balzic said, whirling on Rufee, "you bet your ass on it. One way or the other, you're gonna join the taxpayers. My way's the simple way. You just write a check every week. But if you don't go that way, then we go the bond route. I'll bust your joint every week. It'll cost you twenty thousand dollars to forty thousand dollars a month. I'm giving you a bargain. And no hassles."

"Oh I understand," Rufee said. "PR value will probably be worth twice what I pay." He chuckled hugely. "All you have to do is get your mayor back among the conscious living and explain it to him." Rufee's chuckle became a roar. "That's all," he cried out through his laughter, spittle flying. "That's all. . . . "

"Shit," Balzic said, taking Mayor Strohn by the right arm—Carlucci still maintained his grip on the left—and starting down the stairs. "Why's everything have to be so goddamn hard? I mean it. Just one thing could be simple once in a while. That's not too much to ask. . . . "

"Hey, Balzic. Ho," Rufee called out.

"What now?" Balzic stopped.

"Listen," Rufee said, shaking with laughter, "I don't care. I mean, I be thinking this over, man, and I don't care. I may write the damn checks myself. Cause you know why? Huh? I mean, every time I write a check to wherever you want me to write it to, man, I'll be thinkin' 'bout chu, man. I mean, I got over on some white cats in my life, Balzeek, but never nothin' like this, man. Never. I mean, you the best, Balzic. You the bad-ass mommafuckin' bes' and I got over on you so good I could come, man. I mean, I could jusssssst come!"

"The more you talk, you sonofabitch," Balzic said under his breath, "the more it's gonna cost." He motioned with his head to Carlucci to start walking again, but he couldn't bring himself to look at him.

They were out in the parking lot in the sunlight before the mayor seemed to come to a clearer mind. He stopped walking and pulled his arms away from Balzic and Carlucci, and shrugged this way and that and stretched his neck, pointing his chin up and to both sides.

"Is this the way it's done? Is this what we've come to? I don't believe it. I *can't* believe it."

"This is just one of the ways it's done, Mr. Mayor," Balzic said. "There isn't only one way. And most of them are pretty greasy."

"But, my God, Balzic, this, this dealing, this trading, this, this—I don't know what to call it, it is greasy! Worse than greasy. To accomplish what? What, in God's name? What?"

"Well," Balzic said, looking at his shoes and stuffing his hand in his pockets, "we never did find out what the girl's name was who got shot and killed, and so we never notified her family—if she has one—but, uh, we do know the name of the man who killed her. And if we get any luck at all we may get him out of circulation for, oh, hell, maybe seven years."

"Seven years," Mayor Strohn said, closing his eyes and shaking his head.

"Yes, sir. That's with luck."

"And Rufee? He just keeps on?"

"Yes, sir. But he's got to share a little bit. He doesn't get to keep it all to use as he sees fit."

Strohn dropped his chin and rubbed his eyes.

"Mr. Mayor," Balzic said, after Carlucci had gone to his car and Balzic was standing beside his own, "uh, Mr. Mayor, it's spring and the sun is shining and I think it's about time you and I went somewhere and sat down and drank some wine together. I know just the place. Okay?"

Balzic didn't wait for a reply, but gently steered the mayor to the passenger side and got him in, and then got in himself and drove back to Rocksburg to Muscotti's. He waved away those few people who recognized the mayor and wanted to approach him to complain or to ask favors. To Vinnie, who also recognized Strohn, Balzic touched his index finger quickly to his lips, as one would do to warn off someone who was going to intrude on another's grief. Vinnie instantly lowered his voice.

"Got any good wine, any of Dom's stuff out here?"

Vinnie nodded and brought a bottle of Pinot Chardonnay. "You gotta replace this, you know," Vinnie said, under his breath. "His daughters got him a case for his birthday. So I ain't sellin' it, you just gotta replace it."

"I understand," Balzic said. "Here, Mr. Mayor, try some of this. This is guaranteed."

"To do what?"

"Why, hell. Whatta you think? To make the world a little better place to live in."

"After what I've heard, it'll take more than this," the mayor said. "A lot more."

Balzic was going to say that it wouldn't take too much, that no matter how bad it got, there was always wine, and that it never really took too much wine to make the world seem just a little more bearable, but he didn't. If there was one thing he knew about this mayor, it was that Strohn insisted on having things his way in his time. There wasn't any point in trying to rush things, no matter how deeply the mayor stared into his glass at every lull in the conversation. There were times to tell people and there were times to shut up. Balzic knew, the older he got, the better thing most times was to shut up. Beyond that, beyond just being there, Balzic knew there wasn't anything more he could do for the mayor. One of these days Strohn might want some explanations, but for now all Balzic could sensibly give was his company.

After four glasses of Pinot Chardonnay—it took that many—Strohn seemed to brighten a bit and to start to relax, and then Iron City Steve came shuffling in, elbows flapping and proclaiming to no one, "What's graver than gravity? Show me a man serious enough to answer that!"

Then Mo Valcanas came in, and he was humming and had his hat set low over his right eye and went straight to the juke box and put in much change and punched some buttons and told one of the girls from the community college to play the rest of the songs he'd paid for, and then he came and sat on the other side of Balzic.

Balzic stared after Valcanas and watched him, and then watched as Valcanas approached and sat.

"You're lookin' pretty goddamn spry."

"Spry. Huh. That's an interesting word. But I somehow don't think it applies to me."

"Well, you came in humming and snapping your fingers and playing the jukebox and—"

"It's all a front, my friend. A front. Innkeeper!"

Vinnie rubbed his lower lip. "Weren't you just here a little while ago, huh?"

"You care how many times I come in?"

"Hey, I was just sayin'—"

"Well. So you were. Hm. Double gin on the rocks."

Vinnie poured as directed, took the money, and retreated.

"Must've been a long day, you drinkin' doubles this time of day—"

"What is this?" Valcanas said. "The bartender counts my visits, you analyze my drinking, what next?"

"I was just saying—"

"So don't say. Anyway, I have heard that your brightness has been somewhat diminished."

"Huh?"

"You heard me. The word is, a certain cop was handed

a certain bill of goods by a certain preacher and—"

"Don't know what you're talkin' about."

"How about you and Rufee? Rufee giving you that story about those little girls all mutilated by that narc, what's his name? And you just, uh, getting sloppy. Christ, Mario, that's not like you. Not at all."

"Where'd you hear this?"

"Hell, it's becoming famous down at the courthouse. Even as I speak."

"What? Huh?" Balzic thought a moment, then he sagged. "That sonofabitch. That big-lipped, no-nation, sonofabitch. . . ."

"I beg your pardon?"

"Aw knock it off, Christ. It's bad enough—"

"Mario, I didn't repeat this story to anybody. You're the first to hear it from me."

"That sonofabitch called the courthouse as soon as I was out the door."

"Uh, what sonofabitch?"

"Rufee. Who else? That sonofabitch bad-mouthed me as soon as I left. He's probably got somebody in the DA's office—oh Christ, what's the use."

"Uh, so it's true."

"Aw fuck you yes it's true." Balzic lowered his head and studied his trousers. "Certainly it's true. I knew it when I heard it the first time. But there wasn't a goddamn thing I could do about it. Rugs checked out hospitals, but, hell, he was just goin' through the motions. There wasn't any way we could check that out. How do you check out a story about two black girls getting misused by a white cop? I mean, that's the perfect con. Perfect hustle. You can't get one any better. I was so fuckin' anxious to believe this particular white cop did this shit, you know, I really didn't push it. I should've never never never never never forgot Rufee's flag."

"His what?"

"Yeah. Remember that Revolutionary War flag, that one with the rattlesnake on it, it says, 'Don't Tread On Me'?"

"Sure."

"Well. Rufee's got a flag, black, with a gold rattler on it and gold letters—or maybe it's gold with black letters, I forget—but anyway, it says, it's got this rattlesnake on it just like the original, only it's got the words, 'Don't Get Over On Me' on it."

"Hey, hey!" the mayor piped up. "I saw that. I saw that flag. What does that mean? What does that mean? Don't get over me. Don't get over me. . . . "

Valcanas leaned close to Balzic. "Does he say everything twice?"

"No, that's something new. I guess that's what four glasses of wine does to him."

"Well what does it mean? Huh? What does it—"

"It means the same thing the original one meant. It's just the way black people talk, that's all."

"Don't get over me. Don't get over me."

"It's not 'Don't get over me.' It's 'Don't get over *on* me.' " Balzic looked intently at the mayor's eyes and saw the dullness too much alcohol produces. He put his face close to the mayor's face and said loudly, "Three and a half more years. Three and a half more years. . . . "

After enough time passed to satisfy Coroner Wallace Grimes that no one was going to claim the body of the girl shot by Michael Franks, Grimes, at Balzic's request, turned the body over to Donelli's Funeral Home, where it was embalmed, dressed, and laid in the most expensive bronze casket on the premises. Balzic impressed five of his men to act as pallbearers with him. He got

Father Marazzo of St. Malachy's to perform a graveside service, despite the priest's earnest doubts that the girl was Roman Catholic. Balzic ordered a basket of lilies, a sheaf of wheat, and a potted geranium to be brought to the grave, the lilies to be left on the surface, the geranium to be planted, the wheat to be put atop the coffin as it was lowered. He arranged with a monument-maker to carve into a square marble headstone these words:

> Jane Doe
> Murdered January 20, 1979
> By A Corrupt
> Law Officer.

Then he took the bills from the funeral home, the florist, the monument-maker, and he added a bill for a hundred dollars—twenty dollars for each of the other pallbearers—and he had them delivered to the Reverend Rutherford Feeler, with a note that said: "I have told these honest businessmen that they will be paid in cash by a black man in a white tuxedo with a fur collar. I know you won't disappoint them. S/Mario Balzic."